Occupation:	"Owner of the most prosperous ranch in Conard County, Wyoming."
His Reputation:	"Some say I'm a bit of a risk taker. But never where my heart is concerned."
His Ideal Woman:	"Well, the woman I *should* pursue would be a nice small-town girl from Conard County—someone used to the rigors of ranching life. But I keep being drawn to the mysterious woman staying on my ranch. A beauty I know will have to leave."
Marriage Vow:	"Marriage? That's one mistake I don't plan on making. Though this city woman could make me take the ultimate risk."

Dear Reader,

We are proud to present the very first WORLD'S MOST ELIGIBLE BACHELORS book. This brand-new series combines some of the finest authors in romance with the sexiest heroes anyone could ever imagine.

Here's the concept: *Prominence Magazine* (Yes, it's a fictitious publication, but doesn't it sound fabulous?) has hand-picked twelve of the most eligible bachelors in the world. Each month we'll follow the story of an utterly sexy, overwhelmingly desirable male. *And* you'll get all the juicy details about the romance that lands him on the road to Marriageville.

This month, beloved author Rachel Lee brings us our first incredible bachelor. Jeff Cumberland, a to-die-for cowboy—and also immensely wealthy, don't you know?—hails from Conard County. CONARD COUNTY is Rachel Lee's bestselling series that centers around characters who live—and love—in the Wyoming county that lends its name to the series. We just had to bring you the story of one of those heart-stoppingly handsome men. And just wait till you read what kind of lady lassos that Jeff!

Next month, RITA Award-winning author Marie Ferrarella continues her delightful THE BABY OF THE MONTH CLUB series with the story of a gorgeous millionaire detective. This *Detective Dad* finds himself delivering a baby in a car, and the new mom has lost her memory, and... Oh, you'll just have to come back next month to see what happens!

Until then...here's to romance wishes and bachelor kisses!

The Editors

Please address questions and book requests to:
Silhouette Reader Service
U.S.: 3010 Walden Ave., P.O. Box 1325, Buffalo, NY 14269
Canadian: P.O. Box 609, Fort Erie, Ont. L2A 5X3

World's Most
Eligible Bachelors

Rachel Lee

The Catch of Conard County

Silhouette Books

Published by Silhouette Books
America's Publisher of Contemporary Romance

For my daughter Heather, with love.
I'm so proud of you, sweetie.

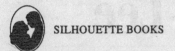 SILHOUETTE BOOKS

ISBN 0-373-65018-3

THE CATCH OF CONARD COUNTY

Copyright © 1998 by Susan Civil-Brown

Printed in U.S.A.

A Conversation with...
Bestselling author RACHEL LEE

What hero have you created for WORLD'S MOST ELIGIBLE BACHELORS, and how has he earned the coveted title?

RL: Jeff Cumberland's business sense, his wealth and his good looks, as well as a certain recklessness, have combined to make him the man of any woman's dreams—except that he lives in an isolated place in Wyoming. *Prominence Magazine* considers him eligible, but the women he considers eligible usually do not, because they don't want to sacrifice their lives to the isolation of ranch life.

This original title is part of CONARD COUNTY, a Silhouette Intimate Moments miniseries. What about this series so appeals to you? Do you have spinoffs planned?

RL: From the moment it was born in my mind and heart, Conard County has been the home I have always yearned to find. It's a creation of my hopes, my dreams, my values and my needs. Two future books are currently in the pipeline, one a book of novellas. I will continue to write Conard County, because each book in the series is a trip back home for me.

What modern-day personality best epitomizes a WORLD'S MOST ELIGIBLE BACHELOR?

RL: Warrick Dunn, of the Tampa Bay Buccaneers. This young man not only took full responsibility for his younger siblings when their mother, a police officer, was killed in the line of duty, but he has since shown a remarkable generosity for the less fortunate. His strong work ethic, his love and devotion to family, and his generosity make him a man to be admired by anyone.

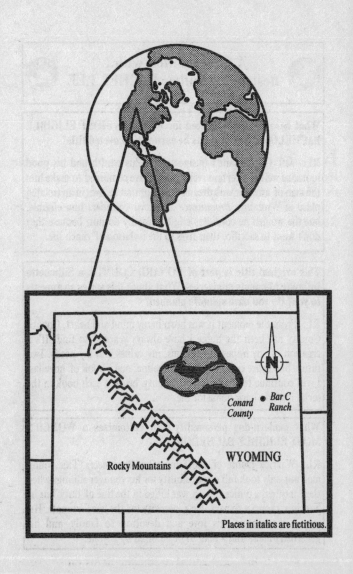

Conard County

Bar C Ranch

Rocky Mountains

WYOMING

N

Places in italics are fictitious.

Prologue

Harriet Breslin sat in her agent's office and stared at Marcie Finkelstein as if she had just suggested Harriet should go to the moon and take pictures of the Sea of Tranquility.

"It's not the moon, Harry," Marcie said, as if the thought were printed in large type on Harriet's face. "It's Wyoming."

"It might as well be the moon."

"Don't exaggerate. The moon is a quarter million miles away. Wyoming is, what—two thousand?"

"It's two thousand too many."

"It's also where they keep the hunky cowboys."

Harriet shook her head. "You can't fool me, Marcie. They have cowboys in Florida, too. What's wrong with a Southern cowboy? At least it'll be warm and I can take a bathing suit."

"If you really want, you can take a bathing suit to Wyoming, too. Look, these guys want photos of the real thing. Real cowboys, real cows, real ranches…and I don't think they'd be thrilled if palms trees got in the way."

"So I'd be careful to keep away from palm trees. They don't move or anything, you know. I could shoot around them."

"And get palmettos instead." Marcie's expression was adamant. "They specified Wyoming."

"I don't want to go to Wyoming. My God, Marcie, the last time I heard, they don't have enough people in the whole state to make up a single large town!"

"So? What's so great about people?" Marcie waved a hand toward the window. The sound of honking horns on the street below was audible even through the glass. "You got mugged out there two months ago. My best friend got beaten up in the lobby of her apartment house just last week. People are not so great. Especially when they're crowded together."

Harriet threw up a hand. "I don't believe you. Last week you said you'd die if you couldn't go to Zabars. You go to concerts and plays all the time. That's what's so great about people, Marcie. Wherever they congregate in large numbers, there are all kinds of things to do! Damn, I bet they don't even have cable TV in Wyoming. Or shrimp. You can't expect me to go someplace where I can't get shrimp scampi or Chinese food!"

Marcie frowned and pushed her dark curly hair back from her face. She drummed her fingers on the desk and blew out an exasperated breath. "I wouldn't be so sure they don't have Chinese food. Hell, you can buy bagels most places these days."

"Frozen, in the supermarket!"

"How would you know? You grew up here! You haven't been out of the city in years."

"Have you?"

"Yes! I go to Florida all the time, which is how I know about palmettos. And I went to Arizona five years ago. And I bought bagels."

"They have more people in Arizona."

"Look, Harry, it's a good job. They're going to pay very well. And they're determined that you go to Wyoming. Conard City, to be exact."

"Conard *City?* Talk about delusions of grandeur. Why does it have to be this particular place?"

Marcie reached into a drawer and tossed a copy of *Prominence Magazine* across the desk. "Look at the 'World's Most Eligible Bachelor' article."

Sighing loudly, Harriet did as she was told. The first thing she noticed was the full-page photo of a man who looked better in cowboy drag than anybody except maybe Robert

Redford. Tanned, lean, tall. Brown hair and blue eyes. She was a sucker for brown hair and blue eyes. Definitely a hunk, she admitted reluctantly.

And underneath was the caption, "Jeff Cumberland, 39, one of Wyoming's most successful ranchers." Mr. Cumberland, it seemed, had been selected as one of the world's most eligible bachelors by the magazine. On looks alone he rated, Harriet decided. But give her a JFK Jr. and NYC any day.

"So?" She tossed back the magazine.

"Keep it," Marcie said. "They like the look of the guy. They like the wild country in the background. It's the kind of stuff they want for their book covers. Romance readers *love* American cowboys."

"Romance readers must be out of their minds. This guy probably smells like cow poop."

Marcie scowled in exasperation. "Cut it out, Harry. Look, I realize the fresh air will probably kill you, and I know you don't want cow dung on your shoes, but this is a big money deal. Money, Harriet. That green stuff that keeps you supplied with film and cameras and keeps me in this office."

"Is this an ultimatum?"

"I didn't say that. But *you* could."

Harriet looked at the magazine on the desk between them and the contract Marcie had shoved toward her. "I hope this place has an airport."

"Just don't forget to get yourself a pair of boots. And look out for rustlers."

Glumly, Harriet leaned forward and signed the contract.

One

Good Lord, that was a tumbleweed! Harriet watched in amazement as the huge ball of brush tumbled slowly across the dirt road in front of her and bounced into the scrub beside the road, where it was detained by a barbed wire fence. In the strengthening wind, it bobbed in vain, trying to break loose.

The thing was half as big as the car she was driving, bigger than she had expected a tumbleweed to be, and she craned her neck as she passed, staring at it.

A sudden pothole dragged her attention back to the uneven road in front of her. She'd taken a wrong turn. Somehow she had managed to miss the intersection she was looking for, and the two-lane blacktop had become a poorly graded dirt road, barely wide enough for two small cars to pass. She had driven the last five miles hoping to come across another intersection, but she was ready to give up.

Time to turn around, she decided, and slapped her palm irritably against the steering wheel. Bad enough that she'd had to fly into Laramie and rent a car to get the rest of the way to Conard City, but this was the pits. What should have been a shortcut was taking her into the wilderness.

She hadn't seen a house for miles, not even another vehicle since she'd made that last turn. And the isolation was beginning to unnerve her. Even though she had known how under-populated Wyoming was, she had never imagined such vast expanses with no sign of human habitation except endless miles of barbed wire.

Turn around, she told herself again, then she carefully jockeyed the rental car through a three-point turn. Once she got back to the state highway, she ought to be able to find a more conventional path to Conard City.

She drove past the huge tumbleweed again and thought about stopping to free it from the fence so it could continue its journey. Then she thought of rattlesnakes and decided the tumbleweed would just have to deal with its own problem.

The sun had vanished behind the western mountains and twilight gripped the world. Night would fall before much longer. The last thing Harriet wanted was to be all alone on this godforsaken track in the dark. Five miles, she reminded herself. Just five miles back to the blacktop.

She hit a pothole that was invisible in the shadowless world, and the jolt rattled her teeth. Instinctively she glanced down at her speedometer and saw with horror that a red warning light was on.

The car was overheating. She swore and considered risking it in the hopes that she could make it back to the highway before the engine seized up. But then she came to her senses and stopped, turning off the ignition. She'd have to wait for the engine to cool down. Then maybe she could make the highway before it overheated again.

When she lifted the hood, steam poured out at her. Great. Just great.

Not only did they not have enough airports in this god-awful place, but they couldn't even maintain a rental car properly. In frustration, she kicked the tire, then leaned back against the car with her arms folded, surveying the emptiness that surrounded her.

Not good. She felt an intense yearning to be back in the city, where, if all else failed, she could walk. This was scary. In fact, it was downright terrifying. She thought of walking back to the highway, but as soon as she envisioned herself tromping down the dark, deserted track, she wondered about wolves and coyotes and bears.

Hell.

It was getting darker by the minute. In the eastern sky a blanket of stars had appeared, more stars than Harriet had ever imagined the sky held. The wind continued to blow steadily, and it was growing colder by the minute. She shivered and decided to get back in the car. At least she'd have some protection from the cold and from whatever wild animals roamed the darkness.

It was going to be a long night.

Jeff Cumberland turned off the highway onto the back road to his house. He was carrying bags of cement for the new shed he was going to put up. The steel building would be delivered next week, but he wanted to pour the slab himself to make sure it got done right.

Old Hoss, as he called the ancient battered pickup he was driving, zipped down the pavement, then bucked violently as it hit the dirt road. From time to time Jeff thought about getting himself a new truck, one with a pretty paint job and better suspension, but Old Hoss just refused to die, and he couldn't quite see his way to spending nearly thirty thousand dollars when he already had reliable transportation.

He hit a pothole, and all that kept him from banging his head on the roof of the truck was his seat belt. Better suspension, he thought. Maybe it would be worth it just to have better suspension. He could certainly afford it. At the very least he was going to have Buck bring the grader out here and smooth the damn road. In the meantime, he'd just have to slow down.

Not that he was in any big rush to get home. There was no one waiting for him, and lately that circumstance seemed to be looming large in his life.

Midlife crisis, he told himself. He was pushing forty and feeling dissatisfied with just about everything. Especially since Lisa had left with the children last spring.

Lisa was his brother's ex-wife, and after George had abandoned her and the kids, Jeff had taken them in. But one winter on the Bar C was enough to convince Lisa that life on a ranch would be the death of her. She felt too isolated, too trapped, too lost in the empty spaces of Wyoming. And she felt her children were being deprived of social interaction with other kids.

He supposed she was right, but her departure had only served to remind him of why he was never going to marry. He'd watched his mother drive his dad nearly to death with her constant complaining about hardship and loneliness, and Lisa merely proved the point: women weren't cut out for ranch life. Especially the kind of women that had always attracted him—women with interesting careers and interesting lives. Why would one of them want to be buried on a ranch?

But still, he did occasionally wish he was going home to a family. Of course, he wished for a lot of things he'd had to do without. That was just a fact of life.

He suddenly stomped on the brake, bringing the truck to a bucking halt as he saw a car off to the side of the road with its hood up. What the hell? He was about the only person who ever used this back road, and he didn't recognize the vehicle as belonging to one of his employees. Must be some traveler gone astray.

He set the parking brake and left the engine idling as he climbed out and walked over to the vehicle. His headlights were shining directly on it, but the hood blocked most of the light from getting into the passenger compartment. Dimly he could see a person inside. He tapped on the driver's window with his knuckle.

The window rolled down a bare inch. "Hi," said a woman's husky voice.

"Howdy. You havin' car trouble?"

"My engine overheated. I was letting it cool down so I could try to drive back to the highway."

Jeff shook his head, wishing he could see her better. "Let me take a look. Maybe all you did was bust a hose. If that's all, I might be able to fix it."

"Thanks."

He supposed he couldn't blame her for staying in the car while he went to get a flashlight and look under her hood. It seemed unfriendly, but she was a stranger and the world wasn't what it used to be.

It didn't take him long to figure out that a piece of duct tape wasn't going to fix the problem. The water pump was leaking antifreeze. He slammed down the hood and came around to her window.

"The car needs a new water pump," he told her.

"Well, doesn't that just figure."

He could make out that she was drumming her fingers on the steering wheel. "I can tow you into town, ma'am. I'm pretty sure they can fix you up in the morning."

"It isn't my car," she told him. "It's a rental. I don't suppose there's a car rental place in Conard City?"

"We don't have much call for one around here."

"How did I guess. Damn."

He hesitated. "If you like, I can take you into town to a motel. You can call the rental company from there. I'm sure they'll get a new car out to you."

"They damn well better. Of all the godforsaken places to have a breakdown!"

Jeff didn't especially like having his corner of the world referred to as godforsaken, but he decided not to point out her error. Instead he said, "Come on, I'll take you into town and you can let the rental company worry about the car."

Harriet watched him walk back toward his truck, apparently assuming that she would follow. He cut quite a Western image, she realized, and wished she had her camera ready to catch his silhouette against the headlights. He had an easy, loose-jointed walk, and he was a perfect archetype in his jeans, checked shirt and cowboy hat. Her clients would probably drool.

But she hesitated to follow him. All her street smarts said it would be crazy to get into a car with a man she didn't know. She'd always been reasonably cautious about such things, and since her mugging, she had become almost paranoid. On the other hand, it was highly unlikely that a cab would drive by on this deserted road in the middle of nowhere.

The man, realizing she hadn't climbed out of her car, turned around and came back. He was big, she thought with a sudden qualm. Why couldn't he have been a short, little old guy?

"Look, lady," he said, a touch of impatience in his voice, "if you want to stay out here by yourself, I'll go up to the ranch and call someone to come get you."

That didn't sound a whole lot more inviting, she realized. It would just mean another stranger.

"I can understand you're uneasy about getting in a car with a stranger," he said after a moment. "But I really don't want to spend all night out here while you think about it, so could you make up your mind?"

She had a canister of pepper spray in her purse, she remembered. Not that it had done her much good when she'd been mugged. Hell, the thing had been buried so far down under all the junk she carried that even the thief hadn't found it. But if she moved it to the top, where she could reach it quickly if necessary...

"Thanks," she said. "I'll take the ride to town."

When he saw her suitcases and camera bags, he came to help her carry them to his truck. He had to move a bag of cement to make a little space to tuck her belongings so they wouldn't fall out, and she was impressed that he didn't complain about it. The men she had known so far in her life had all been complainers. Maybe these Wyoming types were stoic. Or maybe she just hung around with the wrong men.

She climbed up into the cab, feeling sorry for him because he had to drive such an old, beat-up truck. He even had those off-the-rack seat covers, and they, too, looked pretty worn-out. Surreptitiously, she stuck her hand in her bag and felt around for the pepper spray. Once she had it, she held on to it and hoped it was still good.

The dash lamps didn't offer much light, and all she could

see of her rescuer was a strong profile against the darkness beyond the mud-spattered driver's window. Something about him seemed familiar, but she couldn't place it.

"Are you on vacation?" he asked.

"No."

He was silent for a while. "Just passing through?"

"Not exactly."

He turned toward her, and her sense of familiarity grew. "I'm just trying to make friendly conversation. Don't they do that where you come from?"

Harriet felt a hot flush sting her cheeks. He was right; she would have been friendlier with a cabdriver. "Sorry, it's been a long day."

"I can connect with that."

She supposed he could. Here it was after eight in the evening, and he was driving around with bags of cement. "I caught a 6:00 a.m. flight out of New York, had this really awful layover in Chicago, and then I had to drive out here from Laramie." She sighed. "I looked at the map, but I have to tell you, no map prepares you for the distances out here."

"I reckon." He turned onto the highway and picked up speed. "You're not the first Easterner I've heard say that."

"Probably not. Next time I'll read the mileages before I make assumptions. I should have spent the night in Laramie."

"It would have been less tiring."

"Anyway, I was already exhausted when I made that last turn. I thought it was going to be a shortcut to Conard City."

He gave a little chuckle. "You wanted the turn about two miles up the road here. I'll show you."

"Where *does* the road I was on go?"

"To my place."

His place. She imagined some ramshackle old house that would be in keeping with his truck. The Wyoming version of the South Bronx.

"So," he said, "are you just visiting?"

"I guess you could say that. I'm here on a job."

"What do you do?"

"I'm a photographer."

He looked her way quickly, and she got the definite impression he wasn't pleased. "Don't tell me you work for some damn magazine."

"No. I'm working for a book publisher." She didn't want to go into details.

"Why didn't they hire somebody out in these parts?"

"Good question." She looked out the window and thought that she had never seen a night so dark. It was creepy. "Actually, they hired me because of what I do to the photos after I take them. I do color enhancements and textures and things, so that by the time I get done, the picture looks like a painting, only more real. I can't really describe it."

"Sounds interesting. I'll bet you go to all kinds of different places."

"No, I've always done my work in the city."

"Oh. So this is a big adventure for you."

"Actually, I'd rather be anyplace else on earth."

He was silent for a few seconds. "You know, this really is a pretty good place to be. And telling people it's the last place on earth you want to be isn't going to make you any friends hereabouts."

"I don't want any friends hereabouts."

He shook his head but didn't say any more. Which was just what Harriet wanted. She *didn't* want to make any friends here, and she certainly didn't want to be given lectures on manners by some broken-down cowboy in a beat-up old truck. What would he know about manners, anyway?

She returned her attention to the dark world outside her window and decided it would be easy to develop agoraphobia out here. The wide-open spaces were daunting enough in daylight, but at night it was like looking over the edge of the world. She felt a sudden, sharp longing for the high concrete walls of the city, a place that was bright even at night. Fortress walls, she thought. The tall buildings were like the walls of a fortress. Out here, she felt as exposed as a gnat on a giant pane of glass.

Yes, city walls held dangers, but they were dangers she knew. Here she had no idea what the threats might be, and worse, there didn't seem to be any place to hide from them.

She turned again to look at the man who had rescued her and felt a twinge of conscience. She might have had a beastly day, but that didn't excuse her rudeness. And she *had* been rude. After all, her hackles rose every time she heard somebody run down New York, which was a lot nicer than most outsiders thought.

By way of apology, she offered a conversational opening. "I had no idea there were so many stars."

He kept his gaze fixed firmly on the road. "It's something, isn't it? The sky out here is so dark and deep, sometimes you can get dizzy looking up into it."

Harriet nodded and wondered how she'd managed to hook up with a poetic cowboy. "It feels like looking over the edge of the world."

He looked at her then and smiled. "I like that. That's exactly how it feels. There's nothing better than lying back on your bedroll and staring up at the stars until you feel like you're falling...." His voice trailed off, as if he were embarrassed to have said so much.

"I'd probably spend the whole time worrying about bugs in the grass."

He shot her an amused glance. "You don't look that fastidious."

His use of the word *fastidious* caught her attention. Apparently he was a well-read cowboy.

"After all," he said, "rumor has it they have cockroaches as big as mice in New York City."

"I think you're confusing us with Florida. My pet roach isn't any bigger than my thumb."

He laughed at that, a comfortable, hearty sound that caused

her to smile. All of a sudden, the Wyoming night didn't seem quite so strange or lonely.

"Here we are," he said a few minutes later. "Conard City, Wyoming."

Harriet looked out the window, waiting for the big event. She wasn't sure exactly what she had expected, but it wasn't this. They drove down what appeared to be the main street, past houses, then past shops that were already closed for the night. The traffic lights—there were only two on the entire street—were blinking red.

Almost before she knew it, they were on their way out of town, passing a stockyard and railroad terminal.

"That was it?" she heard herself ask.

"It's all we need."

"You sure don't need much."

"What more could you want?" he asked, a faint edge in his voice. "We've got a supermarket, a movie theater, two hardware stores, a department store, a couple of diners and a community hospital...."

"I'm impressed," Harriet said, letting him take it however he would.

"You should be. We've only got five thousand souls."

Harriet stifled a sigh and hoped that twenty-five hundred of the five thousand were cowboys, or she was going to have a devil of a time finishing this assignment.

"Here we are," he said, swinging off the road into a half-empty parking lot.

Harriet looked at the Lazy Rest Motel with glum resignation. Beyond any shadow of a doubt, there wouldn't be room service. She just hoped she didn't spend the night fighting bedbugs.

"Not what you're used to, I'm sure," the man said. "But it's clean. Lucinda makes sure of that."

"Lucinda?"

"Lucinda Schultz. She and her husband run the place."

"Oh."

He climbed out and began to heft her luggage and equipment out of the truck, setting it carefully by the front door of the motel office. "You can manage by yourself now, right?"

Harriet's voice grew sharp. "Of course I can!" After all, she survived in New York all by herself. It wasn't as if checking into a motel were beyond her capabilities.

But he didn't respond to her tone. "I'll say good-night then, ma'am." He touched a finger to the brim of his hat, climbed into the truck and, with a spray of gravel, disappeared down the highway.

She hadn't even thanked him, Harriet realized with sudden discomfort. Feeling unbearably frustrated, she stomped her foot on the gravel. He'd been disapproving of her from the start, and now she'd given him good reason for his attitude.

But what the hell did it matter? she asked herself. He didn't matter at all. He was just some country cowpoke, and she'd never see him again.

A middle-aged woman with hair the color of iron sat behind the desk. She looked up with a warm smile as Harriet staggered through the door with her bags and equipment.

"Can I help you?"

Harriet dropped her suitcase, then lowered her camera equipment with considerably more care. "I'd like a room for the next couple of weeks, if that's possible."

The woman rose and came to the edge of the desk, where she placed a white card and a pen. "You poor dear, you look as if you've had a terrible time of it."

"I'm just tired," Harriet answered, warming to the woman's ready sympathy. "I've been traveling all day and my car broke down."

"What a shame."

Harriet gave the woman her credit card, then began filling out the registration card. "Is there any place I can get a meal nearby?"

"Right across the highway at the truck stop. They serve

round the clock. Pretty good food, too, if you like home cooking.''

Home cooking. That could be anything from watery omelets to hamburger stew. Oh, well. She accepted her credit card back and tucked it away.

"If you have any complaints about your room," the woman said, "just call and let me know. I'm Lucinda."

"I'm sure there won't be any trouble. The man who gave me a lift said you keep a clean place."

Lucinda beamed. "I pride myself on it."

Clean or not, the room gave Harriet the willies. The rough-hewn wood walls were probably considered to be Western in style, but the floor was bare wood planking, and the bed looked old enough to have been retired several generations ago. The chintz curtains on the window were homey but hardly reassuring. Apparently the Lazy Rest didn't redecorate on a regular basis.

The bathroom, however, was spotlessly clean, even if the fixtures were old. For thirty bucks a night, she could hardly complain. The bed, old as it looked, proved to be comfortable enough. For two weeks, she could handle it.

Then she set out to find food, wishing like mad she was just heading around the corner to Weissman's deli.

This morning, if anyone had told her she would be eating at a truck stop tonight, she would have laughed in his face.

TWO

Harriet awoke in the morning determined to improve her attitude. What did it matter that she was stuck in a small town in the back of beyond? She didn't have anything against hick towns, and anyway, the world was probably full of people who would love an all-expenses-paid getaway to the middle of nowhere. Her last boss had been one of them. How many hours had she spent listening to him talk about escaping to a mountaintop aerie where he wouldn't have to see another human being unless he wanted to?

She looked at herself in the bathroom mirror and shuddered. Overnight her short blond hair had taken on a punk style, sticking up in spikes every which way. Her blue eyes looked bloodshot enough to belong to a wino. Groaning, she turned on the shower and stepped beneath the hot water.

So she should count her blessings, right? So maybe it wasn't a trip to Miami, or better yet, Venice, but it *was* a trip. New sights, new sounds, new people, a complete change of pace. That practically made it a vacation.

She could live without scampi, the corner deli and Chinese food for a couple of weeks. She'd managed to live without all that stuff back when she'd been a starving beginner, right? At least until desperation had made her take a regular day job with a boss who spent ninety-five percent of his time thinking about escape.

And here she was, on a major assignment, a moderately successful, self-employed photographer. Should she cry because it wasn't a safari in Kenya? Hell, she'd have had to do without a lot more than Chinese food and the deli if she'd been sent there.

So count your blessings, Harry, she told herself sternly as she ruthlessly scoured the travel dust from her body. There were blessings, and she could count as well as anyone. What was a little scampi?

Scampi she could live without, but the car was another matter altogether. She had a feeling she wouldn't catch many cowboys in their natural habitat without wheels. Of course, she could always rent a horse, she supposed. That was probably easier than renting a car around here.

Except that the thought of riding a horse made her turn green. The one and only time she'd ridden had been at summer camp the year she turned thirteen. The horse had hated her on sight and had managed to throw her—breaking her pelvis and putting her into the hospital for six weeks. Her hip still twinged at the memory.

So horses were out of the question, even if they were the usual mode of transport here. Which they probably weren't.

She sighed, turned off the water and grabbed a towel, drying herself vigorously. Something warned her that she'd better shed her John Wayne-Clint Eastwood notions of the Wild West. People in Conard County probably depended on cars, not horses. Especially since she doubted they had anything as civilized as taxis, city buses or subways.

Which didn't solve the problem of the broken rental car.

She dressed in her usual work outfit of khaki slacks, blue pullover and a many-pocketed safari shirt, which she kept unbuttoned unless it grew chilly. Then she sat on the edge of the bed and dialed the number of the car rental company.

They were, as expected, so sorry that she had had a problem, but no amount of sorry could get her a replacement car before the late afternoon. They were a whole lot less pleasant when she told them she didn't have any idea where the broken car was because she had taken a wrong turn and a stranger had brought her into town.

"This is *not* acceptable, Ms. Breslin," the manager told her. "We can't give you another car until we know what you did with the first one!"

"I didn't *do* anything to it! It did it to me. Anyway, I'm sure somebody out here can tell you where it is. Why don't you check with the cops? They've probably driven past it a couple of times."

"No, Ms. Breslin, *you* check with the police. Get a local garage to tow it in. We'll pay the bill. The new car will arrive this evening, but it won't be turned over to you until you can provide the whereabouts of the one you rented."

"Look, you don't have to treat me like a criminal!"

"I'm not treating you like a criminal. But you did accept the responsibility of returning that car to us. Nowhere in the lease does it say you can abandon it any old where and expect us to hunt it up!"

He had a point, Harriet thought as she slammed down the phone, but it didn't make her feel any better.

Lucinda Schultz suggested she walk into town for breakfast. "It's really not that far, miss, and it's a nice day. You can get a far better breakfast at Maude's than anyplace else around."

Lucinda obligingly sketched a map on a piece of scratch paper and marked both Bayard's Garage and the sheriff's office. Harriet figured she could hit the sheriff, find out if anyone had seen the car, have breakfast, then go to Bayard's to see if they could find the vehicle and tow it in. All very efficient— if walking a couple of miles could be considered efficient.

But she was a city girl, and she was used to walking to the places she wanted to go, and city blocks could quickly add up into miles. She had on a pair of sturdy walking shoes, and the weight of the cameras around her neck and rolls of film in her pockets was something she hardly noticed anymore.

It was a fine September morning. The air was clear and wonderfully dry, drier than she was used to in New York. It invigorated her and put a spring into her step.

She passed the railroad station and cattle pens, which reeked

of manure. Maybe this place didn't look as bad as parts of
New York City—how could it with a background of slate-blue
mountains topped by a light powdering of snow—but it beat
anything in the city for stench, except when there was a garbage strike.

Despite the odor, she found herself stopping to take pictures.
The pens were picturesque with a cattle car in the distance
and the mountains behind. The station itself looked as if it had
been built in the last century and warranted another series of
shots.

Farther down the road she came to a residential area populated by small, slightly ramshackle homes with old vehicles
in the driveways. The wrong side of the tracks, she thought
with amusement.

Next she came to Bayard's Garage. It was on the corner of
the main street and a cross street that hadn't been paved. Right
between the bays and the door to the office, a huge old shade
tree grew. The leaves were already turning yellow, but that
hadn't prevented a couple of old men from setting up a folding
table and playing dominoes, even at this early hour of the
morning.

Harriet paused to ask if she could take their picture. They
assented eagerly, scrawled their signatures on a release, then
gave her toothless smiles. She snapped a photo, then asked
them to go back to playing their game while she took a couple
more.

Just as she was about to resume her stroll, a tow truck pulled
up dragging a blue rental car that looked all too familiar.

Harriet stopped and watched as the driver deftly backed the
car into a parking slot. When he climbed out of the cab, she
approached him. "Uh…I think that's my car." She wondered
if he was planning to sell the thing for scrap or chop it up for
parts.

The man stopped and looked at her, taking in her cameras.
He probably wasn't much older than forty or forty-five, but
he was grizzled-looking and dressed in grease-stained overalls.

"Could be," he said. "I guess you're the lady photographer from New York."

"That's me. What are you doing with my car?" She sounded suspicious and saw a frown crease his brow.

"Jeff called this morning, said he gave you a lift last night."

Harriet nodded, feeling her suspicions ease.

"Anyway, he asked me to tow the thing into town since the rental company will probably want it back."

Harriet couldn't help herself. Suddenly she smiled. "They were kind of insistent about that."

He turned his head aside and spit tobacco juice into the dirt. Harriet closed her eyes a moment, telling herself she hadn't seen that. But of course she had, and hell, she'd seen far worse in the city. Somehow, though, out here in this clean, clear air, the spitting seemed more repulsive.

"Figured they would be." He stuck out a large hand. "I'm Dirk Bayard."

She shook his hand and resisted an urge to wipe her palm on her slacks. "Nice to meet you. Harriet Breslin."

"Well, Miss Harriet, I'm just going to park the car here until they come get it. I reckon they'll pay for the tow, and maybe they'll want me to fix it so they can drive it back. Whichever, there ain't no need for you to be worrying about it."

"Well, thank you very much! I really appreciate it."

He shrugged and gave her a slight smile. "That's what neighbors are for. Now, you get into town and get Maude to make you a nice big breakfast before she puts the eggs and bacon away and starts making lunch. Be sure to get the home fries. That dang woman might have the mouth of a poison snake, but she makes the best dadburn home fries in the whole state."

Harriet thanked him again and headed into town, wondering how he had known she was headed to Maude's. Must've been a good deduction, given that she'd stayed at the motel last night, she decided. Surely Lucinda Schultz wouldn't bother to call anyone with the information. On the other hand, maybe Dirk Bayard had just been making a friendly recommendation.

She was being entirely too suspicious. Reminding herself to take a positive attitude, she walked past the sheriff's office and turned onto First Street toward Maude's diner.

When she got there, she discovered it was actually called the City Diner, but since it was the only diner around, she assumed it had to be the place everyone called Maude's. Inside, it was full of people and bursting with delicious smells that instantly made Harriet's mouth water. Maybe it would be easier to live without fresh bagels than she thought.

There was a vacant booth near the back, and she slid into it, aware that all eyes had fixed on her as she wended her way through the room. It was something like being in a fishbowl. New Yorkers in a similar situation wouldn't have even looked up, but then New Yorkers were surrounded by strangers.

A large, gray-haired woman approached. "I'm Maude," she said. "You must be that photographer gal from New York."

Harriet stared at her in astonishment, but Maude didn't explain how she'd heard. The woman slapped a menu down with as much panache as if she were throwing a gauntlet.

"You can get anything on the breakfast menu," Maude continued, "but I ain't cookin' lunch for another hour yet. If you don't like your eggs runny, tell me so, because I don't want to be throwing them away. If'n you don't like sourdough, don't order the flapjacks. Blueberry syrup is homemade. Coffee?"

"Uh...yes, please." Feeling a little overwhelmed, Harriet decided perversely that she liked this blunt woman with her sour expression. "Mr. Bayard says you make the best home fries in the state."

Maude snorted. "He damn well better. I make the best home fries in the *country*. Pepper and onions, that's the secret, plus frying them right. You want home fries?"

"I'd like to look over the menu first."

Maude gave her a nod and stalked away toward the coffeepot. Harriet gave her attention to the menu, thinking she might actually enjoy the people around her.

"Don't mind Maude," said an unfamiliar voice.

Harriet looked up to see a handsome middle-aged man in a sheriff's uniform standing beside the booth. He had dark, graying hair, friendly eyes and a weathered face.

"I'm Sheriff Nate Tate," he said. "Mind if I join you for just a minute?"

"No, not at all."

He slid in across from her just as Maude returned with Harriet's coffee. She slammed the steaming mug down and looked at Nate. "You want coffee, too, I suppose."

"If it wouldn't be too much trouble, Maude," he said, a hint of amusement in his tone.

"Well, you coulda told me that before I got all the way back across the room."

"Maude," he said in a wounded tone. "Do I ever come in here when I don't want some of your fine coffee? I thought you had it all figured out by now."

The woman harrumphed and stalked back to get another cup.

"Don't mind her, like I said," Tate said with a smile to Harriet. "She grumps and growls, and if she got in a fight with a bobcat my money would be on Maude, but she's all right. Just don't tell her anything you don't want broadcast from one end of the county to the other."

"I like her."

His smiled widened. "I guess you New Yorkers are used to all kinds of characters."

She looked at him, shaking her head. "Does everybody in town know who I am and where I'm from?"

"Probably." He chuckled. "Except we don't know your name yet. Only because Lucinda hasn't been on the phone much this morning."

"I'm Harriet Breslin."

He nodded. "Nice to make your acquaintance. From what Jeff told me, you had some car trouble."

"My, word *does* get around."

He laughed again. "Like wildfire. We all know just about anything there is to know about one another, so when a stranger comes to town, it's like getting a new show on TV after a season of reruns. Everybody's interested."

"And the law checks them out?"

He shook his head. "That's not why I'm here. I just wanted to introduce myself so you know we're here if you need anything. And maybe I can give you some information you need. I take it you're here on a job?"

"That's right. Photos for a publisher to use on book covers."

He smiled. "I bet they want the real Wild West."

She had to smile. "Cowboys. Hunks."

He leaned forward a little, resting his elbows on the table. Maude slapped a mug of coffee in front of him before he could speak.

"Are you ready to order?" she asked Harriet.

Harriet glanced quickly at the menu. "Um…I'd like to try the pancakes and some of your homemade blueberry syrup, please."

Maude nodded, then looked at the sheriff.

"Nothing for me, thanks. Marge topped my tank with a huge breakfast this morning."

"Bet you still got room for a jelly doughnut. Never knew a cop who didn't."

Nate shook his head and patted his stomach. "I'm trying to protect my waistline."

"Can't imagine what you need it for," Maude snorted. "You're too old for the pretty young things, and too damn married besides." She stomped away, leaving Nate looking rueful. Harriet had to stifle a laugh.

He shrugged and looked at her with amused eyes. "It would

never occur to her I'm trying to keep my waistline for my wife.''

Harriet grinned.

"But back to the subject at hand,'' he said. "Cowboy hunks.'' He shook his head. "We got a few of 'em around, but you can't always judge a book by its cover.''

"What do you mean?''

"There're two types of cowpokes. There's the guys who grew up around here and do what their daddies did before them. They don't make much money, but when they come to town, they cut up for all it's worth—stay away from the road-houses on payday, by the way. Things can get pretty wild.''

She nodded. "I didn't plan to visit them at any time.''

"Good. As for the other type—well, they're drifters, not too trustworthy. They work when they have to and hang around between times getting into more than their share of trouble. Shiftless. They do the work because it's easy to get a job when the pay's so lousy.''

"There are always people like that around.''

He nodded, regarding her steadily. "And no way to tell them from the next guy. But they're the types you're most likely to run into, unless you hang out around the bigger ranches. The bigger places tend to pay better and keep people a lot longer. Step over to my office after breakfast and I'll give you a map and show you the best places to look.''

"Why, thank you!''

"Least I can do. I suggest you talk to the ranchers first. I'm sure some of 'em will be glad to help you out. Besides, you don't want to be trespassing and getting in the way of work.''

"No, of course not.'' And that, she thought, was the real reason he was here, to warn her about trespassing. She wondered what they did to trespassers around here. Shoot them?

"You won't be able to see much from the road, anyway.''

"I suppose not.''

He smiled. "We're getting on to the time of year when the ranchers are going to round up the cattle and bring them down from high pastures. You ought to be able to get some really good pictures."

Maude returned with the pancakes and syrup and pointedly put a jelly doughnut down in front of the sheriff. "Call it lunch," she said shortly, and walked away before he could say a word.

"She's a real character," Harriet commented, looking after her.

Nate Tate sighed. "Damn the woman. If I don't eat it, she won't speak to me for a week. I don't suppose I could persuade you to take it."

Harriet glanced down at the huge stack of flapjacks in front of her and shook her head. "I won't be able to eat half of what I've already got."

"I swear Maude is on a mission to make every last living soul in this county as big as a barn. Cheap good food, and plenty of it. It might be okay if I were a ranch hand, but I spend too much time sitting behind a desk these days." Nevertheless, he bit into the doughnut.

The pancakes were perfect and the blueberry syrup was delicious. Ravenous, Harriet dug in with great pleasure. The restaurant had begun to empty out, and it wasn't long before Nate excused himself, as well, reminding her to come to his office for the map. She thanked him again and watched him walk away, thinking that he would make a great subject for one of her photographs.

And he hadn't mentioned a word about rustlers. Boy, was she going to rub Marcie's nose in that. At least rustlers would have offered the possibility of some excitement. She had a strong feeling this job was going to put her to sleep.

Three

Harriet slept through most of the day. She blamed it on having nothing to do in such a small town, but Lucinda insisted it was just her body trying to get used to the higher altitude—and lower levels of oxygen.

The next morning was bright, cool and sunny, the kind of day that Harriet felt she could become addicted to. She breakfasted at Maude's again, this time having ham and eggs, then set out in her new rental car, a four-wheel-drive Jeep. Apparently the car rental company felt she needed something more rugged to get around in her current neck of the woods.

Armed with the map Nate Tate had given her, she set out for the Bar C Ranch, where Nate felt she was likeliest to find what she wanted.

"Cumberland's an obliging type," he'd told her. "He'll probably go out of his way to help you."

She hoped so.

The last few miles to the Bar C were down another empty narrow county road. It seemed strange to drive for miles and not see another car. Almost as soon as the thought formed, Harriet came upon a small group of men loading cattle onto cattle trucks pulled off to the side of the road.

Slowing down, she took a better look, surprised at how easily the cows—or maybe they were steers—allowed themselves to be shepherded up the wooden ramp and into the truck. She also got an eyeful of cowboys. They weren't exactly the cowboys she'd had in mind, but some touch-up would fix the problem with paunches and no chins.

She drove on past them, keeping in mind what the sheriff had said about checking first with the ranchers before taking pictures. But a half mile up the road, she turned around to go back. She wouldn't do anything to interfere with their work, she told herself. And when they were done, she'd ask if they'd sign a photo release. But while they were working she could get some great shots, and she couldn't imagine that those dusty cowboys would mind having their pictures taken.

She parked the Jeep about fifty yards away from the cattle trucks, not wanting to be intrusive. She had a good telephoto lens that would make the pictures look like close-ups. After she uncased her camera, she climbed out of the Jeep and checked the settings and the light. Moments later she was taking pictures almost as fast as she could snap the shutter.

She'd taken a whole roll when she noticed one of the men walking toward her. Not good. She'd stopped their work. But no, two of the cowboys were still loading the cattle as rapidly as they could. Maybe this guy was just curious about what she was doing.

Harriet lowered her camera and smiled at him.

"What're you doing?" he asked. Too roughly, she thought, but maybe cowboys were rough types.

"Taking pictures," she told him pleasantly. "I'm out here on an assignment to get photos of cowboys at work. I hope you don't mind. What you're doing looks so interesting."

He was standing within two feet of her now, and she looked up at him, thinking that while he had a good chin, his narrow, beady eyes would disqualify him from hunkdom. But with a little computer work… Her mind was already spinning ideas for transforming this rather unpleasant-looking man with a square chin into something women would drool over.

"Give me the film."

She gaped at him, hardly believing her ears. People only said that in movies. "But…but why?"

"You didn't ask if you could take our pictures. We don't want 'em taken. How many rolls did you use?"

"Just this one...." She gestured with her camera, wondering how she could talk him out of this. Not that it mattered if his mind was made up, because she wouldn't be able to use the pictures without his consent.

He reached out and grabbed her camera, yanking it hard enough to snap the leather strap around her neck. She stumbled, feeling the back of her neck shriek a protest. Then something clobbered her on the side of the head, and everything went dark.

Harriet's head ached as if it were gripped in a vise, and her shoulders throbbed and burned. Feeling sick to her stomach, she wanted to roll to the side and vomit, but when she tried to move, she realized her arms were tied to the fence post behind her. Groaning, she opened her eyes and winced at the bright light. The sun had risen much higher and seemed to glare off the tall brown grasses that formed a barrier between her and the rest of the world. Dizziness swamped her, and she closed her eyes again, waiting for it to pass.

Gradually she became aware of more than her pain and nausea. She felt the skin on the side of her face prickle with the early stages of sunburn, felt the sharp stalks of grass beneath her cheek, heard the wind soughing gently through the grass.

She had to get untied. A shaft of panic speared her as she realized she could die here, tied to this fence post, only a few feet away from the road. No one would be able to see her through the tall grass, and chances were that by the time the barbed wire fence needed fixing, she'd be nothing but bleached bones picked clean by buzzards.

Some were already circling overhead, she realized as she opened her eyes again and twisted her head to look up at the sky.

She pulled at her bonds, feeling her wrists grow raw as they twisted against the stiff, rough rope. Those bastards had done this on purpose, she thought, her anger growing to white heat.

They'd left her here to die of exposure and thirst and were probably laughing about it as they drove away.

She tried to wiggle into a sitting position in hopes that she would become visible from the road, but that only tightened the ropes around her wrists. Finally she lay back down and began to pull against her bonds with all her might. If she did nothing else, she was going to break free just so she could go to the Bar C and tell its owner exactly what she thought of the men who worked for him.

She had no idea how long she struggled. It seemed like hours but was probably no more than twenty or thirty minutes. Just as she was about to give up, she gave a last mighty tug and felt one of her hands slip free.

Sobbing with a sudden rush of relief, she sat up and looked at her unbound hand. As she'd expected, it was rubbed raw and bleeding in places. It hurt like the dickens, too, but she figured it would hurt even more when the adrenaline wore off.

Feeling another surge of anger, she twisted around so that she could look at her other hand. It, too, was rubbed raw. Hardly caring that it hurt, she struggled with the knot, breaking two nails in the process, until finally she worked it loose and freed herself.

When she tried to stand, dizziness swamped her again, causing her to grab on to the fence post. Damn it, she thought. She had to get away from here in case those creeps came back to finish the job.

The pounding in her head eased a little and she straightened all the way. So far so good, but the car, which was only ten or fifteen feet away, looked as if it were at the far end of a football field.

Her head continued to pound as if there were a loose anvil rolling around in it, and her wrists throbbed and burned with increasing persistence. When the earth tilted again as if it were floating on stormy seas, it occurred to Harriet that she probably needed medical attention. But first she needed to get out of here.

Staggering like a drunken sailor, she managed to make it to the car without falling. She sank gratefully onto the seat and waited for her shakiness to ease.

Boy, was she going to have some words for the man who had hired these jerks. Another wave of anger cleared her vision and she switched on the engine. A three-point turn proved difficult to accomplish when it hurt to turn her head, but she managed it. But she drove slowly to the Cumberland place, figuring that she couldn't really trust her reflexes. Besides, her eyes kept jumping around, as if they didn't want to focus on anything.

It was a relief when she found the turnoff, just as Nate had described it. With each passing minute her simmering anger seemed to cool down, giving way to fear about her own condition. But before she asked somebody to take her to a doctor, she was going to have words with the man who employed such criminals.

Sharp words. Her tongue was going to leave him feeling skinned.

Jeff Cumberland sat at the desk in his large office, running over the week's payroll. A bookkeeper handled everything, but Jeff made a point of checking up on the books once a week. A few years ago a woman had tried to embezzle from him, and since then he'd made a practice of watching the accounts with an eagle eye.

But, God, it bored him. There were a dozen other things he'd have been happier doing, such as riding the range or taking his first skydiving lesson—still a week before he could do that—or just getting into his plane and buzzing around.

He stifled a sigh and focused on the green account sheets. That was life, he told himself. The have-tos always came before the want-tos.

"Mr. Jeff?"

His housekeeper, Sylvia Applegate, stood in the doorway of his office, holding the door open. "What is it, Sylvia?"

"There's a young lady to see you. I don't know what's wrong, but she looks like she's been in a terrible accident and she insists on talking to you."

A number of possibilities occurred to him—first among them that a tourist had probably climbed into one of the bull pens and had had to run for her life. It wouldn't be the first time some idiot had failed to realize that bulls could be dangerous. As it was, he had a hard time keeping the local boys out of the pens. They'd get sauced up and dare one another.

"Can she walk?"

Sylvia nodded. "She drove up in her car. But she's kind of shaky."

"Maybe you should call a doctor."

"Not until she sees you, she said." Sylvia shook her graying head. "Something bad happened to her, all right."

Jeff hesitated, then decided to go out to meet the woman. He rose. "You go back to whatever you were doing. I'll take care of her."

Sylvia nodded and vanished.

He found the woman sitting on the oak deacon's bench in the foyer. She was a mess all right, with scraped-up hands and dried grass tangled in her hair. But when she turned to look at him, he recognized her and shock caused his heart to slam.

"My God, what happened to you?"

"Your men hit me over the head, tied me up and left me to die!"

"My men?" His shock ballooned.

"You're Mr. Cumberland, aren't you? The owner of this place?"

"Yes, I am." It was apparent to him that she didn't connect him with the man who had given her a lift the other night. Of course, judging by the bruising on the side of her face and the slight bruising around her eye, he imagined she had a concussion. It was a wonder she'd managed to get here. "I'm Jeff Cumberland, but my men don't do things like that."

"Hah! All I did was stop to take some pictures of them

while they were working. On *your* property, I might add. If that's the kind of hooligans you hire—''

''I don't hire hooligans,'' he said shortly, anger knotting the pit of his stomach. ''And if my men did this, they're going to be facing criminal charges.''

''I should hope so!''

''Where were they working?''

''Along the road back there.'' She gestured with a raw hand and winced. ''Damn, my camera. I forgot about my camera! What did they do with it?''

''Along the road? How far back?''

''A mile. Maybe two. I don't know. It was hard enough to concentrate on just driving here....''

''What were they doing?''

She blinked at him as if he were stupid. ''Working. Then they beat me up.''

''I mean what kind of work?''

''Putting cows on trucks.''

''Hell and damnation!'' He turned, grabbing his hat from the coat tree beside the deacon's bench. ''Damn rustlers...''

''Rustlers?''

''Rustlers!'' He slammed the cowboy hat on his head and headed for the door. ''I don't have anybody loading cattle for transport right now. Nobody. And if they were working on my property...'' He left the thought incomplete and turned to look at her. ''You stay here and let my housekeeper call a doctor for you.''

''No!'' She stood up and grabbed for support as the world started to spin. ''I have to look for my camera!''

''If I find it, I'll bring it to you.''

''No! Besides...besides, I can show you where it happened.''

He hesitated, then called, ''Sylvia! Sylvia!''

''Yes, Mr. Jeff?'' The housekeeper looked down at him from the gallery above.

''I'm going out to look into some rustling, then I'll take

this lady to the hospital. Tell Dean I probably won't be back until suppertime.''

"Okay.''

Reaching out, he took the woman's arm to steady her. "Come on. What did you say your name is?''

"I didn't. It's Harriet. My friends call me Harry.''

"That's right. Harriet. Come along, Harriet. And watch your step.''

When she saw the battered old green pickup truck, she remembered him. "You gave me a ride the other night!''

"That's right.'' He opened the door and helped her climb in on the passenger side. "It's beginning to feel like a habit.''

He moved around the front of the truck and climbed up beside her, then drove more slowly than was his wont, mindful of her injuries. "What in the name of heaven is a young woman doing wandering all by herself in isolated places?''

"I told you,'' she said truculently. "Taking pictures. What's a big rancher like you doing driving this rusty old pickup?''

"It runs,'' he said shortly. "You shouldn't be wandering around all by yourself. Things could happen.''

"Things *did* happen. Hey, it's supposed to be safer here than on the streets of New York. How was I supposed to know you were going to get rustled? I thought that only happened in movies.''

"It happens all the time, and it *is* safer than the streets of New York out here.''

"You can't prove it by me. I was mugged two months ago, but that's the only thing that's ever happened to me, and I've lived there most of my life. I've only been here two days and already somebody tried to kill me! I'll take New York, thank you very much.''

He figured she would. Women weren't much for isolated, wide-open spaces. Must be a nesting thing, he thought. They wanted the security of caves.

"There!'' She lifted a sore hand and pointed. "That's where my car was parked.''

"I see the spot." He could also see the marks left by big cattle trucks backing up to the pen. He wanted to slam his hand on the steering wheel in frustration but restrained himself, figuring the gesture might frighten her after what she'd been through.

He stopped in the middle of the road, not wanting to mess up any of the tracks. "You stay here while I look around. We don't want to destroy any evidence before I get the sheriff out here to take a look."

"Okay, but see if you can find my camera, please?"

He nodded. "Glad to."

Harriet leaned her head back and watched him from beneath lowered lids as he walked alongside the road, pausing frequently to look toward the fence and pens. She felt as if her nausea were at last subsiding, and the world didn't seem to be rocking quite so much, but her head still pounded. Every little sign of improvement heartened her, though.

She hadn't been nearly as sharp with Cumberland as she had wanted to be, but something about the man made her reluctant to read him the riot act. It wasn't that he intimidated her, because he didn't.

No, she assured herself, she wasn't afraid of him. Maybe it was just because she felt so rocky right now. Angry or not, she didn't feel up to getting involved in a verbal duel. In fact, she wasn't all that angry anymore. She was too tired to be angry, too pained to rustle up the energy.

And wouldn't Marcie die laughing when she heard that Harry'd had a run-in with rustlers.

Jeff returned a few minutes later, carrying her camera. Harriet sat up eagerly, reaching for it, then gave a dismayed cry when she saw it. "They smashed it!"

"I'm afraid so." He climbed in beside her.

"Do you know how much a really good Leica costs? And where am I going to get another one out here in the middle of nowhere?" She clutched it to her breast, forgetting her other pains for the moment as she tried to absorb the dimensions of this catastrophe. Her Leica. The best camera she had ever had, one she cared for like a baby. The camera she had scrimped and saved to be able to afford.

"I'm sorry," he said.

She barely heard him, she was so upset. She had the sudden feeling that she was watching her entire life being sucked down into a huge black whirlpool.

"I'm taking you to the hospital," Jeff said.

"No…" She looked at him then, but hardly saw him as she battled with tears. "No, really. Just the doctor. I don't have insurance.…"

"Don't worry about it. But I think you have a concussion and you need to be kept under observation."

"Don't worry about it! That's easy for you to say. I don't have that kind of money."

He glanced over at her. "Let's just see what the doctor says, all right?"

"I need to go back and get my car. I can drive myself."

He shook his head. "Are you always this argumentative? I'll have somebody from the ranch bring your car into town. And you're in no condition to drive yourself. Look at you. It's a wonder you're not still unconscious."

Arguing was taking too much energy. Besides, she didn't think the hospital would take her as a patient once they heard she didn't have medical insurance. Deciding that would settle the whole issue, she gave in to her fatigue and allowed her eyelids to droop closed. Why was she so very tired? she wondered drowsily…then slipped off.

Harriet roused to find herself being lifted out of the truck onto a gurney. "I can walk," she said querulously.

"No need to, miss," said a soothing voice. "You just let us handle everything."

She looked up into a smiling dark face that evinced gentleness, causing her to relax.

"That's the way," he said. "We'll have you inside in no time."

The world seemed to spin again, but not so much because of her head as because of the effortless way she was lifted and settled onto the gurney. She was rolled up a small incline, through pneumatic doors and into a short hallway. She wondered if she would have to wait hours to be seen, as she would in any city emergency room, but hardly had she formed the thought when she was wheeled into a curtained cubicle. Moments later, a woman doctor stepped into the room.

"What have you been doing?" she asked pleasantly. "Arguing with a truck?"

"Some guy beat me up," Harriet told her.

"That would explain it. I'm Dr. Renee Wilson, Ms. Breslin. Are you having any dizziness or nausea?"

"I was. The nausea's gone, though. The dizziness I'm not sure about."

The doctor nodded. "How long were you unconscious?"

"I'm not sure." She thought back. "Maybe an hour or so?"

"That's not good. It'd be my guess you have a pretty nasty concussion here. We're going to need to take X rays at the very least, and then do some neurological testing. Don't worry. Nothing will hurt."

"But I don't have insurance."

Renee Wilson smiled at her. "Sure you do. You were injured on Bar C property. That's all the insurance anybody needs."

Puzzled, Harriet watched her walk out of the room, but before she figured out exactly what the doctor had meant, she drifted off again.

The rest of the day passed in a miserable blur. Every time she drifted off, someone was there to call her sternly back to wakefulness. They wouldn't even give her anything for her headache, which made her wonder what use all these medical people were.

Finally, after a series of tests and X rays, she was deposited in a private room and asked to sit up in a chair.

"You can't sleep," the nurse told her. "You're drifting off far too easily and we have to keep you awake for at least twelve hours."

"Buy why?" Harriet asked plaintively.

"Because you've had a serious concussion. Your drowsiness is cause for real concern and might indicate some bleeding in your brain. We have to keep you awake and functioning so we know instantly if things are getting worse."

"But I'm so tired...." She sighed the words, not really arguing.

"I know," the nurse said sympathetically. "But maybe we can do something to help. Do you like to play cards? Checkers? Or the two of us could put together a jigsaw puzzle."

Harriet chose the jigsaw puzzle, figuring it would interest her a lot longer than cards or checkers—assuming she could focus on the pieces.

But her eyes didn't seem to be as bad as they had been earlier, and she didn't feel dizzy any longer, so she and the nurse sat facing each other over a table and talking casually as they tried to assemble pieces.

During the early evening, Nate Tate showed up, greeting her with a smile.

"Jeff Cumberland tells me you had quite an adventure this morning."

The nurse excused herself and Nate settled in the chair across from Harriet. "Well, little lady, you look like you got some rough treatment."

Harriet didn't like being called "little lady," but the way the sheriff said it took some of the sting away, and she let it pass. "I was knocked out and tied to a fence post."

Nate nodded. "You've got a pretty good shiner there. Bad concussion?"

"Bad enough they won't let me sleep."

He tsked. "I'm real sorry about that. Jeff says they were rustlers."

"That's what he told me. I suppose you want to know about it."

"It would be a real help."

She settled back in her chair, blinking away another wave of drowsiness. "There were three men and three cattle trucks. Big ones. Now, since I'm a city girl, I don't know whether they were bigger than usual or just average for cattle trucks."

He smiled at that. "Don't worry about it. They were separate cabs and trailers, though?"

"Yes. Definitely. And as big as the semis you see on the highway."

He nodded and wrote in a small notebook. "It's a big operation, then. Those trucks don't come cheap. Were any of the trucks loaded when you saw them?"

She thought about it. "I think so. Two of them. They were loading the third one. I didn't pay much attention, since I was more interested in the cowboys. For my pictures," she added, in case he misunderstood.

"Of course. Did you get close to these men?"

"Not until one of them walked up to me. I guess I was standing between forty and fifty yards away when I started taking pictures."

"So you could describe only the one man to me?"

"Oh, no, Sheriff. I saw them all plainly through my telephoto lens. As clear as if they were standing right in front of me."

"Well, hot damn. If I have an artist come by in the morning, could you help her draw pictures of them?"

"Sure, I'd be glad to."

At that moment, Jeff Cumberland walked in carrying a shopping bag. He greeted the two of them and perched on the edge of the bed that Harriet hadn't been allowed to get into.

"Good news, Jeff," Nate said. "Ms. Breslin says she saw

all the rustlers clearly. She's going to help Esther draw pictures of them.''

"That's great!" Jeff looked genuinely pleased. "Thanks, Harriet.''

"I want to see these men in jail as badly as you do," she said.

He smiled. "Probably even worse. I lost some cattle today, but that's not personal. What they did to you was.''

"It sure feels that way.''

"I reckon so," Nate said. He rose, holding his hat in his hand. "I'll have some more detailed questions in the morning. Maybe you can recall something else about the trucks after you've thought it over. As it is, they're probably half the way to Omaha by now.''

Jeff shook his head. "I don't expect to see those steers again, but I intend to make damn sure they don't take any more. I'm going to round up early.''

"Might be a good idea." Nate said good-night and left.

Jeff came to take the seat Nate had vacated. "I got something for you," he said, passing the bag to her.

"You shouldn't have!''

"It's the least I can do.''

Harriet tried not to look at her bandaged wrists as she pulled the bag open and took out the first of two large boxes. What she saw made her gasp.

"It's a Minolta," he said apologetically. "The guy didn't have any Leicas, but he said this is as good. He also said he can fix your camera. The lenses aren't damaged, by the way, and he figures he can have it ready in about a week. Will that be okay?''

Harriet was almost too stunned to speak. "Oh…oh, you shouldn't have. Really. It's so expensive.…''

"It's nothing," he said uncomfortably. "I feel responsible, you being assaulted on my land and all. Besides, you have a job to do.''

She stared at him. "But you *weren't* responsible.''

"It happened on my land," he said stubbornly.

Harriet leaned back in her chair and studied him thoughtfully. "Are you a closet romantic?"

He looked startled, then laughed. "What makes you say that?"

"This is so...so quixotic. I was just wondering if you joust with windmills, too."

He smiled. "No, but I mean to joust with some rustlers if I can find their hairy hides."

For the first time that day, Harriet actually felt like laughing. She repressed the urge, though, because her head still hurt. "I'd like a turn myself."

"I bet you would." He hesitated. "Nate said you were coming out this morning to ask my permission to take pictures around the ranch."

"I was."

"Well, that's fine by me. When you get out of here, we'll set it up. With the roundup, you ought to get lots of good shots."

"Thanks. Is it going to cause a problem, rounding up early?"

"Not really. The lower pastures are in pretty good shape, and it's only a difference of a week or so, anyway. But I want to make sure those guys don't get any more of my head. And I want to know just how big a bite they've taken out of me. I have a feeling this wasn't the first time they pulled this operation."

"They were certainly brazen about it. I mean, there it was, broad daylight. Anybody could have come along."

"Most people would figure they were working for me."

"Like I did."

"Like you did," he agreed. "The people who would have known they were up to something bad are all my employees, and they were too busy working to be running down that road at midmorning. Nope, those rustlers figured it pretty well. And it's a whole lot easier to load those trucks by day than by night.''

"I guess it makes sense, then. But I couldn't imagine doing something like that when anybody could see me." She gave him a little smile. "Me, I'd go for the darkness."

"I probably would, too. Not that I'd ever pull a stunt like that."

"No, you seem entirely too honest and upright." She gestured to the camera. "I don't know of anybody else who would have felt responsible for what happened to me, or who would have tried to make it right like this."

He shrugged, looking embarrassed. "Like I said, it's the least I can do."

She could tell the discussion was making him uncomfortable, so she turned her attention to opening the box and admiring the camera. It was a beautiful piece of equipment, top of the line, with every feature she could have asked for and a couple she would probably never need. He had also bought her a telephoto lens to fit it and a wide-angle lens. There was even a bag full of various filters. "This is incredible."

He shrugged again. "I just asked the guy at the camera shop what a real professional would need and want. I don't know much about it. My picture taking is pretty much limited to snapshots, and I don't even do much of that."

"Why not?"

"Well, there isn't a whole lot I want to take pictures of, and nobody who'd want to see them. Although I did take a bunch of snapshots of the archaeological dig."

"What dig?"

"Oh, the university runs a site on my land. I found some arrowheads and other stuff out there a few years ago, and they came in to take a look at it. They're finding out all kinds of interesting stuff about the people who camped there over the last eight thousand years."

"Eight thousand years. I can't begin to imagine it."

"The site's right near the creek, so I guess it was a favorite campsite. Apparently it was used over and over again. And there's a couple of guys running around looking for dinosaur bones. Wouldn't surprise me if they find them.''

"I hear there are a lot of those around here.''

He nodded, looking comfortable for the first time. She decided archaeology must be a hobby of his.

"They've found a few really good sites. No reason to think they won't find more.''

"I guess not. What are they finding at the campsite?''

"They found some early burials. The bones were taken to the reservations for reburial. Some cooking pots. Some beads that suggest there was a wide trading network even seven, eight hundred years ago. It's amazing to me how much you can tell from the things that were dropped in and around a campfire or buried with a body. The beads they found were turquoise that had to have come from a certain place in New Mexico. The clay in a couple of the pots is not native, either, so they're trying to trace its origin right now.''

"That's fascinating.''

He smiled. "It sure is. Would you like to go out to the site someday when you're better?''

For some reason, Harriet caught her breath. It was just a casual invitation, she reminded herself. It didn't mean anything. It *couldn't* mean anything. She'd be going home in a couple of weeks, and he wasn't her type anyway. "Sure,'' she said.

She had absolutely no idea what she was letting herself in for.

Four

Harriet continued to improve throughout the night. Her dizziness was gone, although not her desire to sleep. When the doctor finally told her it was okay to sleep, she crashed.

She heard the nurses come and go throughout the next day, but hardly stirred more than it took to turn over and go back to sleep. When she awoke in the early evening, there were flowers on the bedside table. The card said they were from the Bar C.

The sheriff stopped by again, this time with a lovely auburn-haired woman he introduced as Esther Nighthawk.

"We came by this morning, but you were zonked," Nate said. "Figured we'd try again this evening."

"They kept me up all night," Harriet said by way of explanation. She reached for the control and raised the head of the bed so she could look at them.

"That'll do it all right," Nate agreed. "Esther is an artist, and she's going to sketch those guys you saw, if you feel up to describing them."

Harriet had gotten enough sleep by now to feel a spark of her original anger. "Anything I can do to help, I'll do. Anything. I want those creeps behind bars."

"So does Jeff," the sheriff said. "He figures they must have made off with close to a hundred head yesterday. He's also wondering how many other times they pulled this stunt this summer."

"Surely somebody would have noticed if large numbers of cattle kept turning up missing."

"You'd think so, wouldn't you. Except with as big an operation as Jeff is running, and as spread out as his cattle get in summer pastures, it's not always easy to know."

"I guess. *Prominence Magazine* listed him as one of the state's biggest ranchers."

Nate grinned. "I wouldn't be mentioning that article to him if I were you. He didn't want to do it, but the city commission kind of twisted his arm. They thought it would be good for the county and wanted to know why he was afraid of a little bitty picture. So he did it. Since that magazine hit the stands, he's been getting calls from women all over the world. A couple of 'em even turned up at his front door. He's not really happy about it."

"I can imagine." Harriet smiled, having a sudden vision of Jeff Cumberland barricading his doors against hordes of determined fortune hunters.

"It'll settle down," Nate said. "The magazine will feature some lawyer or doctor or business tycoon next month, and nobody'll remember Jeff Cumberland."

Harriet spent the next couple of hours with her head bent close to Esther Nighthawk's as they worked on the sketches of the rustlers. The sketches Esther drew had a lot more detail and vitality than the sketches Harriet had seen in the newspapers.

Of course, Harriet was an artist, too, with a fine eye for detail developed during all her work with retouching and enhancing. That probably contributed quite a bit to the lifelike sketches that Esther produced.

"Good job, ladies," Nate pronounced as he studied the finished product and Esther began to pack up her materials. "It's as good as a photograph would have been.

"By the way," he said to Harriet, "Jeff asked me to tell you your car is in the visitors' lot in front of the hospital. And the medical bills have been taken care of. He says it's the least he can do."

Harriet didn't know whether to be annoyed or grateful. The man took a lot upon himself, but the truth was, she had no idea how she would have paid those bills herself. "He seems to do an awful lot and call it the least he can do."

Nate nodded. "That's the way he is. The man has a big heart, Ms. Breslin. A real big heart."

As soon as the sheriff and the artist were gone, Harriet reached for the phone and used her credit card to call Marcie Finkelstein at home.

"You'll never guess where I am, Marcie."

"Mmm..." Marcie drew her response out, sounding mischievous. "You've been abducted by a sheikh with oodles of oil wells."

"Nope."

"Okay. You've run off to the Caribbean with a billionaire businessman."

"I wish. Try again."

"You fell in love with an ax murderer on death row."

Harriet sighed. "Close enough, I guess."

Marcie's tone changed. "What's wrong, Harry? Cow dung on your boots? You want to elope with a cowboy?"

"Actually, I'm in the hospital."

"Good God!" Marcie sounded shocked. "How in the world did you manage that?"

"I had a run-in with some rustlers."

"You're kidding, right?"

"I wish."

"Oh my God, Harry! Are you all right?"

"I look like I did a couple of rounds with the heavyweight champion of the world—whoever he is."

"Oh, Harry! They beat you up?"

"Well, I got a concussion, I have a gorgeous black eye, and one side of my face is about twice as big as normal. I figure I could get myself cast as the monster in a horror movie."

Marcie clucked sympathetically. "But it's not serious, is it? I mean...you're going to be all right?"

"They'll probably parole me in the morning. But you know, Marcie, this wasn't one of your brighter ideas."

"Are you blaming *me* for what some rustlers did to you?"

"I'm blaming you for sending me to the ends of the earth! I wanted to turn down this assignment, if you remember."

"Right. I remember. But I don't remember the part about how you were going to pay your rent if you didn't take this little job. Don't be a whiner, Harry."

"I'm not whining! I'm complaining. There's a difference."

"Really? I guess something must be wrong with my ears."

Harriet seethed. Marcie could be so…so…*unsympathetic.* "Have you no heart?"

"I have plenty of heart. And I really do feel awful for you, Harry. I'm also beginning to wonder how you do it."

"Do what?"

"I haven't known many people who manage to get themselves mugged twice in the space of two months."

"That's because most people who get mugged once have the sense to stay at home with their doors bolted and don't go running off to the wilds of Wyoming."

"Wyoming is hardly wild. Empty, yes, but wild, no. I imagine you can't find one other soul out there who's been mugged by a rustler."

"I don't know. I haven't taken a poll."

"I don't believe it's an everyday occurrence."

Harriet refused to give ground.

"How did it happen, anyway?"

"Oh, you know. The usual. I just stopped to take some pictures of these men who were loading cattle onto trucks by the roadside, and for some reason I just can't fathom, one came over, beat me up, smashed my camera and left me tied to a fence post to die."

Shock silenced Marcie for a moment. Then she said briskly, "Well, I still don't understand how you do it. You got attacked by those swans the time you—"

"Hey, wait a minute! Swans are nasty birds. Very aggressive."

"Right. And then there was the time the pigeons dumped all over you when you were taking photos of that new fountain."

"Pigeons dump. There were thousands of them."

"Mmm. And what about that time on the Staten Island Ferry—"

"Oh, for heaven's sake, just shut up, Marcie. You'll have me convinced I'm jinxed."

"Aren't you?"

Harriet fell into a seething silence.

"Anyway," Marcie continued, "you're going to be all right, aren't you?"

Harriet spoke between her clenched teeth. "Presumably."

"But what are you going to do without a camera?"

"The rancher on whose land I was hurt was kind enough to buy me a new one."

"So you'll get the job done. Good."

"Marcie, you're inhuman."

"No, I'm not. Trust me, I'm worried about you. I'm also worried about what will happen to you if this contract doesn't get fulfilled on time. The client was very insistent that the deadlines be kept, because they have deadlines, too. There's no leeway here, Harry. If I tell them you can't perform on time because your camera is broken—"

"How about mentioning I have a concussion?"

Marcie sighed. "They'll just give the contract to someone else. Since you're arguing with me, I have to assume that you're not that sick, so naturally I'm worried about whether we can keep our part of the agreement."

"Oh, I'll keep it, all right."

"I knew you would. Especially since failure to perform involves some pretty expensive penalty clauses. It's time for a stiff upper lip, Harry. I'll break out the tea and sympathy when you get back."

"Gee, thanks."

Marcie's brisk tone softened. "I really am sorry this happened to you," she said. "I was hoping you'd have a lot of fun doing this job. It looked so simple and straightforward."

"Mmm."

"Maybe this rancher who bought you the camera will help out. He must have tons of cowboys working for him."

"I'm not feeling too kindly toward cowboys at the moment."

"I expect not."

"Oh, heck," Harriet said. "Forget it. I *was* whining. I'm not usually a whiner."

"No, you're not. But I can't say I blame you, not when you're so far from home. I'd be whining, too. Take care, Harry. And don't mess with any more rustlers."

With those words of caution, Marcie disconnected. Well, what had Harriet expected? Marcie wasn't her mother, after all. She was hardly going to fly into hysterics and insist that Harriet come straight home. And she wouldn't have been doing her any favors if she had.

"Knock, knock."

She looked up from the gloomy contemplation of her hands and saw Jeff Cumberland standing in the doorway. "Hi."

"Mind if I come in?"

She gestured with her hand, indicating the chair. "Take a load off."

He smiled and sat. "I wanted to tell you that your car is parked in the visitors' lot out front."

"The sheriff told me. Thank you."

"You're welcome. How are you feeling?"

"Not too bad, actually. My headache's almost gone."

"That's good."

An awkward silence filled the room. "It's nice of you to stop by," Harriet finally said. She hated awkward silences. "And don't tell me it's the least you can do."

He laughed quietly. "Well, it is."

"And I still say you're not responsible for what happened to me." That sounded ungracious, so Harriet amended her statement. "I appreciate your concern, though. I guess nobody's found out anything?"

"Not yet. I saw the drawings you helped Esther Nighthawk with. They're very good, Harriet. It ought to be easy to pick those guys off the street."

"If they're stupid enough to walk down the street around here." She wanted to get out of bed and sit in the other chair, but she was wearing a hospital gown that opened down the back. Keeping the sheets modestly tucked around her, she sat up cross-legged. "I'm jinxed, you know."

"How so?"

"Every time I do a major commercial shoot, something goes wrong. I was hired once to do an advertising campaign for a cigar manufacturer. Some dweeb account executive thought it would be great to have this hunk in a three-piece suit photographed smoking a cigar on the stern of the Staten Island Ferry, silhouetted against the skyline. I managed to fall overboard."

"How did that happen?"

She shrugged. "I was off balance, leaning to one side over the rail to get the angle just right. They'd even turned off the engines so the vibrations wouldn't ruin the pictures. Somebody bumped into me and the rest, as they say, is history." She shuddered. "I don't even want to think about how dirty that water was."

"It could have happened to anyone."

"Right. Ruined the camera and film, too. Then there was the time I was on a shoot at the airport. You know the setup—busy executive striding down the concourse, briefcase in hand, expensive coat draped over his shoulder."

"I can see it."

"Yeah. Clichéd, huh? Well, there was a bomb threat, and security took me in to search because of my cameras and bags. Time is money so they got someone else to take the shots."

"Too bad."

"Mmm. Of course, not everything winds up with me losing the job. There was this one where they wanted a kid walking down this freshly poured concrete sidewalk, leaving his little footprints behind. The stuff was pretty well set, so the kid just left these tiny footprints. But I wasn't watching, and I stepped to one side and went right into a wet spot up to my ankle." She shook her head. "I got the picture, but it took two people to pull me out and I lost my favorite hiking boot."

"You do have some interesting luck."

"Oh, I've got all kinds of stories. I was bitten by a dog. Scratched in the face by a supposedly friendly parrot. Rained on during an outdoor fashion shoot on a day when there wasn't supposed to be a cloud in the sky." She shook her head.

"But this doesn't happen *every* time you do a commercial shoot, does it?"

"No. I'd be out of work if it did. But count on me to be the first person attacked by rustlers in recent memory."

"Well, we can turn your luck around a little bit. Why don't you come out to my ranch the day after tomorrow. We're rounding up the cattle and you should get lots of good pictures of cowboys doing cowboy things."

"If I show up, you'll have a stampede."

"I don't think so. My men are better at their jobs than that."

"You hope." But it would sure make things easier for her, she thought. "Thanks a lot. I think I will. Maybe I can get this job done in a couple of days instead of a couple of weeks."

"If you feel up to it, you might even come out tomorrow afternoon. My men should be bringing one of the herds into the lower pasture around midafternoon. There might be some good opportunities."

"Maybe I'll do that." For the first time, she was beginning to feel positive about this assignment. "This is great! I can't thank you enough."

He rose, brushing aside her gratitude. "I have only one proviso. No pictures of me."

"Fair enough."

After he left, she wondered why he was so camera-shy. And then she wondered how she could get him to change his mind. He was exactly the kind of hunk *she'd* want to see on a book cover.

Appalled at herself, she cut off that train of thought. No. Absolutely not. She wasn't going to dally with some hick cowboy, even if he did own the ranch.

Five

The Bar C Ranch looked deserted when Harriet arrived there the next afternoon. The other day, after she'd been attacked, she had vaguely noted people moving around near the barns and corrals, but today no one was in sight. There weren't even any horses in the corrals. Everyone must be busy on the roundup, she thought.

The door was answered by the same gray-haired lady who had answered it before. This time, however, the woman smiled at her. "Miss Harriet! How are you feeling? Mr. Jeff told me what happened to you. It's a terrible, terrible thing!"

"I certainly thought so." Harriet returned her smile. "Mr. Cumberland asked me—"

"To come out and take pictures of the roundup." The woman nodded. "He told me. I'm Sylvia, by the way."

"Nice to meet you, Sylvia."

"Why don't you come on in and have a cup of tea? I've got something on the stove I need to take care of before I drive you up to the pasture."

Harriet followed the housekeeper across the polished wood floor of the foyer, down a narrow hallway and into a gleaming kitchen that would have done a small hotel proud.

"I'm making fudge," Sylvia said as she motioned Harriet to take a seat on a stool at the center island. "Those boys do love their sweets, particularly after a day in the saddle. Of course, nobody has an appetite like a hardworking cowboy."

"Except maybe a construction worker."

The older woman laughed. "Them, too. And roustabouts. I

worked for a while in Gillette feeding those oilmen when they came in from drilling. Talk about appetites.''

"How long have you been here?"

"Oh, maybe twenty years, I guess. It's the best job I ever had.''

She put a cup of steaming water in front of Harriet along with a couple boxes of tea bags. Harriet chose an herbal blend.

Sylvia stirred the fudge gently and checked the candy thermometer. "Won't be long now.''

"I don't know why, but I thought this pasture would be near the house.''

"At one time it would have been, I expect, but Mr. Jeff's mother didn't care for the smell of cattle, so his father built this house on a parcel of land that was too poor for grazing. Wasn't until after she died that Mr. Jeff even brought the horses down here.'' She shook her head. "That woman was a piece of work. I can't think of anything more inconvenient than having to drive to get to your horses. The cattle are one thing, but the horses?''

Harriet didn't quite know how to respond to that. "I guess. I'm surprised that a woman would marry a rancher if she couldn't stand the smell of cattle.''

"Nobody was asking her to have them right outside the window. Nobody wants *that* smell in their faces all the time. But she claimed she couldn't even stand a whiff of it.''

"A hard woman to please.''

Sylvia glanced her way and nodded. "She wasn't a happy woman.''

"That must have been hard for Jeff.''

"He never complained. But I can still remember him coming home after working all day and her telling him he smelled like a pig and to get into a bath before he came anywhere near her. It got so he was taking his showers in the bunkhouse and changing before he got home.''

Harriet thought that was a little excessive and said so.

Sylvia nodded emphatically. "But I'm talking out of turn.

I will say there weren't too many tears shed the day she passed on. Except for Mr. Jeff, of course. He loved her dearly. But then, she was his mother.''

She bent again to look at the candy thermometer. ''Another minute or two. It always takes longest for the last little bit.''

''I hate to take you away from your work like this.''

Sylvia laughed. ''There's nothing so pressing it can't wait a little while. It's a good excuse to get outside on a beautiful day. That's one thing I have to say for working on a ranch. Nobody minds if I run outside for a while. Sometimes I even take one of the horses for a ride. Mr. Jeff is easy to look after, of course, and that helps.''

Harriet sipped her tea. ''Delicious. Do you cook for everybody, then?''

''Not quite everybody. We've got a couple fellas who go home to wives and kids, but I cook for the ones who are living in the bunkhouse. It's not as hard as it sounds.''

Harriet couldn't imagine it. No wonder this place had a kitchen like this. ''Cooking for three or four is about my limit.''

Sylvia checked the thermometer again, then removed it from the pot, setting it on a spoon holder. She lifted the pot and began to pour the thick chocolate mixture onto a huge, buttered cookie sheet. When she finished, she put the pot in the stainless steel sink and filled it with water.

''There, that can wait,'' she said. ''Just let me get a sweater. The breeze can get chilly this time of year when it blows off the mountains.''

They drove a couple of miles along a rutted track, past stands of cottonwoods and open expanses full of browning grasses. Finally they pulled over near a large fenced area with a wooden chute leading into it.

''They should be here soon,'' Sylvia said, glancing at her watch. ''Mr. Jeff's going to bring them from over there.'' She pointed to the left. ''Then tomorrow they're going to run them through this chute, count them, and check them for disease and injury. I think this herd is all steers. If it is, he'll probably be shipping them out to feedlots within a week or so."

"Why doesn't he just keep them here all the time?"

"Economics. Grazing is better in the high pastures in the summer. More cattle can feed in a smaller area. It's cooler, the growth is thicker, and there's more water. Once he brings them down here, it won't be long before he has to start feeding them, especially this time of year. There won't be much new growth now. In the spring he lets them graze out the new growth, then moves most of them up again."

"But they can't stay up there all year?"

Sylvia shook her head. "Winters are bitter around here, and worse up there. He'd have to feed them whether he kept them here or there, and it's a whole lot easier to feed them down here."

The day was quiet. Harriet was still having trouble with the silence. She could hear the wind blowing through the grass and an occasional birdcall, but that was it. She was used to a far noisier environment, and it seemed almost eerie to hear nothing but the wind.

Desolate, she thought. This place is desolate.

The mountains looked as if they had more snow on them today than the last time she had seen them. The white sprinkling had turned to a thicker coat in the last few days. And Sylvia had been right. The breeze blowing off them was chilly.

It wasn't long, though, before she felt a rumble in the ground, and then a dark, moving stream became visible in the distance.

"Here they come," said Sylvia needlessly.

Gradually the moving stream began to resolve into individual shapes. Harriet was able to pick out cowboys on horses riding at either side of the flowing river of cattle. From time to time, one of them would wave his hat.

As they came closer, her amazement grew. She hadn't imagined so many steers. In her mind she had envisioned maybe fifty head, but there were hundreds, possibly even a thousand head of cattle moving toward the pens. And this was only a part of his holdings?

It suddenly struck her that there was a reason Jeff Cumberland had been featured in *Prominence Magazine*. And no wonder he thought it possible that the rustlers might have taken more cattle without him being aware of it. Nobody could count thousands of the beasts on a regular basis.

She climbed out of the car with her cameras, took the cap off her telephoto lens and climbed up onto the fence railing of one of the pens. From there she had an unobstructed view of the approaching herd, and she began to take photographs of the riders and their charges.

Most of the cattle seemed content to move in a steady forward direction, encouraged by two riders at the head of the herd. Every now and then, however, a steer would wander a little away from the rest. A cowboy would cut away and drive it back, his cow pony doing most of the intricate work involved in convincing the steer to rejoin the herd.

She'd heard about the value of a good cow horse, but now she was seeing it, and it was breathtaking. The cowboys themselves seemed to be almost part of their mounts, bending and twisting easily with the horses' movements.

These men, she thought, were highly skilled and graceful. Talented.

As they drew closer, she was able to get better shots of the cowboys, and she was sure she'd be able to use at least some of them. One of the leading cowboys was Jeff, and she found herself taking pictures of him, even though she'd agreed not to.

They were just for her, she assured herself—and then wondered why she should want pictures of him. *Because he was beautiful in the saddle,* she assured herself. He was a handsome man, and she realized now that she'd been stubbornly refusing to notice that fact since they first met, probably because he wasn't her type. She preferred three-piece suits to checkered shirts and jeans. Unlike many of her friends, she had never swooned over the cigarette cowboys.

But Jeff...well, to be honest, he was a man to turn any woman's head. And reluctant as she was to admit it, she liked his bronze, weather-hardened face a whole lot better than the softer, paler city faces she was used to.

Don't be stupid, she told herself, and trained her camera elsewhere. It wasn't long, though, before her lens found Jeff again. He looked as if he'd been born in the saddle, she found herself thinking almost dreamily. And there was no mistaking the athleticism in his movements. Alarm bells started clanging in her head, but she ignored them.

It didn't matter whether she thought he was a beautiful figure of a man. It didn't matter how it made her feel deep inside when she watched his powerful thighs ripple as he tightened them around his horse. It didn't matter that he had an incredibly broad pair of shoulders. Nope, that was all window dressing. She was too mature to fall for that.

But it didn't hurt to enjoy the view.

As the herd and riders drew closer, she got a number of great action shots of Jeff and the others. Then, suddenly, the riders changed direction and began to steer the herd in a circle. Slowly, lurching a little like a vehicle with uncertain brakes, the herd came to a milling halt.

Harriet took a few more shots, then looked up from her viewfinder to discover that Jeff was riding toward her. Inexplicably embarrassed, as if she'd been caught doing something she shouldn't, she began to fumble a fresh roll of film into her camera.

"Hi there." He reined his horse to a halt in front of her.

The horse was big, and it was too close for Harriet's comfort. When it turned to nuzzle her leg, she forgot she was sitting on a rail and jerked backward. Only Jeff's quick reflexes saved her from tumbling. He caught her elbow and steadied her.

"You're not comfortable around horses?" he asked with a surprise that sounded almost like disapproval to her.

"I'm a city girl, remember?" Annoyed by her reaction as much as by his comment, she tugged her elbow from his grip. "My one previous encounter with a horse ended with me spending six weeks in a hospital with a fractured pelvis."

"Ouch." With a gentle nudge of his heels, he moved his mount a few feet away so she didn't feel quite so intimidated. "You need to get over that. Horses are wonderful creatures."

"Why bother? I'll only be around here a couple of weeks, and as long as I avoid the mounted patrol, I'll never have to deal with one in New York."

Something in his face seemed to alter subtly, but she couldn't read the change. "I guess so," he said. "Well, go on taking whatever pictures you want. I told my men what you're here for, and they all said they'd be glad to cooperate. If you can hang around a little while, you can come take pictures back at the stable."

"Thanks, I will." She supposed she could stand being near horses that long—as long as she could use her telephoto lens. "I really appreciate your help."

His expression unreadable, he touched a finger to the brim of his cowboy hat. "Glad to be of service, ma'am."

Then, with a nudge of his heels, he rode back to join the other cowboys and the milling herd.

"Once burned, twice shy, huh?" Sylvia said.

Startled to realize the housekeeper was standing at the fence to her left, Harriet looked down at her. "I guess so."

"That's the way it is." Sylvia nodded to herself. "Mr. Jeff, he's given up on women, I think. He always went for those highfalutin career types from the city, and not a one of them was going to give up her career to live in the boonies."

"I can kind of understand that."

"I s'pose." Sylvia leaned against the rail, looking out at the cowboys and the herd. "I'm not one to recommend a woman ought to give up everything for a man. God knows, enough of us get left high and dry with a passel of kids.''

"All too often.''

"And a lot of women need a career to feel good about themselves.''

"We certainly do. I know *I* do.''

Sylvia nodded. "Nothing wrong with that.''

"But why doesn't he look for a woman around here?''

Sylvia shrugged. "Beats me. Maybe it's because he knows them all too well.''

It was hard for Harriet to imagine living in a place where you knew everybody. Not that she didn't have her familiar little community in New York. She knew most of her neighbors and even had friends she'd grown up with. But every day brought any number of new people across her path. Out here that was probably rare. The thought made her shudder. The boredom would kill her.

Of course, excitement was overrated, she admitted glumly. Her last few relationships with men had been lousy. The type of man she was attracted to was driven to succeed in his career—much as she was. Unfortunately, those same men were self-centered, thoughtless and often downright childish. Their idea of a woman was somebody who could subsume herself in their careers. Somebody who would be there whenever they wanted, would look decorative on their arms and generally exist only to please.

Harriet wasn't like that. Needless to say, her relationships had been full of conflict, and the last one—well, the last one had left her feeling skinned alive.

Brett had seemed different at first, but she should have known better. He simply had a polished line and knew what women wanted to hear. By the time she realized that he talked the talk but didn't walk the walk, she'd been in over her head and clutching desperately at anything to preserve the relationship.

Well, that didn't matter now, she told herself without quite believing it. Demons would ice-skate in the netherworld before she gave another man her heart.

As if they realized their long trek was over, the cattle were beginning to spread out. They separated from the larger group into smaller groups, wandering farther and farther away as they grazed hungrily.

"Let's go on back," Sylvia said. "They're just talking about how they're going to handle the head count tomorrow. They'll be coming back to the stable before long."

Harriet took a couple more pictures of the changing scene, then followed Sylvia to the car.

Back at the ranch house, she asked Sylvia if she thought it would be all right for her to wander around outside.

"I don't see why it would be a problem," Sylvia assured her with a smile.

The day was absolutely perfect, Harriet thought as she walked around the outside of the huge house. Dry, cool, breezy. She couldn't have asked for better. Flower beds had been carefully tended all the way around the house. Sylvia must have planted those, Harriet thought. It didn't strike her as the kind of thing a rancher would do himself.

Out back there was a huge vegetable garden, apparently so important to the ranch that an underground sprinkler system had been installed along the rows. Healthy tomatoes climbed stakes, cucumbers spilled in profusion from their vines, spinach, radishes, carrots and lettuce filled other rows. Late though it was in the year, the garden was producing with vigor. Harriet wondered if Sylvia canned the produce, too, or if it was all eaten by a mob of hungry cowboys as soon as it was picked.

The barn was a big steel building that housed horse stalls and equipment. Beside it were stacked the bags of cement that had been in Jeff's truck the night he'd given her a ride. Behind the barn, a level area had been cleared and staked out, probably for another slab of concrete.

Farther along the path, past a stand of trees and brush, she found another house and wooden barn, both old but in good condition. Probably the original, she thought, remembering Sylvia's story about Jeff's mother. The barn was painted red and the house a fresh white.

Someone lived there, she realized when she saw the laundry hanging on a line behind the house. Someone with little kids, to judge by the diapers and rompers. A yellow dog came running up to sniff at her ankles, wagging its tail with almost frantic friendliness. A woman's voice came through an open window, singing a children's song. Then she heard a child's gleeful shriek.

And all of a sudden, Harriet felt sad.

Turning, she headed back to the big house, telling herself she was just homesick. She wanted to be home in her cozy little apartment, where the farthest she could see was the building across the street. This place was simply too wide-open for her taste.

Jeff and the others were riding up to the corral and barn by the time she got back, and she took some close-ups as they cared for their mounts. At this rate, she'd be able to go home early. She told herself that was a good thing.

Just as she was finishing another roll of film and trying to decide whether to take any more photos, the sheriff's Blazer came crunching to a halt nearby. Nate Tate climbed out and smiled at her.

"Just the lady I was looking for," he said. "I thought you might be out here."

He offered his hand and she shook it. "Did you catch them?"

"Not exactly." He turned to greet Jeff, who walked over to join them. The two men exchanged a handshake.

"Did you catch them?" Jeff asked, echoing her question.

"No, not exactly," Nate repeated. He put his hands on his hips and looked from one of them to the other. "Actually, what we have is a body."

"A body?" Harriet and Jeff queried in unison.

"Yep. Murdered."

Harriet was used to reading a daily litany of murders in the newspapers, but this was different. This time she might actually have talked to the victim. Her stomach felt queasy as it filled with fluttering butterflies. "You're sure he was murdered?"

"A bullet hole—well, actually, three of them—is pretty unmistakable."

The corner of Jeff's mouth lifted, and to Harriet's amazement, he looked more excited than dismayed. "The plot thickens. Are you sure it was one of the rustlers?"

"Well, that's what we need Miss Harriet for. To identify him. I'd also appreciate it if you could come take a look, too, Jeff, in case you know the guy."

"Sure." The prospect almost seemed to please him.

"We don't get all that many murders around here," Nate remarked. "We sure don't get a whole lot of bodies dumped by the roadside."

"Maybe there was a falling-out among the thieves," Jeff suggested.

"Maybe. Can the two of you come with me right now?"

"Sure," Harriet said, when what she really wanted to do was tell him there was no way on earth she was going to look at a corpse, particularly one that was all shot up and hadn't yet experienced a mortician's magic.

Jeff nodded. "I'll follow right along. Let me just tell Sylvia I won't be here for dinner." He looked at Harriet. "I'll take you to eat at Maude's afterward."

"If I can still swallow."

Nate shook his head. "It won't be pretty, I'm afraid. I wish I could tell you otherwise."

Their small caravan of cars headed toward town as the afternoon sun began to sink toward the western mountains. Harriet drove right behind the sheriff, and Jeff followed in his battered pickup.

That pickup, Harriet thought, must say something about the man, but she wasn't sure what. He had to be wealthy. *Prominence Magazine* wouldn't have featured him otherwise. So why wasn't he driving some great big shiny truck with chrome roll bars, dozens of extra lights and a flashy paint job? In her experience, men loved their cars more than their wives, children and pets. They slavered over high-performance sports cars and lusted after expensive options as if a car defined them.

So if a car defined a man, what did Jeff's say about him? That he didn't care about appearances, only performance? That as long as the truck did what he needed it to do, he couldn't see the point of wasting money on a replacement? Or did it say he was embarrassed by his wealth?

From what she vaguely remembered of the *Prominence Magazine* article, he was a self-made man who had turned around a failing ranch. Nobody should be ashamed of that.

They reached town at suppertime, and the streets were quiet, as if everyone were indoors, gathered around their tables. New York was never quiet, Harriet found herself thinking. Except maybe very early on a Sunday morning. Then the streets could be almost eerie. But any other time there was a continual ebb and flow of crowds. The caravan continued through town until they reached the county hospital and pulled into the parking lot.

Harriet climbed out of her car and looked at Nate. "I thought I just got out of this place."

He laughed. "Sorry, but the morgue is here, too."

The morgue was an adjunct of the hospital pathology lab, and the hospital pathologist, who only worked there part-time, doubled as the medical examiner. He wouldn't be coming until later in the week, so for now the body was in the cooler. Apparently they didn't have much call for this type of thing because there were only four refrigerated drawers.

"We've only had all of them full once in my memory," Nate remarked. "It was a bad auto accident."

The antiseptic smells were sharp, but they didn't quite cover a nauseating odor that Harriet couldn't identify. At Nate's request, a young man in blue scrubs opened the drawer.

A sheet-covered body slid out on a long tray. The first wave of near panic struck Harriet then. She *didn't* want to do this. She had the worst urge to turn and run.

She didn't think she had a thing about corpses. She'd seen a few in her day, but they'd always been nicely laid out in a coffin, and except for an excessive amount of makeup that tended to make them look more like pink wax than real people, she hadn't thought much about it one way or the other. But this was different. She knew instinctively that it was going to be different, and she wanted to get out of here now, before she saw something she'd never be able to forget.

"Are you all right?" Jeff asked.

Harriet looked up from the sheet-draped corpse and realized that both of them were watching her with concern. "I don't know," she said frankly. "I don't want to do this."

"I don't blame you." Jeff reached out and put a hand on her shoulder. "How messed up is he, Nate?"

"Not messed up at all in the face," the sheriff answered. "He was shot in the torso. But he's not going to look very real, Harriet—ashen and waxy because all the blood has run out of his face. He's a little swollen because decomposition had started by the time we found him, but it's not so far along that it's gruesome."

Jeff squeezed her shoulder. "Pretend it's makeup for a horror movie."

"Oh, hell," Nate said, "it's not even as bad as that."

"It's the idea of the thing," Harriet countered.

Both men nodded, but neither of them offered her an out.

"We need to know," Nate said finally. "It's not that we can't identify him, but we need to be sure whether he was one of the rustlers or not."

Harriet closed her eyes a moment and drew a deep breath. "Okay."

Nate pulled the sheet down, uncovering only the man's face.

She stared, swallowing hard. "That's him," she managed to say, and turned away quickly. "That's the guy who hit me."

"You're sure?"

"Absolutely. I remember that scar beside his eye."

"Thanks. Jeff?"

"I'm not sure. I have the feeling I've seen him somewhere before, but damned if I can remember."

"Okay."

From behind Harriet came the sound of the drawer being shoved back.

"That's it, folks," Nate said. "Thanks for your help."

Harriet started walking for the door as fast as her legs could carry her without running. It wasn't like a funeral at all. It had made her acutely aware that death wasn't a pretty thing.

She knew someone was following her, but she kept going, taking the stairs up to the exit that led out to the parking lot. Only when she stepped into the fresh air and could gulp down its sweetness did she stop.

"Are you going to be all right?" Jeff asked again. She could feel him standing right beside her.

"Sure. It was just a corpse." She sucked down more air, wanting to get the stench of that room out of her lungs.

"A pretty ugly one at that." He paused a moment, then said, "I imagine he found it hard to get a date."

Harriet's head snapped up and she found herself looking into Jeff's smiling eyes.

"Well, he was an ugly cuss, wasn't he? I doubt he looked a whole lot better alive."

"He didn't."

"So you see? There was just no way to improve the view."

Maybe it was the sudden release of tension, but for some reason Harriet found herself laughing, and the laughter seemed to cleanse her. Jeff joined her with a chuckle.

"Well," he said a few seconds later, "it appears his career as a dastardly villain is over. He won't be hitting any more pretty young women on the side of the head."

Harriet caught her breath, wondering if he meant that or if he was just being nice. *Pretty.* She wasn't used to hearing herself referred to that way. Her erstwhile beaux had always been trying to improve her somehow. *Can't you grow your hair longer, Harry? Can't you wear more makeup? Can't you get someone to help you choose your clothes? Didn't anybody ever teach you how to dress?*

Could she help it if she liked to dress casually and makeup made her break out? As for short hair—she loved being able to wash it, finger comb it and forget about it. Long hair would be in the way, especially when she was on an outdoor shoot. Men didn't seem to understand these things.

But Jeff was already turning away, so she couldn't try to find out if he really thought she was pretty. Besides, how could she ask him? Nate Tate had come to join them, and he and Jeff seemed to exchange significant looks.

"What's going on?" Harriet asked.

They looked at her. "Going on?" Nate repeated.

"There's something more about this guy we just looked at. What aren't you telling me?"

Nate shrugged. "I told you everything I know for sure, Harriet. I can't say any more until after the autopsy. But it looks like this guy was killed deliberately."

"Well, people don't usually shoot three times when they don't mean it," she said tartly. Then understanding dawned. "You mean they killed him because I saw him?"

"We don't know that."

"Right." She clenched her teeth. "I'm not a child, you know. I can take it."

Nate shook his head. "We really don't know that, Harriet. Besides, you saw the other two, also."

"Yeah, but they might not realize how much I could see through a telephoto lens."

"So put the best spin on it," Nate said. "Maybe they killed him because of what he did to you."

Harriet shook her head, aware that a kernel of dread was

beginning to take root in the pit of her stomach. "You don't believe that any more than I do."

Nate didn't seem to have an answer. It was Jeff who broke the silence. "We really don't know, Harriet. Maybe they had a falling-out over money and he lost. It's not going to do any good to read too much into this right now."

"Except that I should be careful and keep my room and car locked, right?"

"That would be advisable under any circumstances," Nate said. "It never hurts to be cautious. But Jeff's right—we don't know why this guy was killed, so it'd be a mistake to read too much into it right now. Maybe he got in trouble with his drug dealer."

"You have drug dealers out here?"

"Not very many, but I'd be astonished if we didn't have any. Our problems are the same as those in bigger cities. We just have a lot fewer of them."

"I guess." Nate was right. It would be a mistake to read too much into this.

"I'll let both of you know if there are any further developments," Nate said, and bade them a good evening.

Harriet watched him walk away to his Blazer and found herself once again wishing she was home in New York, where she at least understood the threats she faced.

"Come on," Jeff said. "Let me buy you dinner."

She turned to him and tried to smile. "At Maude's? Is that the only place people eat around here?"

"If they want the best food." He cocked his head. "Of course, I could always drive you to a fancy seafood place, if you don't mind traveling about a hundred miles."

"I'll skip it. I'm too tired tonight. Maude's will be fine." Imagine having to drive a hundred miles for seafood. Goodbye, scampi.

"Another time then."

Another time? Why did her heart skip a beat when he said

that? Good God, in less than a couple of weeks, she was going to leave this place forever and never see this man again. Besides, hadn't she learned her lesson where men were concerned?

Six

"Sylvia mentioned your mother today," Harriet told Jeff. They were eating a positively sinful meal of prime rib, onion rings, sautéed mushrooms and baked potatoes. Harriet reluctantly admitted she had never had better.

"She probably didn't have much good to say," Jeff replied. He added a spoonful of sour cream to a potato that was already drenched in butter. "Sylvia didn't like her."

Harriet didn't know how to respond to that and wondered why she had brought up the subject in the first place. It was probably a sensitive issue and not a place a virtual stranger ought to be prying. "She just mentioned the reason the house is so far from the pastures."

Jeff looked up, a twinkle in his eyes. "And mentioned that Mom wasn't real fond of ranch life."

"Well..."

He laughed. "It's okay. It's not a sore subject with me. She *wasn't* happy. In fact, it'd be fair to say she made my dad's life a living hell. If she'd had her way, Dad would have sold the place and taken a job in town. But that would have killed him. He was a real cowboy at heart. One of those guys that are never happier than when they're sleeping on a bedroll under the stars."

"And your mom?"

"She was a rancher's daughter, but apparently she had bigger dreams. She married the wrong man. I'm just glad that during her last few years I was able to give her some of the luxuries and travel she wanted."

"Did she travel alone?"

"Oh, no. My brother, George, went with her."

"Did you ever want to go?"

He tilted his head to one side and gave her a look that was surprisingly wistful. "Sure. But a ranch isn't something you can walk away from for weeks at a time. At least it wasn't back then. Now I suppose it could run itself for a while."

His wistfulness touched her and she gave a little smile. "Unless there are rustlers."

"Unless," he agreed. He ate a forkful of potato and cut himself another bite of steak.

"I imagine it would be hard to be a rancher's wife."

"I guess. I don't really know. Some women seem to be happy with it, but..." He shrugged. "I had my brother's ex-wife living with me for a while, her and her two kids. After a year, she called it quits. Too isolated, she said. And she was worried the kids didn't get enough social interaction with other kids. Maybe she was right."

"But surely she could drive to town, get the kids involved in activities, that kind of thing."

"Oh, sure, when the weather's good. Sometimes in the winter that's more of a wish than an option, though."

Harriet nodded and ate a couple more pieces of steak before she spoke again. "I saw the house and barn up the track from your place. Is that your property, too?"

"That's the old ranch house. Ben Tweed, my foreman, and his family live there now. They have a thirteen-year-old and a pair of two-year-old twins. Cute as buttons."

"So there are other people around."

He nodded. "There are always people around on the ranch. It's just not—well, I guess you'd say it's not society. There are always the hands to talk to and there's always something going on. It's not boring. It's just not..." He hesitated. "Exciting, I suppose. No excuse to dress up, no fancy places to go."

Except for the scampi shortage, that didn't sound especially bad to Harriet. "Are you happy with it?"

"Ranch life?" He shrugged, but she wasn't deceived. "I never really thought about it."

That was a lie, and somehow she knew it. Somehow she knew this man had a bit of his mother in him and wished for more exciting things. "So you never wanted to visit Scotland? Or the Far East?"

"Well, yes. I also wanted to be a fighter pilot." He smiled. "If wishes were horses…"

"Even a poor man would ride." She laughed quietly and realized she liked this man's attitude. He might have made a lot of sacrifices, but he wasn't wallowing in regrets.

"Remind me before you leave to take you up in my plane and show you the Bar C from the air."

"You have a *plane?*"

He looked a little embarrassed. "Well, yes. Just a small one. Twin engines, four seats."

Maybe that was why he couldn't afford a new truck, Harriet thought. She couldn't imagine owning your own plane.

"It's almost a necessity," he said after a moment. "Keeping an eye on things in the winter can get difficult."

"I imagine."

"Besides—" his eyes twinkled with amusement again, "—I told you, I always wanted to be a fighter pilot."

"Just don't tell me you've got a machine gun on board."

He laughed outright. "No, nothing like that. Although a few years ago when we were having some trouble with cattle mutilations, I sure wished I had one."

"Cattle mutilations? I've heard about that. Aren't some people claiming those have something to do with flying saucers?"

"So I hear. But our mutilations were more mundane. Some kind of cult moved into the area. Nate cleaned them out and I haven't had any trouble since. Thank God. Nobody should treat a beast that way." He shook his head. "There was a while there when *I* was ready to believe in UFOs."

"But cults can't account for all the mutilations, can they?"

"I wouldn't think so." Again that humor glimmered in his gaze. "I'd much rather believe in little gray men. The idea has so much more appeal than the thought that it's just another crazy bunch of humans doing a terrible thing."

"Doesn't it, though? The whole idea of being visited from outer space offers so many possibilities."

"And much more opportunity for speculation." He smiled. "I'm a great speculator. When you spend a lot of days on horseback, pretty much by yourself, you do a lot of thinking and speculating."

Harriet nodded. "I tend to do that when I'm on the subway or bus. Otherwise I just stew about life."

"You must travel at least a little in your job."

"Not really." She was almost embarrassed to admit it. "As I said the other night, almost all my work has been in the city. Frankly, I didn't realize there was still so much open space left. It's overwhelming."

He looked interested so she continued, giving a self-deprecating laugh. "When my car broke down and I got out of it, all I could hear was the wind, and all I could see in any direction was grass and the mountains. It seemed almost surreal, as if I had been suddenly transported to another world. Weird, huh?"

He shook his head. "I'd probably have a similar reaction if I went to New York. Do you still feel that way?"

"From time to time," she admitted. "But I'm getting over it."

Before long, conversation moved back to the rustling.

"Is there anything you can do?" Harriet asked. "To keep more cattle from being stolen?"

"A little. I can bring the cattle in, as we did today, so I can watch them in a smaller area until I'm ready to ship them out. And I'll put more men out to watch over them. But I don't think the robbers will come back, Harriet. They know they've been seen. They'd have to be fools to come back."

"In my opinion, they'd have to be fools to do it the first time, but they did."

"That's true. I'll do what I can, but there's no way I can be a hundred percent certain to prevent further rustling." He shrugged ruefully. "It's like putting a burglar alarm in your house or extra locks on your doors. You've done what you can, but there's no way you can absolutely prevent a burglary."

"I guess." She pushed her plate aside, her dinner only half-eaten. Maude was excessively generous in the portions she served. "It's a depressing thought."

He smiled. "Not really. But if I catch those so-and-sos, they're going to be sorry." He made a graphic wringing motion with his hands. "Stealing the cattle was bad enough. Beating you up is unforgivable."

"I'm inclined to agree with you." Harriet found herself returning his smile and sinking into the warm depths of his eyes. Quickly she looked away. *Watch it, kiddo,* she sternly warned herself. *Quicksand ahead.*

"So you've never married?" As soon as she asked the question, she wanted to strangle herself. One minute she was warning herself about quicksand, and the next she was putting her foot firmly into it. Maybe the concussion had killed a few critical brain cells.

"No," he said easily, as if he weren't at all bothered by the direction she'd taken. "I've thought about it a couple of times." Again he gave her a self-deprecating smile. "I seem to be drawn to women who would have to give up too much if they married me. You know, little things like careers and life-styles."

"Oh." Definitely quicksand, she thought. He spoke of women giving up things, but not of giving up anything himself. "So you couldn't modify your own life-style?"

"I'm not really keen on the idea of a commuter marriage. I guess it works for some people, but I want a closer relationship than that."

"So you'd expect some woman to give up everything and become a housewife?" Harriet found the idea annoying.

"No. Of course not. But I'm kind of tied to my location, and if she's equally tied to hers, why get married? One weekend a month is hardly even dating."

"So what would be ideal for you?"

"Somebody who could work from home, or who could move her base of operations here even if she still needed to travel." Another rueful smile. "I don't ask for much, do I? What about you?"

Harriet made a face. "I always fall in love with the wrong guy."

"Wrong how?"

"Oh, I don't know. How about selfish, self-centered, egotistical schmucks?"

He laughed. "That probably describes a lot of men."

"It seems to. Oh, well." She had to laugh at herself. "I've decided not to get involved again. I've got too much going on in my life to take time out to play sycophant to some guy who needs perpetual ego stroking."

Considering their agendas, Harriet decided, they were both safely immune to each other. Which was a good thing, right?

Why, then, did she feel so deflated?

"Listen," Jeff said suddenly. "Why don't you come out to the ranch again tomorrow. I can take you up in my plane and show you the Bar C from the air."

"Sounds good to me."

"Say around ten?"

"I'll be there."

Harriet felt her stomach plummet the next morning when she saw the plane sitting on a grass airstrip a half mile from Jeff's house. It was so *small*.

"There she is," Jeff said with all the pride of ownership of a kid with a fancy toy.

Harriet's feet seemed to have become rooted to the ground, and her mouth was suddenly dry. "I can't go up in that."

He looked at her. "Why not?"

"It's so...so tiny."

"Not really. Two engines, four seats. They make planes a lot smaller."

"Not one I'd ever get into."

"It's perfectly safe, Harriet. I fly it all the time."

"Maybe you're crazy."

One corner of his mouth quirked upward. "That's one thing I've never been accused of before. Really, it's no different than driving a compact car, and it's a whole lot safer."

"I can get out of a car if something goes wrong."

"And I can land this thing if something goes wrong." He patted a wing. "She's great on an unpowered glide. That's one of the reasons I bought her. I could lose both engines and still set her down as light as a feather."

Somehow Harriet didn't find that reassuring. "What if you run into a chicken or something?"

"Chickens don't fly. But if you're worried about geese and ducks, don't. I can avoid them."

"Mmm."

He grinned. "Come on, Harriet, be a sport. Once we get up there, you'll fall in love with flying, I promise."

"How can you promise that?"

"Because I'm unscrupulous?"

Nervous or not, she had to laugh. "Are you sure you don't have a death wish?"

"Positive. I'm planning to make my first parachute jump later this week. Now, *that's* dangerous."

"No kidding." She looked at the plane again and took a deep breath to calm her fluttering stomach. "You won't do any fancy flying?"

"Straight and level, I promise."

Well, thought Harriet, a little adventure was good for the

soul. Besides, Jeff was standing here talking to her and he'd flown many times. It probably *was* safe. "Okay."

"Okay?"

"Okay."

He showed her where to step to climb in, then he helped her buckle herself into the right-hand seat. He passed her a headset. "It'll make it easier to talk," he told her. "We won't have to shout over the engines."

Then they were rolling down the length of the grassy strip, past a wind sock that was blowing steadily in an easterly direction. The field wasn't nearly as smooth as a paved runway, and Harriet felt her teeth jolt together a couple of times, but then they were airborne.

After the first wave of panic as the ground fell away—and to be fair, she felt the same panic on a large airplane—she began to relax. She could feel the power in the engines, and that managed to reassure her as nothing that Jeff had said could.

When they leveled out, they were low enough that she was surprised by how much she could see. A rider crossing a huge expanse of browning grass was discernible, as were the occasional dark shapes of what she thought must be cattle.

"This is a great way to keep an eye on things," Jeff said, his voice coming clearly through her earphones. "Are you doing okay?"

"I'm fine."

"The ride won't be as smooth as on a big plane, but it's a good day for flying. We shouldn't experience too much turbulence."

As she relaxed, Harriet felt more comfortable about leaning to the side so she could look down directly. The plane didn't tip, so she guessed it was okay.

"See over there? That's where they're rounding up today."

The river of cattle that had so impressed her yesterday impressed her even more today. It was a dark stream moving very slowly across the rolling terrain. She could even make out the cowboys who were guiding it. "This is fantastic!" she heard herself say.

"It is, isn't it? I love to get up here on a clear day and just fly."

He pointed out the site of the archaeological dig he'd mentioned to her, and she could see small specks that must be people working there. He showed her the men he had patrolling his fence line wherever it came near the road. They were driving trucks, though, for speed.

Maybe, thought Harriet, that was why he couldn't afford a new truck. Maybe he owned all those down there that were driving back and forth to prevent further rustling.

"I won't take you near the mountains," he said as an air pocket caused the plane to drop suddenly. "The turbulence is a lot worse."

"Thank you." Wrapping her arms around herself, she wondered if her stomach was on the ground below as Jeff banked the plane and flew them farther from the mountains.

He showed her other herds of cattle, still in their summer pastures, spread out and grazing contentedly. He pointed out the creeks and streams that were the lifeblood of the ranch, bringing water down from the mountains.

But finally, the one thing that overwhelmed her was the sheer size of his ranch. She couldn't imagine one man owning all of that.

"It's huge," she told him. "I can't believe how big this ranch is!"

"More than four times as big as Manhattan," he told her, flashing a smile.

More than a hundred square miles. She was awed.

"It runs into the neighboring county," he said. "It didn't when I was a boy."

"So you've made it bigger?"

"Considerably. I also lease a lot of grazing land from my neighbors. Raising cattle is big business these days."

And he was a big businessman, she found herself thinking.

Not really all that different from the driven, upwardly mobile men she had dated. He was probably consumed by his ranch and the possibility of making it even larger. So much so that he had never married. He seemed nicer, but what did that mean? They all seemed nice enough at first.

All of a sudden he banked the plane, giving her a strong case of vertigo. "Can you see what that is down there?" he asked.

"Where?"

"Over there to the right, near the creek bank."

She squinted, but all she could see was a dark blot that didn't look like much. "I'm sorry, no."

"I'm going to bring us down a little lower."

Oh God, she thought, the trees already looked too close. She closed her eyes for a moment and clenched her jaw, hoping she didn't look as frightened as she felt. The sense of safety their altitude had given her vanished as she thought of those trees coming closer.

"Can you see it better now?"

Clenching her hands in her lap, she opened her eyes and forced herself to look. At first there was simply a dizzying sense that the ground was entirely too close and moving entirely too fast. Reluctantly, she forced herself to look around and get her bearings. There was the creek. They were coming up on it fast, and she had the terrifying conviction that their wing was going to hit the tree growing beside it.

And then she saw the dark blot again. Only this time there was no mistaking it.

"It looks like a person," she said. "Someone sleeping on the creek bank."

"That's what I thought." His voice was grim. "I'll take you back now, Harriet. I need to check this out."

She looked at him. "Do you think something's wrong?"

"I'm not sure. It might be nothing."

But from the set of his chin, she could tell he didn't really think so.

The landing was the worst part. She'd never seen the view from the cockpit as a plane landed, and she finally closed her eyes so that she didn't have to watch the ground rushing up.

The wheels hit, but not too hard. They bounced a couple of times, then rolled to a halt. When Jeff switched off the engines, the silence was suddenly loud.

"Are you all right?" he asked.

She looked at him. "I don't think I'll ever be a pilot."

The smile he gave her was fleeting. "I'm going to take you back to the ranch house. I need to go out and see who or what was lying there beside the creek."

"Do you think it could be one of the rustlers?"

"I don't know. Maybe it's just some wanderer camping out. Maybe somebody got lost. But it's not one of my men."

"How can you tell that?"

"He didn't have a horse."

Jeff asked Harriet to wait at the ranch until he got back. "I want to treat you to lunch, but I wasn't planning on this interruption. Do you mind?"

"Of course not. I'm in no great hurry to go back to town and eat a hamburger at the truck stop. Besides, I can always take more pictures."

He laughed, resisting the urge to give her a quick hug, and headed out to the stable to saddle his horse.

Harriet Breslin was some woman, he thought as he saddled Wilbur, named in a moment of whimsy after the character who had owned Mr. Ed, the famous talking TV horse. Wilbur's ears pricked eagerly and he moved impatiently, eager to be out of his stall.

Some woman, Jeff thought again. An appealing mixture of traits, at times tough and difficult, at other times scared and brave all at once. He liked the way her blond hair blew about in the breeze and she didn't seem to care that it was getting messed up. He even liked the sensible way she dressed in slacks and that safari shirt. She seemed approachable.

On the other hand, she was a career woman who lived in New York, and he'd be a fool to think about her as a woman at all. He'd been burned more than once by her type.

He saddled a second horse so he could bring the trespasser back to the house with him, then set out across the open range the way he had always loved to do. Today was no different. It was the kind of day he could have ridden until sunset and then camped happily beside a stream.

He was usually in no rush to get trespassers off his land. People liked to hike and often they wandered onto private property. They rarely did any harm, and all he ever asked when he found them was that they be careful about building fires. This time, though, his cattle had been rustled, and he wasn't comfortable about any strangers being on his land un-invited.

And this time, he wanted to get back to Harriet so he could have lunch with her. This time, he found himself resenting the intrusion.

Jeff knew his ranch like the back of his hand and knew exactly where to look for the trespasser. Instead of taking the leisurely ride he would ordinarily have taken, he kept his mount to a quick canter. Wilbur seemed delighted to work off the energy he had stored up since yesterday and needed little encouragement.

When Jeff arrived at the creek and saw the intruder, he wished he'd taken his merry time getting there. The man was dead, shot through the back.

"Damn," he muttered as Wilbur shied and backed up. "Double damn it all to hell. What do you think, Wilbur? Is this another one of the rustlers?"

Wilbur nickered and backed up another couple of steps, clearly unhappy in the presence of death. Flies buzzed noisily around the corpse, and Jeff gave thanks he hadn't invited Harriet to ride out here with him. She didn't need to see this.

What was she going to think of Wyoming? he wondered,

then dismissed the question. Why should he care? It didn't matter at all.

"Let's go back and call the sheriff," he said to his horse.

Wilbur needed no encouragement. He took off for home as if the hordes of hell were on his heels. Jeff kind of felt that way himself.

Seven

The yard between the ranch house and the barn was full of police cars. Harriet stood on the kitchen porch, feeling forgotten and out of place. She was a little surprised at the number of vehicles. For some reason she hadn't thought there were so many lawmen in this isolated part of the country. This was a regular convention.

And all of these thoughts were an attempt to ignore what she feared—that the murdered man was another one of the rustlers. She didn't want to think about the possible ramifications if someone was murdering the men she had seen. She didn't want to think about how far that person might go.

Since Jeff had returned tight-lipped and called the police, she'd been having nightmare visions, all of which seemed to revolve around her being a small hunted animal. A mouse being stalked by a cat.

Stupid, she tried to tell herself now as she waited for the police to bring the body back. There was no reason to think any such thing. If the victim *was* one of the rustlers, then it had probably just been a falling-out among thieves. They weren't going to come hunting her in New York. All she had to do was wrap up this job quickly, and she felt she had almost enough photos right now to do so. She could be out of here in another twenty-four hours, safely on her way.

Maybe.

She wished Jeff would get back. He'd taken the police out to the murder scene and it might be hours before he returned to the house. Maybe she should just go back to town instead of standing here, uselessly waiting.

But every time she thought of striking out on her own, she hesitated. It might be best to wait until she could follow the cops back to town. At least then she wouldn't be alone on an isolated road.

Sylvia stepped out onto the porch. "It'll be a while yet, Harriet. Those cops are going to go over the whole area with a fine-tooth comb. Are you getting cold? Would you like something hot to drink?"

Harriet realized with a start that she *was* getting chilled. From a cool morning, the temperature seemed to have been dropping steadily. "I'd love some coffee or tea, Sylvia."

"Well, come on in and get warm. It's about time you ate something anyway. You can't wait all day for Mr. Jeff to show up for lunch."

The kitchen was warm and full of delicious aromas. "I figure the deputies are going to be hungry and cold by the time they get back," Sylvia said. "I'm making chocolate chip cookies."

"I *love* chocolate chip cookies."

Sylvia grinned. "Help yourself—after you finish lunch."

Sylvia served her hot clam chowder with crackers and a ham salad sandwich.

"Aren't you going to join me?" Harriet asked.

"I've been nibbling on cookie dough. I couldn't eat another thing." She turned back to the counter and began to put spoonfuls of dough on a cookie sheet. "This is terrible, what's been happening. Bad enough the cattle were stolen, but murder beats all, doesn't it?"

"It's awful."

"Coming from New York, I expect you're more used to it than we are."

Harriet almost laughed. "I've never known anyone who was murdered before. I read about it in the papers, of course, like everyone else, but it's not a part of my life."

Sylvia looked abashed. "I didn't mean anything by it. It's just that you have all that organized crime and everything. We used to be safe from it, but not anymore. I can tell you stories about things that have happened here in the last few years that just astonish me."

"So all those stories I heard about the Wild Wild West weren't exaggerated?" Harriet asked dryly.

Sylvia looked at her in astonishment, then laughed. "You're right. I shouldn't make assumptions about places I've never been. As for here...well, we get mostly rustling from time to time. People all over steal. But murder—that's something rare in these parts, unless it's some guy getting into an argument with his wife. But it happens everywhere the same, I guess."

"People are people everywhere."

Sylvia pulled two sheets of cookies out of the oversize oven and popped in two more. The delicious aroma grew even stronger, and good though the chowder and sandwich were, Harriet would have cheerfully pushed them aside in favor of a few of those cookies.

The sudden thud of booted feet drew the attention of both women to the kitchen door. It opened and Jeff stepped in, looking grim.

"I'm sorry," he said when he saw Harriet sitting at the island, finishing her meal. "We were supposed to have lunch together."

"Murder has a nasty habit of getting in the way of social engagements," Harriet replied with a dismissing wave of her hand.

Jeff stared at her a moment and then laughed. "You're right. It does."

"Lunch?" Sylvia asked, waving a ladle at him. "Don't even think about touching those cookies until you've eaten decent food."

Jeff snatched one anyway and popped it into his mouth. "Just let me wash up. That chowder sure looks good."

He disappeared through the door to the rest of the house.

"That man!" Sylvia said with a shake of her head. "If it weren't for me, he'd live on junk food."

"Men are absolutely helpless without us," Harriet agreed. "They can build bridges, fly to the moon, fight wars—"

"Run ranches," Sylvia interposed.

"Run ranches," Harriet agreed. "They can even run major cities—although not very well. But they sure can't take care of themselves."

Sylvia smiled. "To be fair, Mr. Jeff can do most everything for himself. He certainly has when I've been sick. But why should he when he pays me to do it for him? His eating habits, though!" She shook her head. "I gave up asking him what he wanted for dinner. It was always steak and potatoes or meat loaf. It took me the better part of two years to get him to like salad, and he still won't eat brussels sprouts."

Harriet grimaced. "I *hate* brussels sprouts."

"You won't get any around here. Spinach, though, I can hand out by the bucketful."

"You have a nice garden out back."

Sylvia beamed proudly. "That's my pride and joy. Nothing makes me feel better than digging in the dirt and watching things grow."

Well, thought Harriet, returning to her soup, Mr. Jeff certainly didn't need a wife for any of the traditional reasons. Not when he had Sylvia. She could easily imagine that the women Jeff might have been interested in could have been overwhelmed by Sylvia. Could have felt threatened.

Do I feel threatened? No, of course not, she assured herself. In the first place, she wasn't applying for the position. In the second, she had absolutely no interest in cooking, cleaning or gardening beyond the occasional houseplant. Sometimes she wondered if all her ex-boyfriends had been right. Maybe she wasn't very feminine.

But so what? She had her career and her interests, and she didn't need to give them all up so she could wait hand and foot on some man.

Jeff returned a short while later wearing a fresh shirt and jeans. He joined Harriet at the island and complimented Sylvia on the chowder.

"Do the police know anything yet?" Harriet asked.

Jeff shook his head. "Nate's of the opinion the guy was shot in the back."

"Nasty."

"No accident, that's for sure. They'll be out there for a while looking for evidence. Nate wants you to stay here until he has a chance to talk to you."

"Me?" Harriet didn't like the sound of that. "I didn't have anything to do with it!"

"I don't think he believes you did."

"Oh." The wind stolen from her sails, Harriet calmed down reluctantly. "I have a job to do."

"I know. So does Nate. He'd still appreciate it if you don't go running off by yourself until he talks to you."

Harriet's attention caught on the phrase "by yourself." A chill trickled down her spine. "He thinks it's another one of the rustlers, doesn't he?"

"I'm afraid so."

Harriet totally lost her appetite and she pushed her soup and sandwich aside. "He thinks I might be in danger."

"He didn't say that."

"He's going to. I can read between the lines."

Jeff didn't argue. "Look, I'm sure there are other things you can take pictures of around here for your book covers. We can spend the rest of the afternoon doing that. And how about tomorrow I take you out to the archaeological dig? Maybe we can find a few bones, or a dinosaur footprint."

She scowled at him. "I'm not a child, Jeff. You don't have to distract me."

"I'm not trying to distract you. I'm trying to help you do your job and entertain you." Exasperated, he threw his napkin on the butcher block beside his plate. "Sometimes you are just the sweetest, nicest person. Then you get all prickly, like you won't be happy unless you can start a fight. I'm only trying to be a good host.''

"You're not my host!"

"No? See, that's exactly what I mean!"

Sylvia interrupted. "The two of you sound like a couple of three-year-olds. Cut it out. You're both upset because of the murder.''

As one, Jeff and Harriet turned to glare at her. Sylvia lifted her hands in surrender. "Okay, okay. Have your stupid little fight.'' She started taking the cooling cookies off the sheet and putting them onto racks. "But neither of you gets another cookie until you behave.''

Jeff and Harriet exchanged looks and then burst into laughter.

"I'm sorry," Harriet said.

"No, I'm sorry. I don't blame you for being upset about this, and I'm not going to make it any better by acting like a tour guide. But really, if you want, I'd be happy to show you around and help you find some good shots.''

"Thank you. You're right. I'd be better off staying busy.''

Sylvia turned around with a plate of cookies and set it in front of them. "That's better," she said approvingly, and went back to her baking.

"Do you feel properly put in your place?" Jeff asked Harriet.

"Absolutely.''

"Now, don't start on me," Sylvia said over her shoulder. "I'm the cook here, remember. I might get a mind to make brussels sprouts for dinner.''

Harriet hadn't had time to notice before, but when she walked around with Jeff that afternoon, she realized there were a lot of animals on the ranch other than horses and cows. Three dogs greeted her as ecstatically as if she were a long-lost relative. A half dozen cats regarded her suspiciously from various perches in and around the barn and house. Behind the barn, hens pecked at the ground under the baleful eye of a huge rooster that sat on a fence post.

"I always thought of chickens in a coop," she said.

"We keep the laying hens in a coop up by the foreman's house. These birds are for breeding. The young ones are good for frying or roasting."

Harriet shook her head. "I'd rather pick them out at the supermarket."

He flashed a grin. "Hey, by the time I bring 'em to the kitchen, you can't tell they didn't come from the supermarket."

"No feathers?"

"I clean 'em first. My mother didn't want any part of it, so it just seemed easiest to do it myself. Sylvia probably wouldn't mind, but it's not all that difficult to take care of it."

"Do you use the feathers, too?"

"We used to. Not anymore. I prefer a polyester pillow."

There were flocks of geese and ducks by a pond. The ducks swam sedately on the water while the geese—surprisingly large geese—came up to them honking and demanding food.

"Sorry, gang," Jeff told them, "I didn't bring anything today."

"You eat them, too?"

"For special occasions. I prefer a good roast duck myself."

Harriet, who was used to finding her food already dead and packaged in plastic, wasn't sure how she felt about eating something with which she had a relationship. The realities of ranch life had never been more apparent.

Jeff looked up at the sky. Clouds that had been fluffy white balls of cotton around noon had become thick, silvery thunderheads that blotted the sun. The cooling breeze had grown chilly, and the low rumble of thunder could be heard to the west.

"It might be wise to go in, Harriet. This looks like it's going to get nasty."

"I love thunderstorms."

He smiled at her. "So do I. But see that circulation over there? And that low-hanging wall of cloud? We might see a tornado."

"*That* I don't like."

"Not my favorite thing, either."

The chickens had vanished, she noted as they passed by the barn. She wondered where they hid when the weather was bad. Even the rooster had relinquished his proud perch.

They entered the house through the front door, stepping into a foyer darkened by the day's cloudiness. Jeff led the way to the living room, a spacious, airy place with a high, beamed ceiling and enough curios in cabinets and on the wall to give it the feeling of a museum.

Harriet sat on a window seat so she could watch the storm, and Jeff sat in a recliner with a view out the large front windows. The designer of the house had taken full advantage of the mountains to the west, and right now they had a spectacular view of the towering peaks and a sky that was steadily turning darker and greener.

"Do you want a light on?" Jeff asked from the gloom.

"Oh, no. Not unless you do. I don't often get to see this much of the sky." She hesitated. "I must be keeping you from your work."

"If there's any advantage to owning this operation, it's that I can take time off when I want to. That's why I have a foreman."

She nodded and leaned back against the window embrasure, turning her attention to the outdoors. "I'd hate to be one of the cops out there with the body right now."

"They're probably on their way back in. Once it starts to rain, there won't be much evidence left, anyway."

Harriet shivered, thinking of the body and what it might mean to her. "I don't mind telling you I'm a little afraid."

"I don't blame you."

A streak of lightning, almost hot pink in color, stabbed

downward in the distance. Moments later they heard the rumble of thunder.

"Lightning scares me, too," she admitted, giving an embarrassed laugh. "Ever since I was a kid. I don't know why. I never knew anybody who was struck by it. And it's really silly when you consider that I love storms. I especially love to be outside right before they hit, when the air gets so fresh and the wind picks up. It makes me feel alive."

He made a sound of agreement. "Although I have to admit I prefer being near shelter. I've spent some cold afternoons and nights out in downpours."

There was another flash of lightning, and the thunder boomed hollowly.

"I guess this wasn't the trip you bargained for when you came west," Jeff remarked.

Harriet had to laugh. "Not exactly. I didn't want to come, but all my reasons seem silly in retrospect. Things like not having a corner deli and not being able to get shrimp scampi."

"Shrimp scampi I can arrange. That seafood restaurant I mentioned makes a good one. And Sylvia could probably manage it, too. You'd think she might stick with good home cooking, but the woman has a gastronomic streak. Or maybe it's an artistic streak. She has me eating things I can't pronounce. In fact, I'd almost bet she can't pronounce them, either."

"She mentioned something about your preference for steak and potatoes."

His laugh rolled across the room. "It was all I ever ate around here before Sylvia showed up. My mother hated cooking, and that was about all I knew to do for myself. That and roast a bird. You should have seen the look on the men's faces the first time she served sukiyaki." He chuckled again. "Now they look forward to Japanese food. Chinese, too. They aren't too keen on French stuff, though, so she doesn't cook it anymore."

"Sylvia seems like a gem."

"She is. I couldn't ask for a better housekeeper."

Thunder cracked loudly, making Harriet jump. She looked out the window, watching low, dark fingers of cloud sweep the treetops. "I've never seen the clouds so low!"

Before Jeff could respond, there was a pounding at the front door. He rose from his chair. "I'll get that. If you want to turn on the lights, be my guest."

But Harriet didn't want to. She enjoyed watching the storm from her safe little window seat. It gave her a chance to avoid acknowledging the shadows of doom that hovered around the edges of her mind.

But then she heard Sheriff Tate's voice, and a moment later he stepped into the living room. Her heart slipped into high gear and she pivoted around on her seat as Jeff flipped on the lights. The room was immediately bathed in a warm, bright glow that seemed to hold the storm at bay.

"Howdy," Nate said to her. His clothes were damp but not soaked, and he declined Jeff's offer of a seat. "I'll just make it wet." He looked from Jeff to Harriet. "Well."

"Yes, well?" Jeff said. "Did you find out anything?"

Nate shook his head. "As near as we can tell, he was killed somewhere else and dumped there."

"Why would anyone do that?" Jeff asked.

Nate gave a crooked grin. "Oh, I suppose because you have to get rid of a body somehow. You sure don't want to keep it at your place or in the trunk of your car."

Harriet had to laugh, despite her nerves. Jeff smiled and shook his head.

"I meant why all the way out there. A roadside would be handier."

"But all the way out there, maybe scavengers would get rid of the evidence before the bones were found." Nate shrugged. "What were the odds that you'd fly over that place today— or any day in the next couple of weeks?"

"Higher since the rustling, but not all that high. Point taken."

"Do you know who it is?" Harriet asked.

Nate's dark eyes settled on her. "It looks an awful lot like another one of your rustlers."

"Oh, God!" Harriet's stomach and heart lurched, leaving her feeling sick and hollow. "Maybe I'd better go back to New York."

"Well…" Nate drew the word out. "I've been chewing that over. It seems like if you go away, the rustlers might be less nervous about being identified. On the other hand, they might be smart enough to know it won't make any difference. As long as you're alive, you can testify against them."

Harriet could hear the pounding of the blood in her ears. She was afraid, more afraid than at any other time except when she'd been mugged. "But there's only one of them left," she heard herself say, not sure what she meant by that.

"One's enough." Nate sighed and pushed back the damp hair from his forehead. "And there might be more."

Harriet felt a fresh stab of fear.

"More?" Jeff repeated. "You think this is a big operation?"

"Well, I don't have any proof of it, but I got this feeling. I'm afraid I'll need you to take a look at him, Harriet, to make sure he's one of the rustlers."

Harriet nodded. She was too worried about her own situation to be upset about having to look at another dead body.

"Okay," Nate continued. "We've got three known rustlers, two of whom are now dead. One I might explain as a falling-out, but two—" He shook his head. "No, two makes me think there's somebody higher up in this operation, and he's trying to get rid of everyone who might link him to it."

Harriet seized on that. "I can't link anything but those three men to the rustling."

"Maybe. Maybe not. You *did* see the trucks."

"Well, yes. But there wasn't anything identifiable about them. I must have passed three just like them on my way here from the airport." She spread her hands. "I'm a city girl. I couldn't tell one cattle truck from another. All I know about them is that they stink.''

A smile flickered on Jeff's face.

Nate chuckled. "Don't they, though? You should have been here for the hullabaloo before they ran the state road around the town. Back when it came right down Front Street, the cattle trucks would be running through day and night. Anyway, they'd drop manure on the streets and folks would get real temperamental about the smell and the mess. City sanitation had a fit and wanted me to ticket the drivers...like they had any other way to go. Closest I ever came to losing an election." He shook his head. "I gave thanks when they rerouted the highway.''

"But if she can't identify the trucks," Jeff said, "she shouldn't be in any danger."

"Right. Except that the rustlers might not know she can't identify them."

Harriet's eyes met Jeff's. She read a concern there that mirrored her own.

"I'll just go back to New York," she said again. "They won't follow me."

"Well..." Nate drew the word out once again. Harriet felt her mouth go dry. He didn't think she'd be safe nearly two thousand miles away from here? "I wish I could guarantee that," he continued. "But everyone knows where you're from. It's not like this is some big city where no one knows anything about you. Unfortunately, the word is out that you're from New York City, that you're a photographer, that you're taking photos for book covers. With your name being known, you'd be real easy to find if somebody got a mind to. And I can't protect you all the way out there."

Harriet felt a flare of anger. "Look, I have a job to do. As soon as I finish my photography—and I'm almost done—I need to get back and work on the pictures. I have a *deadline*. You can't expect me to hang around here and twiddle my thumbs until you catch these guys."

"You may have to do just that—at least until we think the heat is off."

Harriet jumped to her feet and started pacing before the large windows. "I don't believe this! I come all the way out into the middle of nowhere to do an assignment I don't particularly want, and now you're telling me I'm tangled up with rustlers and I'm a prisoner in this godforsaken place!"

"It's not godforsaken," Jeff said quietly. "I realize we don't have all the wonderful amenities you're used to having right around the corner, but we've got fresh air, open spaces and good people."

"Good people! For heaven's sake, in New York we have the Mafia, but it didn't run my life!"

"It might have if you'd witnessed a mob operation," Jeff said. "This could have happened anywhere. It's just unfortunate."

"Unfortunate doesn't begin to cover it! I feel like I've slipped into a time warp to the 1880s! Cowboys, horses, cattle and rustlers, for God's sake!"

"It could have been Uzis, drugs and gangs." His voice had taken on an edge Harriet couldn't miss.

"What do you know about it? You've never lived in the city!"

"And you've never lived *here*. You're rushing to pass judgment and you don't even know what you're talking about."

"I know what I'm talking about! I was beaten and left for dead, remember? At least when I got mugged, the guy didn't tie me up and leave me to die!"

Jeff and Nate exchanged looks, but it was Jeff who spoke. "They might have if you had tangled with organized crime."

"So you're telling me I'm in trouble with organized crime?"

"Our version of it, anyway," Nate said. "Look, I'll make you a promise. The instant I can confirm that they're not after anybody else, I'll let you know."

"Just how are you going to confirm that?"

He shrugged. "Maybe by putting them all in jail."

Harriet stopped in front of the windows and looked out at the stormy day. It was still dark out there, a deep bottle green that made her feel as if she were underwater. Another roll of thunder echoed across the shallow valley, and lightning flared, leaping from cloud to cloud.

"So," she said, "I'm supposed to be safe sitting all alone in a room at the Lazy Rest Motel?"

"Well, that's another problem," Nate said.

"She can stay here," Jeff offered. "We can put it around that she's gone back to New York, but she can stay right here. I've got men I'd trust with my life to keep an eye on things. They won't talk. And with Sylvia here, she'd never be alone."

"Marcie's never going to believe this," Harriet said to no one in particular.

"Who's Marcie?" Jeff wanted to know.

"My agent. The one who thinks I'm jinxed. Now she'll be sure."

"You're not jinxed. You're just having a run of bad luck."

"The run started when I was thirteen and—" She broke off abruptly, embarrassed that she'd almost told these two men she hardly knew about her first date. Harvey Beddoes, the big junior varsity jock, the school dance—and her first period. All over the white skirt she was wearing. Yep, she'd been jinxed for a long time.

"You were saying?" Jeff prompted from behind her.

"Never mind. It doesn't matter. Oh hell, I don't want to stay here. I want to get back to my life."

"Not just yet," Nate said. "Soon, but not now. I don't want to be getting a wire from the NYPD telling me you've been found shot to death along some city street."

"Neither do I." She was beaten and she knew it. Sighing, she looked down at her hands as lightning flickered again. "Okay. I don't have any choice. But I have to be back in two weeks at the latest, so I can use my equipment to enhance these photographs. Two weeks, Sheriff. That's all the time I can spare for this."

She noted unhappily that neither of them agreed with her.

"Come back to town and pick up your stuff from the motel when this storm is over," Nate said. "Tell Lucinda Schultz you're going home on a morning flight, so you're driving to Laramie tonight. I'll have one of my deputies stop you just outside of town. You can switch cars with her and come back here. I'll have the deputy return your car to the rental place."

"I don't want her wandering around out there after dark all alone," Jeff said. "How about I ride with your deputy so I can be with Harriet on the trip back out here?"

"Sounds good. And now I have to ask you to come out and take a look at the body. They should have it in the back of the ambulance by now."

Harriet hoped to find the corpse was a total stranger, but there was no mistaking the face, even though it was bloated in death. Harriet had seen it too clearly through the eye of her camera.

The noose was drawing tighter, she thought grimly. And her neck was stuck inside it.

Eight

"How'd you like to go to Denver today?" Jeff asked two mornings later.

Harriet looked up from her breakfast of waffles, across the top of the *Los Angeles Times,* which to her surprise Jeff received every day along with the *Wall Street Journal* and the *Washington Post.* They were a little out-of-date—they came by mail—but she didn't care. It was a touch of the outside world. If she didn't get her daily dose of politics and mayhem, she didn't have anything to be irritated about. Besides, there was something elevating about being able to look at the mess the rest of the world was in, curl her lip and think how much wiser she was.

"Denver? Am I allowed?" She couldn't help the edge in her voice. Thirty-six hours here had felt like thirty-six hours in a prison cell. Jeff had plenty of good books, plenty of videotapes, plenty of music to listen to, but she wasn't happy with nothing constructive to do.

"I don't see why not. We'll fly down on my plane. Who'll even know you're there?"

"Are you going down to look at cows or something?" She didn't think a day spent wandering around looking at bovines offered much improvement over her current circumstances.

"Actually, I was thinking about having a vacation day. No business involved. I know a great deli—they even make bagels, if you like them—and a place where we can get a wonderful shrimp scampi for dinner."

"Sold," Harriet said, putting her fork down. "When do you

want to go? And I hope I don't have to get dressed up. I didn't bring anything but work clothes.''

"Denver's casual enough, but you can always buy something when we get there, if you want to."

She *did* want to. For some weird reason—probably because she was going stir-crazy, she actually liked the idea of putting on a good dress and going out to dinner. "I *would* like to look at clothes, if that's all right."

He smiled. "Fine by me. While you buy dresses, I can always wander through the electronics store." He glanced at his watch. "Half an hour? And bring something to spend the night. I can fly us back after dark if you really want, but you'd enjoy it more if you could see the scenery."

She looked suspiciously at him. "I get my own room at the hotel, if we stay."

"Of course!" He seemed surprised. "Damn it, Harriet, I haven't even made a pass at you. You're safe with me."

For some reason that didn't make her feel any better.

He went on without waiting for a reply. "I need to be back tomorrow, though. I have my first skydiving lesson the following morning."

"You're nuts!"

He smiled. "Probably. You can come watch me splat, if you want. Although I guess we ought to disguise you if you do."

Harriet shrugged. "A wig and sunglasses will do it." In spite of herself, she was intrigued. "Can I take pictures?"

"As long as you don't identify me. I'll never again let anybody put me in a magazine. Do you know I'm actually getting cheesecakes and pies by mail? Yesterday, I got two dozen fudge brownies from a woman in Des Moines."

Harriet laughed. "It's the money, cowboy. Some women have a nose for it."

"Too many women," he said glumly. "Sometimes I feel like a wallet with legs."

"Poor little rich boy, hmm?"

He made a face at her. "I'd like to be appreciated for my other qualities. My sterling character. My gorgeous mug."

"You *do* look a little like Robert Redford."

He blinked, startled. "Oh, come off it, Harriet. I look ordinary. No, it's my money they want."

"Probably," she agreed. *But ordinary?* she thought. *Not by a long shot!*

"Thanks for the vote of confidence."

"Oh, for Pete's sake, Jeff!" She pushed her plate aside and tried not to laugh at his pretense of being crushed. "How could they be going for anything else? They don't know anything about you except that you have money."

"Exactly. I'm thinking about getting an unlisted phone number. And how did Pete get into this conversation anyway?"

It was nice, she thought a few minutes later as she packed her suitcase for the trip, to be with someone who could actually make her laugh. Laughter had been missing from her previous relationships with men. Maybe that was what had ruined them. She didn't want to spend her life with someone who couldn't make her laugh.

But of course she didn't want to spend her life with anyone anymore, and certainly not a cow farmer from the wilds of Wyoming.

And then she glanced in the mirror and saw her black eye, now turning several shades of green. For a moment she almost changed her mind about going, then decided that Jeff had been looking at it for a week, and nobody else mattered. The thought should have made her uneasy, but somehow it didn't.

She had to get away before she lost her mind!

Flying in a small plane was nicer this time and didn't frighten Harriet nearly as much. In fact, she found she could appreciate the luxury of not having to wait at a terminal and be boarded like a cow onto some cattle truck. The only time she got nervous, in fact, was during some heavy turbulence over the mountains, and when they came in for the landing. Denver had a big international airport, and she was conscious of all the other planes in the sky. Big planes. Planes that could smash their little twin-engine job like a flyswatter hitting a fly. But it didn't seem to bother Jeff any. He assured her he'd landed there countless times, and his communication with the tower seemed calm and in control, even though Harriet didn't understand a lot of what he was saying.

The landing was easier than landing on a grass strip, though. Much smoother, even if the pavement did look a lot harder than grass as it rushed up to meet them.

Jeff taxied to their designated parking area with all the panache of a seasoned pro, and almost before she knew it, Harriet's feet were once again firmly planted on solid ground.

It was early afternoon by the time they took a cab from the airport to town, and Jeff suggested they book into a hotel before they did anything else. "We can spend tomorrow morning doing things, too, if you want, but we'll have to leave by one o'clock."

"Sounds good to me."

They checked into separate rooms at a brand-new motel on the west side of Denver. From her room Harriet had a spectacular view of the snow-powdered mountains rising darkly to the west against the blue sky. It occurred to her that she would like to get out and walk in those mountains sometime. They beckoned to her with their mysterious contours, promising adventure.

"I'm losing my mind," she said out loud. She didn't want to go hiking in those mountains. Not really. It would mean dealing with all kinds of wildlife, whereas squirrels, dogs and cats were the limits of her comfort zone. They probably had mountain lions up there—and bears and God knew what else.

She changed quickly into fresh khaki slacks and a washable blue silk blouse that was the usual extent of her dressing up. If silk wasn't dressy, she reasoned, what was? But she still had a silly urge to buy a dress. Not a dress like the ones she wore when she went out with her ex-boyfriends to their fancy business parties, but something comfortable yet pretty.

In fact, she thought suddenly, sitting down in the chair by the window as realization struck her, she'd never been happy wearing sequins and the slinky black things her upwardly mobile boyfriends had wanted her to wear. She always felt like a fraud when she dressed that way, and besides, she was abysmally uncomfortable in push-up bras, backless dresses and stiletto heels.

In short, she didn't want the life-style that went with the men she had dated. So why the hell was she drawn to men who put her into that position? Why didn't she have the sense to look for some guy who liked her in her slacks and running shoes? Some guy who wouldn't expect her to look like a fashion plate on his arm every Friday and Saturday evening. Some guy who liked her short nails rather than one who wanted her to paste on those ridiculous acrylic things that always got in her way.

"Are we having an epiphany, Harry?" she asked herself aloud. Had she been looking for all the right things in all the wrong places?

And now she was quoting country songs. The smell of manure must be getting to her, fogging her brain cells.

Or maybe, said the quiet little observer in her mind, those brain cells had been fogged all along and were just now clearing up.

Harriet and Jeff took a cab to the mall. It was a mall like any other mall. "The homogenization of America," Harriet commented. "Everywhere you go, these places are basically the same. Or so I hear."

"Probably. Temperature-controlled, climate-controlled, shopping-controlled. Everybody buys the same things in the same stores. Mass-produced culture."

She looked up at him and laughed. "But convenient."

"Exceptionally."

She expected him to wander away into the electronics store as he had promised, but instead he followed her through the clothing stores until she settled on a royal blue silk pantsuit. It wasn't exactly the dress she had been thinking of, but it wouldn't involve wearing panty hose, and she was strongly opposed to them—largely because she never managed to put on a pair without getting one leg twisted, a fact she never noticed until she was in agony. More than once at some fancy soiree she'd had to hide in the powder room trying to figure out the intricacy of getting the hose straight when they didn't even have a seam in them.

Jeff seemed to like the pantsuit. When she stood before the mirror checking the fit, she caught the look of approval gleaming in his eyes and something inside her shivered deliciously. Enjoying the sheer feminine power of the moment, she stood before the mirror longer than she might have otherwise.

"How about some coffee?" Jeff asked when they left the store.

They stopped in the food court and bought cappuccinos.

"I love to watch people," Jeff said as they sat at a small table near the edge of the court. All around them people moved in a colorful swirl. "See that couple over there with the little baby?"

They were hard to miss. Neither parent took their eyes off the little baby in the carrier seat they had set on the table between them. Their faces reflected total absorption and fascination with the child. Harriet was about to say it was their first baby when another child, about nine or ten, joined them, carrying an ice-cream cone.

"I feel sorry for the older kid," Harriet said after a few moments. "Mom and Dad have forgotten he exists."

"Looks like it." He smiled. "I was the oldest child, too. I can identify."

"I was the youngest, which is probably why I'm such a freewheeler. By the time I came along, my parents were taking the hands-off approach to child rearing."

"How many siblings do you have?"

"Four. Two doctors, a lawyer, a chemical engineer and me, the artsy one."

His smile deepened, creasing the corners of his eyes. "You must have been a surprise."

"I was the family rebel. Still am, I suppose."

"Not me. I always did what needed doing. Still do, I guess."

"Says he who is taking skydiving lessons."

He shrugged. "I figure it's my turn."

"How many brothers and sisters do you have?"

"Just one brother. George. He might as well have been four or five of them, though. George was always the one to do whatever he wanted and damn the consequences."

"Which is why you stayed home on the ranch?"

"You got it. Someone had to do it."

"So you really didn't want to be a cattle rancher?"

He shook his head. "Not when I was younger. As I said, I dreamed of joining the navy and flying fighters off carrier decks. Or of being a great lawyer. For a while I even thought of running away with the circus."

"You must have read *Toby Tyler.*"

He laughed. "How did you guess? I used to have such a thirst for adventure."

"I would guess that you still do," Harriet said. "Why else are you proposing to jump out of an airplane?"

"Why don't you jump with me?"

She shook her head. "Not me. I like my feet planted firmly on the ground. I've got all the adventure I need with some bloodthirsty rustler looking for me."

"Maybe he isn't."

Harriet just looked at him. "So George grew up and left the ranch?"

"As soon as he got out of high school. He even ditched his first fiancée at the altar." He shook his head. "I could have killed him for that."

"At the altar? Really?"

"He never showed for the wedding. We got a phone call later that night saying he'd gone to Denver and wasn't coming back."

"Smart move, not coming back after that."

"To say the least. Everybody was pretty much appalled."

"So is he still here in Denver?"

"I don't know. I don't hear much from him. A couple of years ago he left his wife and two kids. I told you about them earlier. They came to stay with me at the ranch but couldn't handle the isolation, so they moved back here. But as far as I know, they haven't seen George since he walked out."

"I hope he's paying child support!"

"No. I am. But I can afford it. George has always been something of a ne'er-do-well. I bought his share of the ranch years ago, and he managed to blow the money within a couple of months."

"So what I'm hearing here is that you got all the sense of responsibility, and he got all the adventure."

"I guess you could look at it that way."

"What other way is there?" Harriet sipped her coffee, thinking about what she had just heard. "Does it gripe you?"

"What? That I'm a rancher?" He looked off into space, thinking about it. "I don't know. Not anymore, I guess. It used to chap me, but..." He shrugged. "You make the best of the hand you're dealt. If you try to do anything else, you'll go crazy."

But he took skydiving lessons and flew a private plane and helped fund an archaeological dig on his property. He was still an adventurer at heart, Harriet thought. Still very much the boy who had wanted to run away with the circus.

"What about you?" he asked. "Are you doing what you want with life?"

"Pretty much." She gave him a rueful smile. "Earning a living gets in the way sometimes."

"Like forcing you to come all the way out here?"

She almost blushed with embarrassment. "Well, I admit I didn't want to come to Wyoming. I even suggested that I could photograph cowboys in Florida."

"Florida, hmm?" There was a twinkle deep in his blue eyes. "So what you really wanted was beaches?"

"It's all your fault I'm here, you know. My client saw your photo in *Prominence.*"

He made a face. "I'm never going to live that damn thing down."

"Sure you will. Next month all the women in the world will be after the new bachelor. In the meantime, you got my companionship out of the deal." She'd been joking, but he didn't seem to take it that way.

"I'd never complain about that."

Something in his look and the way he spoke the words sent another delicious shiver through her. Trouble ahead, Harriet thought. She didn't want to get involved. Of course, who said she had to get involved? There was such a thing as a modern relationship. Not that she was emotionally inclined to them, but maybe for once in her life she could manage it.

Assuming, of course, she wasn't misinterpreting the promise in his eyes. He hadn't done a single thing to indicate he was interested in her as a woman. Maybe she was imagining it. Maybe it was just the lighting here at the mall. Maybe she'd been so long without masculine appreciation that she was inventing it.

And maybe she needed her head examined. Never yet in her life had she managed to live up to that gleam in a man's eye, anyway. Anyone who had ever shown that kind of interest in her had wound up being seriously disappointed.

Her mother was right. She just wasn't sexy enough or beautiful enough to keep a man's attention. Worse, she wasn't very feminine. *You'll never get a man, Harriet, if you insist on dressing like a man and acting like a man.* And wasn't that what her former boyfriends had all said in the end? Heck, the last one had told her he was beginning to feel as if he were dating another man.

So why was she soaring so perilously close to the flame again? And worse, with a man who could only hurt her if for no other reason than that he lived half a continent away from her home base?

Get a grip, Harry, she told herself sternly. This man could have almost any woman in the world merely by asking. What could he possibly see in *you?*

Convinced she was imagining the look in his eyes, she focused her attention on the group of giggling teenage girls at a nearby table. "School must be out for the day," she commented.

He glanced at his watch. "We'd better head back to the hotel. I need to make a dinner reservation."

He didn't look at her that way again.

They sat facing each other across a snowy white tablecloth, bathed in soft candlelight. This restaurant had been a mistake, Jeff thought. It was too intimate, too romantic. Too suggestive of things he wasn't sure he wanted to suggest to Harriet.

Here he was again, getting interested in a woman who was going to pack up and go back to her life in a large city just as soon as she could. A woman who would undoubtedly die of boredom if she had to stay too long on his ranch.

But she was so...intriguing, he decided. She had a brash attitude that had initially irritated him, a hard veneer that he was beginning to feel was self-protective rather than real. Every now and then he sensed a softness at Harriet Breslin's core, and it drew him even more strongly than her lovely face, her tousled blond hair and her sparkling blue eyes.

She was pretty. Some would even say beautiful. If she thought she was hiding it when she tromped around in work boots and shapeless khaki garments, she was sadly mistaken. Her short hair, far from being boyish, merely emphasized the delicate slenderness of her neck and accentuated the graceful curve of her jaw.

She was a mystery, although he had a strong feeling that she considered herself an open book. From time to time he saw the shadow of an old pain in her gaze. It made him angry to think that anyone could have hurt her.

But people got hurt every day, he reminded himself. Every day. He had been hurt plenty of times. That was life.

And he was going to get hurt again if he didn't rein in these knight-errant impulses of his. Women like Harriet didn't need men like him.

None of which was helping him get to the core of his immediate problem—how he could safely lead into the subject.

"If you could do anything at all in the whole world," he asked her finally, "without regard to making a living, what would you do?"

"Anything?"

"Anything."

She hesitated, her glass of wine sparkling in her hand. "Well, I'd photograph things I want to, not things I have to. Does that make any sense?"

He nodded. "A whole lot, actually."

"I like faces. People's faces are so fascinating. You can read entire stories there, if you catch them in the right mood. Sometimes I go to the park and shoot people walking around, sitting on benches, playing with their children." She shrugged. "There's not much of a market for it, though."

"You could find a whole lot of interesting faces around Conard County." He half expected her to disagree, but she surprised him.

"I'd love to get some pictures of Lucy Schultz working in the motel. She has a wonderfully expressive face."

"What about Maude?"

She laughed. "Maude would need an entire book for herself. She'd be like unraveling a ball of string or peeling the layers of an onion. And the sheriff. He has a fascinating face, too. It's seen a lot.''

He nodded. ''Would you change them, the way you do with your commercial work?''

''Not the faces. Their surroundings, maybe. Sort of like a fantasy journey or something.''

''Lift them out of the mundane?''

''Not exactly.'' She hesitated, grasping for words. ''The idea would be to focus on their faces, to create a background in which the face would be the centerpiece, a setting for whatever story their expressions were telling. It's hard to explain. I'd have to do it and show you.''

''I'd like to see that. What kind of equipment do you work with?''

She set her glass down and leaned back to allow the waiter to place a plate of shrimp scampi in front of her. ''You mean the technical description of my system?''

He nodded. ''Or maybe the technical description of the system you'd really like to have.''

She gave him a crooked smile. ''Oh, I have dreams. Big dreams. I'd like to start with a much bigger monitor so I could see details more clearly. I have a great scanner, but my printer isn't so hot. I usually have to take my work to a commercial place to get it printed. It would be neat if I could do it in my studio so I could make fine adjustments without having to wait for my prints.''

He nodded, encouraging her, and finally got her to talk specifically about hardware and software. It tickled him that she seemed to have an intimate acquaintance with the subject, far better than his own approach of simply buying a complete system and plugging it in.

It also gave him a sense of relief to be discussing something so impersonal. Earlier, when they had stopped for coffee in the mall, they had come perilously close to dangerous territory by discussing their dreams. He supposed he shouldn't be so sensitive about it, but his dreams were something he had never dared to discuss with anyone, for fear they would laugh. Exposing himself that way had meant taking a step he had never taken before, and it had left him feeling vulnerable.

He didn't like the feeling. Vulnerability, he had long ago learned, eventually caused pain. When he started talking about his deepest wishes, he left himself open to attack, and far too many people were willing to use that power destructively.

Janna certainly had. She'd been the real estate attorney who had handled his purchase of his brother's share in the ranch years ago. The sparks had flown between them, and as soon as the deal was closed, they had shared a wild, wonderful weekend. They had gone their separate ways after that, until a few years ago, when they had met again over a new real estate deal.

The attraction had flared anew, and Jeff had found himself falling in love. Every weekend he had flown to Denver to be with her—until the weekend he had found her with another man. A man who, she had said, actually lived his dreams. A man who wouldn't take her away from hers. Did he really think she was willing to give up all the power and perks of her position to make babies with a man who had cow dung on his boots?

That had been the last time he had allowed himself to be scalded. It hadn't been the first time, but it had definitely been the last. No other experience had left him feeling quite so raw, as if his soul had been flayed.

Time and again he had tried to lower his sights, but the truth was, he wasn't interested in the kind of woman who could be a ranch wife. He didn't want a woman who would make him the center of her days. He wanted a woman who was as vitally interested in her own pursuits as he was in his. A woman who could discuss her own interests with him, rather than simply discussing his. A woman who could be his equal in all ways. Most of all, he didn't want her to be dependent on him. He had seen what dependency had done to his mother.

Now, here he was, treading dangerous ground with another

woman whose life was miles away from his. A woman who stood on her own two feet in a world that was both dangerous and competitive. It couldn't be easy being a woman alone in a big city, and it had to be even harder making a living as a photographer. He admired Harriet Breslin, and that admiration was a dangerous thing.

But he could flirt with the danger. Flirting with risk was a deeply embedded character trait of Jeff Cumberland, and he was doing it now.

He flirted with risk even more when he suggested they go to a club after dinner. And he was downright putting his foot in it when he asked her to dance.

Harriet hesitated. She was as conscious of the danger as he, and as leery. Somehow the realization made him feel safer. When she finally took his hand and walked onto the dance floor with him, the exhilaration he felt wasn't much different from what he had experienced the first time he soloed in his small plane.

She smelled good, he realized as she stepped into his arms. The fresh scents of a woman mingled with shampoo and soap. No perfume. Harriet wasn't the type to wear perfume, and he liked that.

She felt good, too. He tried not to bring her too close, but every nerve in his body was aware of the warmth of her small hand in his, of the way her slender waist, shielded only by a layer of slinky, seductive silk, felt against his palm.

Inevitably, as they danced, their bodies brushed together, heightening his consciousness of her. The accidental pressure of her breasts against his chest filled him with a nearly forgotten heat. They were firm breasts, and surprisingly full. Being a man, he had noticed they weren't very large, but when he felt them against him he found them ample enough to make him wild with longing.

Her hip touched his, just the lightest of touches, and given the circumstances, the contact shouldn't have seemed so intimate. But it was excruciatingly intimate and, hardly aware of what he did, he pressed his hand against the small of her back and brought her even closer. He needed more, much more.

As he drew her against him, she looked up at him. Her eyes widened a little in startlement, then grew heavy and slumberous with the same heat he was feeling. Joy and a sense of victory tumbled through him like a rushing waterfall, filling him to the brim, leaving room for nothing else.

He shouldn't be doing this. But he couldn't force himself to draw away, not even when her cheek came to rest on his shoulder and her eyes drifted closed as she gave herself up to the pleasure of dancing in his arms.

They danced until the club closed, their drinks forgotten on the table. They stayed on the floor, swaying gently together as if they were the last people in the universe.

It was all they could ever have, and neither of them was willing to let go of it.

Not yet.

Nine

Harriet awoke in the morning with the feeling that everything in her life was at sixes and sevens. She needed a haircut, her feet hurt from dancing in those stupid new pumps she'd bought and—

And Jeff hadn't kissed her. He should have kissed her, she thought miserably. The way they had danced...well, it had been one of the most romantic evenings she had ever spent. She couldn't remember ever having felt as secure and safe in her entire life as she had in his arms last night.

The edgy tingle of sexual desire he had awakened in her while they danced was still with her this morning, leaving her feeling irritable and hurt. Yes, hurt. Hurt because she had thought he had been there with her, feeling what she was feeling, and then he had left her at the door of her room as if nothing had happened.

"No man wants a woman who acts like a man, Harriet." Her mother's voice seemed to hang in the air, as if the words had just been spoken in this room, instead of nearly twenty years ago in another city half a continent away.

No man would ever want Harriet Breslin, she thought miserably. Not for long. Not once he discovered who she really was.

From the start, she had been herself with Jeff. What made her think a silk pantsuit and a pair of pumps would make any difference? Clothes hadn't solved the problems with any of the other men in her life. Why should she think Jeff was any different?

She sat up, pushed her tousled hair back from her face and wondered why it was that nobody in the world could love her just the way she was. And why it hurt so much to rediscover what she had known all along.

But she knew the answer to that. It was because for a few hours last night she had allowed herself to live in a fool's paradise. For just a few hours, she had allowed the wishful Cinderella in her to believe that something magical was happening.

And that had definitely been stupid.

It hurts, Harriet, she told herself. It hurts, and you have to stop playing these stupid games. It's time to grow up and admit there is no Prince Charming out there who is going to see past the cinders and ashes and love the real you.

Although, to be honest with herself, she had to admit Prince Charming hadn't seen the real Cinderella, either. No, he'd seen a beautiful, mysterious woman in a gorgeous ball gown and glass slippers. He never would have noticed the real Cinderella.

Every man in her life had been trying to turn her into a princess when she was really just ordinary Harriet Breslin, who wouldn't wear glass slippers if they were handed to her by Prince Charming himself.

"So if glass slippers don't fit," she asked the empty room, "why do I keep trying them on?"

And why did she keep deluding herself that she wanted Prince Charming? He'd only expect her to wear those damn shoes like all her other boyfriends.

"Grow up, girl," she told herself. "Grow up and get real." She'd be far more likely to find her real mate by looking among the poets, writers and artists who haunted the coffeehouses of the East Village.

The phone beside the bed rang and she reached for it.

"Breakfast on my balcony in twenty minutes?" Jeff asked.

"I'll be over shortly. Thanks."

Maybe, she found herself thinking, she could stay in Denver

for a while until they caught the rustlers and dead bodies stopped turning up. It would be a lot safer to hole up here than back in Conard County with Jeff.

But the idea held no appeal at all, and by the time she had washed and dressed, she knew one thing for certain: she was going back to the Bar C.

If Jeff had any reservations about what had happened last night, he wasn't showing it this morning. In fact, he acted as if nothing at all had happened. And maybe it hadn't. Maybe Harriet had imagined everything and had felt far more than the circumstances warranted.

Mildly depressed, she went with him to an electronics superstore after breakfast. He said he needed a new computer system because his present one was growing cranky.

Harriet's first passion was photography, but computer equipment ran a close second. She couldn't stay depressed long as she looked at superfast computers and high-quality color printers and scanners and drew up a private wish list of software packages. She could have spent a small fortune without blinking an eye, so it was a good thing she didn't have enough money to do what she wanted to.

But Jeff's wishes seemed remarkably similar to her own, and by the time they left in a cab for the airport, he had purchased the kind of system she only dreamed of.

"This is going to be fun," he said, looking as delighted as a kid with a new Christmas present. "I've been wanting a system like this for as long as I can remember."

"Me, too," Harriet admitted.

"Would you mind showing me how to do things?"

"Of course not." It would make her feel like less of an extra wheel. Besides, it would be fun for her, too.

"Thanks." The smile he gave her was heart-meltingly warm. "I've never really had the time to get into this more than the basics I need to do my accounting, but I've always felt that these machines offer so much potential just for fun."

"I play with mine all the time. Games are fun, but I spend a lot of time drawing, too. You feel so free on the computer because you can change anything at all without having to throw away paper—or let anyone else see it."

"So you draw, too?"

She shifted, suddenly uncomfortable. She wasn't as confident of her drawing ability as she was of her photography. "Just a little. I play with it."

"Playing is a good thing, not something to apologize for."

She looked at him and felt herself smiling. "You should hear me sing. I can't carry a tune to save my life, but I sing all the time, anyway. As long as I'm alone."

"I think I'd like to hear you sing."

"No, honestly, you wouldn't."

He laughed. "Come on, I'm sure it can't be that bad. Besides, that's not the point. People sing when they're happy and feeling good about themselves. I'd like to see you feel that happy."

She flushed a little and looked away. "Let's just get these rustlers off my back, then watch out."

"I'll take that as a promise."

"You may live to regret it."

"That's a chance I'll take."

She looked at him again. "You like to take chances, don't you?"

His expression grew wistful. "Not as much as I used to."

Me, neither, Harriet thought, returning her attention to the scenery. Maybe it was a good thing, maybe not, but as she grew older, she found herself thinking of consequences far more than of the fun she might have in spite of them. "Do you think we can fit all this stuff in the plane?" she asked, trying to keep herself from growing gloomy.

"Just watch me."

It took some jockeying, but Jeff loaded all his purchases into the plane. By six that evening they were setting up the computer equipment in an upstairs bedroom that Jeff said he'd been thinking of converting into a second office.

"Why do you need two offices?" Harriet asked.

He shrugged. "I've got all this room I don't use anyway. Besides, I can't feel like I'm playing if I'm working at my desk in my business office."

"It *is* a big house."

"My mother liked to have weekend guests. And I think my dad was planning on George and me both raising our families here."

"Under one roof?" Harriet looked up from the parallel cable she was attaching to the printer. "That could get rough."

Jeff nodded. "That's what I think. George and I never did get along that well. And could you imagine the both of us with wives who might feel the same way?" He feigned a shudder. "It wouldn't last six months. Somebody would have to build another house." He held up two telephone cables. "Which is phone in and which is phone out?"

She showed him, suspecting that he already knew, but not wanting to call him on it.

It was Sylvia's day off and payday for the cowboys, most of whom had headed out to look for some Friday-night excitement. They scrounged together in the kitchen, making sandwiches out of leftover turkey, then carried a bowl of popcorn upstairs to munch on while they loaded the new software on the computer.

It was nearly midnight before everything was ready, and they agreed it was too late to start exploring tonight.

"Tomorrow," Jeff said. "We'll play tomorrow night. I've got work to catch up on in the morning, unfortunately. But if you want to use the system, just help yourself."

"Really?" She was already itching to see what the system could do. "I've got some photos at the drugstore in town. Maybe I could go in and pick them up. But what about your skydiving? You said it was in the morning."

"I changed it. I'll have somebody go in and get the photos for you. Do you have the claim numbers?"

She went to get them out of her camera bag and gave them to him.

"Funny," he said, "I thought you'd develop your own."

"Sometimes I do, but not for this job. I'm going to make so many changes to the pictures, it wouldn't matter anyway."

He glanced at the tags. "Herschel's Drugs opens at eight. I'll make sure you have the photos by nine."

"Thank you. I'll pay for them, of course."

He waved her offer away. "It's what—twenty dollars? Don't worry about it."

He looked at her then, smiling, and she felt a tingle begin inside her that spread all the way to her toes. For just an instant, the merest breath of time, she thought he leaned toward her.

"I've got to get to bed," he said abruptly, and turned away. "Good night, Harriet."

The pictures were waiting for her by her breakfast plate in the morning. Jeff, Sylvia informed her, had already gone to work.

"There's more to do around here than you'd expect," Sylvia said, joining her with a cup of coffee. "He was out at dawn checking on the herd they brought in yesterday. A couple of the cows had some injuries, so he's dealing with those. It sure was a pretty sunrise, though."

"I haven't seen a sunrise in years. I'm a night person."

Sylvia smiled over her mug. "Out here you get to be a morning person."

"Ugh."

"Well, there isn't a whole lot of nightlife to keep us up."

"Bigger ugh."

Sylvia laughed. "You work so hard at not liking this place. Listen, getting up with the roosters isn't so hard once you start doing it every day."

"I'll take your word for it."

Jeff still hadn't returned by the time Harriet finished breakfast, but that was okay. She was eager to get upstairs with her photographs and try scanning them in and working with them.

It was nearly one by the time she emerged from her fog of preoccupation and realized she was starting to get hungry. The computer system was everything she had hoped for, and it was going to kill her to go back to her own slower, more unwieldy system. Horrible to think it, but she was in danger of getting spoiled.

She paused a moment to look over the enhanced pictures she had printed out and sighed happily. This stuff was good, as good as any commercial work she had ever done.

Then, following the dictates of her stomach, she headed downstairs to see what Sylvia was brewing for lunch. Sylvia, she realized, was something else she could get addicted to. It was nice not to have to worry about meals and feeding herself.

"I thought, since it's such a nice day, that I could serve lunch on the porch," Sylvia told her.

"What can I do to help?"

"Just go on out and take a seat at the table. Everything's ready. Jeff said he'll be here in a couple of minutes."

The hands were already gathered at a long table set out under some cottonwoods, passing around heaping plates of fried chicken and bowls of potato salad. Judging by the quantities of food, Harriet suspected they'd be eating leftovers for supper tonight.

Which was fine by her, she thought as she settled at the table on the porch. There was a plate of fried chicken for her and Jeff, a bowl of potato salad and a green salad with several different kinds of bottled dressing beside it. Beads of condensation ran down the glass sides of a pitcher of iced tea.

She caught sight of Jeff down among the men eating beneath the trees, but when he saw her, he waved and came to join her.

Just before he reached the porch steps, however, the sound

of an approaching car drew his attention toward the drive. Harriet could see the familiar outline of the sheriff's Blazer heading up the wide dirt road that was the ranch's driveway. Her heart climbed into her throat. What now?

Nate Tate pulled the vehicle to a halt in the wide graded parking area, along with the assorted pickup trucks that belonged to the hired hands and right alongside Jeff's battered and rusty vehicle.

"Howdy," he called as he climbed out of the Blazer and walked over to them. "Man, something sure smells good."

"Join us for lunch," Jeff said with a smile. "As usual, Sylvia cooked enough for an army."

Nate climbed the steps beside Jeff and greeted Harriet with a smile. "Do you know how lucky you are to be staying here? I swear Sylvia could almost put Maude out of business if she opened her own place in town."

"Don't put ideas in her head," Jeff said with a grin. "I need her too much."

Sylvia, who was coming out the door with a heaping platter of cookies, laughed. "I couldn't compete with Maude's personality."

"Thank God," Jeff remarked emphatically. Sylvia laughed again and carried the cookies down to the men under the trees. "Let me get another place setting, Nate. I'll be right back."

He disappeared inside, leaving Harriet and Nate smiling awkwardly at each other.

"Another body?" she finally asked.

"No." He shook his head. "Nothing like that. You can relax, missy."

Harriet wasn't sure she liked being called missy, but he wasn't asking, so she didn't tell him so. Besides, she didn't think he meant it to be anything other than friendly. Sheriff Tate seemed like the kind of man who had pet names for all the women he knew, and he would never imagine that they could be taken wrong.

He leaned back in his chair and cocked his head a little to the side. "This situation must be really chapping you."

"To put it mildly. See if I ever let my agent talk me into taking a job like this again."

He chuckled softly. "I gotta admit, you're seeing the worst side of the West. It really isn't like this all the time."

Harriet sighed. "I know. Believe me, I know. New York gets a bad rap because of the stuff that makes the news, but it's actually a nice place to live."

He nodded. "It has its good points. I feel too closed in there to be comfortable, but the folks are real nice."

She smiled, making a peace offering. "When I first got here, I kept feeling—oh, I don't know what you'd call it. Agoraphobic, maybe? Everything was so wide-open, I had the craziest feeling that I was going to fall off the edge."

He nodded. "And I feel claustrophobic when I get in the city. Same thing, I reckon. But we don't have cattle rustlings every day of the week around here, and it's been a while since the last murder. The most violence we usually see is between married folks along about February when cabin fever sets in. Although—" He shrugged and broke off. "Sometimes I get the feeling this county is going to hell in a handbasket. We've had some strange troubles here the past few years. Spies, satanic cults, toxic waste dumping..." He shook his head. "Years ago, problems used to be a whole lot easier."

"At least they seemed to be."

He laughed. "Yeah, nostalgia can be so damn misleading, can't it? And years ago, toxic dumping wouldn't have been a crime."

"No, people would have just done it closer to home."

Jeff returned with another place setting, drew another chair up to the table and told everybody to dig in. Nate helped himself to a chicken breast, a huge mound of potato salad and a side plate of the tossed salad. From the trees where the hands were eating, laughter drifted up to them. Sylvia seemed to be having a good time down there with the "boys."

"So, what's up?" Jeff finally asked. "Or did you just come out here because you wanted some of Sylvia's cooking."

Nate shook his head and sipped his iced tea. "Marge packed me her usual lumberjack's lunch. It's out there in the car spoiling. Remind me to throw it away before I leave. Meat-loaf sandwich. That woman makes the best damn meat loaf in the world."

Jeff regarded Nate steadily. "So what's the bad news?"

Nate sighed and put down his fork. "The stockyards in Omaha have seen quite a few cattle with a new brand. The inspector made a note of it, and it looks like it could be your cattle, Jeff."

Jeff sat up straighter. "Are they sure?"

Nate shook his head. "It could be, that's all anyone's gonna say for now. The brand is an *O* inside an inverted triangle."

"Damn!"

"Now, wait. It's a legitimate brand, all registered and everything. It belongs to a cattle company in Montana doing business as the Overland Cattle Company. The only reason anyone paid any attention to it is that it's new. The Overland Cattle Company didn't exist a year ago. And last month was the first time they shipped any cattle to market."

But Jeff's face had settled into hard lines. "How close is it to my brand?"

"Too close," Nate said. "The Bar C could be overlaid perfectly with this brand."

"So what do we do now?"

"I've got a friend up in Montana, a cop, who's checking into Overland. And the brand inspectors are going to take a closer look at the Overland cattle to see if they can detect an overlay. Unfortunately, the last group they sent to market has all been set to slaughter, so they have to wait for another shipment."

"Slaughter? Already?"

"Apparently Overland had them pretty well fattened up before they reached the feedlots. Brought a damn good price, I hear.''

Jeff swore softly.

''Now, we don't have any proof yet, Jeff. It might turn out to be nothing. Some Japanese investors may have opened a big operation up there. You've seen it happen before. They buy out some rancher, pour the money in and bring the operation up to big time real fast. That may be all it is.''

''Maybe. How many head were shipped?''

Nate shifted a little uneasily in his chair. ''Nearly five hundred.''

''Five hundred!'' Jeff sat back as if he could hardly believe his ears. ''They can't be my cattle. I couldn't have lost that many without knowing it.''

Nate chewed his lower lip a moment before saying, ''Maybe you need to get somebody else to do your counting for you.''

Jeff's eyes narrowed. ''What are you saying?''

Nate cocked his head. ''Maybe nothing. Or maybe that somebody around here is kind of falling down on his job. Or maybe somebody didn't want you to know because they'd messed up.''

''You're saying that if those were my cattle, somebody on this ranch is in league with the rustlers.''

''Not necessarily. If they *were* your cattle, maybe somebody around here fell asleep at the wheel and just doesn't want you to know it. How many head do you still have out in the summer pastures?''

''Quite a few. Of the ones we've brought down so far, I seem to be missing only a handful.''

''Interesting.'' Nate scratched behind his ear and picked up his fork again. ''Well, maybe they're not your animals.''

But Jeff clearly didn't believe that. He looked both stunned and angry. ''They filled three trucks with my beef just last week, Nate. They wouldn't have had to pull that kind of operation off too many times to drive away with five hundred head.''

"But in broad daylight? Harriet here wouldn't have been the first person to stumble on them."

"Maybe they did the other thefts at night. Or maybe..." His voice trailed away. A moment passed before he stated the unthinkable. "Maybe somebody on the Bar C is in collusion with them."

"How long will it take you to get the rest of your animals in?"

"Maybe another week. I've been trying to do it in stages so I didn't have to hire a bunch of strangers." His gaze strayed from Nate to the mountains that rose along the western edges of his ranch. "Five hundred head ought to leave a pretty big hole somewhere. Maybe I ought to ride out myself and start checking."

"And maybe I ought to just go home," Harriet said, following her own line of thought. "If somebody on this ranch is working with the thieves, I'd be safer in New York."

"You'll be safe with me," Jeff said swiftly. "You come with me."

"On a *horse?*" She almost squeaked the word. "I don't think so."

"I've got the perfect mount for you," Jeff said reassuringly. "A really gentle mare."

"I don't believe in gentle horses. I've heard *that* line before." Her hip twinged in memory.

"I let my four-year-old niece ride this pony," Jeff said.

"Your four-year-old niece has never been thrown and had her pelvis broken."

"That's true." He almost smiled. "But that's because she rode Maggie."

"Maggie? A horse named Maggie?" Harriet looked disbelieving. She had always thought horses had names like Night Wind, or Devil, or Satan Incarnate.

"Maggie," Jeff repeated. "She's nice, she's old, she's patient, and the joy of her life is being ridden. You'll see."

"I will not! You can't possibly expect me to get on a horse! My God, that's more dangerous than these damn rustlers."

"Don't exaggerate," Jeff said, a twinkle in his eyes. "Maggie hasn't ever shot anyone."

Harriet fell silent, staring gloomily at her plate. "I'll just go home."

"No," both men said in unison.

"This is ridiculous! You can't keep me here against my will. And you certainly can't make me risk my neck on a horse!"

"You'll be safe with me," Jeff promised.

She slowly raised her eyes to his and felt a shiver of quick pleasure run through her at what she read there. Safe with Jeff? She'd never be safe with him as long as they were within touching distance. "No," she heard herself say. "There is no way I'm going to spend my days riding around this ranch counting cows."

"It won't take all that long," he assured her. "If they've taken that many head, I've got a pretty good idea where they must have come from. We'll be out two nights, tops."

"Absolutely not."

"Wouldn't you like to see the wolves on Thunder Mountain?"

"Wolves? There are *wolves?*"

"Very shy wolves. Very nice wolves. This used to be their country, but they were exterminated a long time ago. This group apparently worked its way back here from up north, and everyone's trying to protect them. Just think, you can see a rare gray wolf."

"I don't know," Harriet said uneasily. The idea appealed to her, even as it frightened her.

"I'll show you the archaeological dig, too."

She felt herself weakening, and she made one last-ditch effort. "No."

"Yes," Jeff said. "There are a lot of beautiful things out there, Harriet, and you can't see them except from horseback.

I'll show you places where humans have hardly ever gone. Places where the wilderness still rules. It's just a couple of days, and I'll guarantee you that you won't be thrown by Maggie. That horse couldn't get up the energy to escape a rattler.''

"Rattler? There are rattlesnakes out there?''

Jeff apparently couldn't help it. He started to chuckle and Nate joined him.

"Come on, Harriet,'' Jeff said. "I'm offering you a chance to see things that most people will never see. And believe me, it's a whole lot less dangerous out there than walking through Central Park. *Our* wolves don't kill people.''

Ten

"I can't do this." Harriet stood outside the corral looking in at the huge horse Jeff had saddled for her and was now holding by the reins. Of course, the horse wasn't that big as horses went, but the closer Harriet got to it, the more like a dinosaur it looked.

"Of course you can," Jeff said soothingly. "Maggie is a calm, patient, lazy horse. She's far more likely to stop to nibble grass than she is to walk fast."

"Until I get on her."

The sun was hanging heavy over the western mountains, promising another long twilight.

"All you have to do is try it," Jeff said. "We made a bargain, remember? If Maggie doesn't manage to soothe your fears in a half hour, then you can stay here while I go out on the range."

It was that promise of escape from her rash acceptance of Jeff's offer to take her with him that had gotten Harriet this far. Her feet—heck, her whole *body*—were now refusing to go any farther.

Jeff smiled patiently, apparently not at all frustrated by her reluctance. He gave a gentle tug on the rein he held and led Maggie over to the corral fence where Harriet stood.

"She really *is* a nice horse," Jeff said, running his hand along Maggie's neck. The mare nuzzled him approvingly.

"Her teeth are huge."

"She's never bitten anyone in her life."

"I don't want to be the first."

"You won't be. She's as gentle as a lamb, Harriet. Try touching her nose. She loves it when you pet her like this." He demonstrated, rubbing the horse's forehead, then down to her nostrils. "Maggie thinks she's a puppy, don't you, girl?"

Tentatively, Harriet reached over the fence and stroked Maggie's nose. The horsehair felt coarser than she had expected, but Maggie seemed to like her touch. The mare didn't even bare her teeth, which Harriet took to be a positive sign.

"See?" said Jeff. "I have someone exercise her every day, but what Maggie really likes are long, easy rides on the range. She settles into a nice, gentle pace and can go all day."

"How do you know she likes it?" Harriet dared another stroke, and the horse accepted it calmly.

"You can just tell. She gets this sparkle in her eyes, and her ears prick up. She looks happy."

"Mmm."

Harriet found herself staring into one of the horse's liquid brown eyes. The mare didn't look like a killer beast. Nor was she really that big. The dinosaur image was beginning to fade as the animal accepted repeated pets on the nose.

Maybe she was being silly, Harriet told herself. Her one bad experience shouldn't keep her from trying again. Besides, the more she thought about it, the more she liked the idea of traveling on horseback to places she couldn't go in a car. As a child, riding had been one of her biggest dreams, a dream that had gone sour the very first time she got an opportunity to try it.

She closed her eyes, feeling the mare's warm breath on her skin, and remembered long-forgotten dreams of riding through open country on her very own horse. Now, here was her chance to do something she had always wanted to, and she was going to pass it up because she was afraid?

"You want to do it, don't you," Jeff said quietly. "Come on, Harriet. I'll hold the rein and lead Maggie around the corral. You don't have to worry about controlling her. I'll do that."

Harriet opened her eyes and looked deep into Maggie's big brown one. And somehow she found herself climbing the corral fence.

Once inside the fence, she experienced a moment of sheer fright as Maggie seemed to grow huge again, but the moment passed.

"Grab the pommel with your left hand," Jeff was saying. "That's right. Now, can you get your left foot into the stirrup?"

It was a stretch, but Harriet managed.

"Good, now lift yourself up and swing your right leg over the saddle."

Unlike her first experience on a horse, Maggie didn't sidle as Harriet swung herself up. At most, she twitched a flank muscle as the saddle pulled harder to one side.

And then Harriet was sitting on the back of a horse for the first time in twenty years. She looked around, and a burst of excitement filled her. "Wow!" she said. "Double wow."

Jeff grinned up at her. "Feels good, doesn't it?" He patted Maggie's neck. "Got your other foot in the stirrup?"

Harriet looked for and found the stirrup, sliding her toe into it. "Yeah."

Jeff tethered the horse to a fence rail and took a few moments to adjust the stirrups to his satisfaction. "Okay," he said. "Now, the first rule is to ride with your legs."

"My legs?"

"Keep your feet firmly in those stirrups. Stand in them if the horse's gait becomes uncomfortable. Use 'em to keep your balance if you feel like you're tipping one way or the other."

Harriet nodded. Butterflies were rioting in her stomach, but she was surprisingly eager for the next step. Just getting up here seemed to have surmounted the worst of her fear.

"Whatever you do," he continued, "don't just sit there and try to keep your balance with your upper body. Your feet and your legs have to do most of the work, okay?"

"Okay."

"Think of it as riding standing up, and you'll get the idea. Now, keep your legs snug against Maggie's side. If you squeeze them hard, she'll speed up a little. Each time you squeeze them, she'll go to her next faster pace."

"Got it. I thought she didn't have a faster pace."

He laughed. "Not really. But she can go a little faster than a slow walk. I don't think she's galloped in years."

Harriet nodded, wondering what other little surprises Maggie might have for her.

"Now," Jeff said, "the reins."

"I thought you were going to hold them."

"I'm going to use the leading rein." He pointed to a long rope that was attached to a ring on Maggie's bridle. "But you have to learn to steer her and stop her, Harriet. Whatever you do, don't pull hard on the reins. Maggie's mouth is tender, and I don't like riders who use the bit for control."

"Gotcha."

The leading rein was tied to the fence rail. Jeff passed her up the two long leather reins.

"I'm not a purist," he said, "and you're not riding for show. I don't care whether you hold both reins in your left hand or one in each hand, or both of them in both hands. Do whatever is comfortable, okay? But if you lay the reins gently to the right, she'll turn right. To the left, and she goes left. Say 'whoa' and she should stop. But if she doesn't, give a gentle backward tug on the reins. Don't ever pull hard, okay?"

"Okay."

He untied the leading rein—which was an awfully long rope, Harriet noticed with a sharp qualm—and looked up at her.

"Move the reins gently to the right."

Harriet tried it, and much to her amazement, Maggie kept turning until she slackened the reins.

"Good going," Jeff said with approval. "Now squeeze her gently with your knees."

And Maggie was off. Well, not really off, Harriet admitted

once the first thrill of fear passed. The mare ambled slowly forward, as if she had all the time in the world to make it across the small corral. It was fast enough for Harriet, who was trying to get used to the swaying motion while remembering everything Jeff had said.

She pressed her feet down more firmly in the stirrups, as he'd instructed her, and immediately discovered that she felt much more stable. The feeling gave her greater courage, so she attempted to turn Maggie.

The horse obeyed as if she were perfectly willing to go wherever her rider suggested. And when Harriet said "Whoa," Maggie halted.

"See?" Jeff said. "She's a good pony. I've had plenty of horses I've had to argue with, but Maggie is just naturally sweet-tempered. Try riding her around the outside of the corral."

After three or four turns around, exhilaration filled Harriet, and daring caused her to tighten her knees once more. Maggie picked up her pace a little, still walking, but at a speed that might actually get her somewhere.

"Very good," Jeff said approvingly. "How do you feel?"

"Wonderful!"

"Wanna do this again sometime?"

"You bet!"

In fact, she didn't want to stop. Round and round she went, gradually working up her nerve to try Maggie at a faster pace. Jeff was now standing in the middle of the corral, holding the end of the rope, turning in circles as she rode around. Several times she changed direction, just to be sure she could, and whenever she said whoa, Maggie obediently came to a stop.

But finally Jeff called a halt. "I don't want you to get saddle sore. You'll never want to go with me in the morning if you do."

Harriet felt absurdly disappointed. In a matter of a mere half hour, she had overcome a paralyzing fear and rediscovered a great joy. She didn't want to give it up.

But she knew Jeff was right. In fact, she fully anticipated being miserably saddle sore after her ride with him tomorrow, but now she was looking forward to it, even to the soreness. It was going to be *fun*.

They left at dawn, far too early for Harriet, who kept reminding herself that on New York time it wasn't as early as it felt. But it *felt* early, anyway.

The sun was barely peeping up over the horizon, turning swaths of clouds into arcs of pink and purple. The air was chilly, chilly enough that she could see her breath and the horses blew clouds of steam. In her saddlebags were packed a change of clothes, rain gear and necessary toiletries. Jeff also led a packhorse that carried food, sleeping bags, a tent and supplies for the horses. It seemed like a lot for one night, maybe two, but he explained that at this time of year the weather could turn cold and wet almost without warning, and they had to be prepared.

Maggie was feeling frisky, Harriet could tell. The normally placid mare wanted to move along at a trot this morning.

"Let her have her head for a bit," Jeff suggested. "She's feeling her oats, but she'll settle down in a little while."

Which was how Harriet got introduced to Maggie's trot. At first she felt sure she was going to fly off the horse's back, but it wasn't long before she picked up the rhythm and became comfortable with it. She wondered why no one had told her about standing in the stirrups all those years ago. It made riding so much easier.

Maggie soon settled down to a walk, and Harriet settled down with her, allowing her body to sway gently with the horse's gait instead of fighting it. Before long she was even able to spare attention for the beautiful countryside.

As the day brightened, it grew warmer. Harriet shed her sweater, tying it around her waist, and watched with interest as they slowly climbed toward the mountains.

"Where are we going first?" she asked Jeff.

"To the archaeological dig. It's on the way to the high pastures and it'll be a great place to stop for lunch."

"Are they finding lots of good stuff out there?"

"Actually, yes. But I don't know how much we'll be able to see today. They move the artifacts back to the university at least once a week, so unless they've discovered something spectacular in the last few days, we might not see anything except holes in the ground."

"Open graves." That was how she envisioned these archaeological windows on the past.

"Possibly. Although if there are any occupants, they'll be turned over to the Indians for reburial."

"I've heard so many people say how ridiculous that is," Harriet said. "But can you imagine how they'd bellow if some archaeologist tried to dig up a thousand-year-old graveyard in England?"

"Some of what they're finding here is closer to eight thousand years."

"Eight thousand! Can you imagine it? Is there much left?"

Jeff shrugged a shoulder. "Depends on what you mean by much. They've found some bead necklaces, some clay pots, arrowheads and knives. Some bone needles and awls. I think they learn more from the garbage, though."

"The garbage?"

"The stuff that was burned in the fires. They've found animal bones, of course, and some grains and seeds that give them a good idea of the local diet back then. They were pretty much hunter-gatherers, I guess, except that this village seems to have been a fairly permanent encampment. The fire pits go back a long way."

Harriet nodded, looking around her and trying to imagine what it must have been like eight thousand years ago. "Was the climate the same?"

He cocked his head. "I honestly don't know. I know there's a theory that the first humans came over a land bridge from Siberia thirty thousand years ago, toward the end of the last great ice age, but eight thousand years ago? I'd have to check on it."

"I thought this continent has only been populated for twelve or thirteen thousand years."

"That's what archaeologists used to say, mostly because they hadn't found any artifacts from earlier times. I had trouble believing it myself. The native populations spread too far, too fast if you believed the twelve-thousand-year timetable."

Harriet nodded. "So what changed their minds?"

"Well, the land bridge between Alaska and Siberia had to have been covered with water by the melting of the ice caps at the end of the ice age. No way around it. And that happened thirty thousand years ago. Then, recently, they've discovered bone tools in the Yukon that date back twenty-two thousand years ago, and fire pits in Mexico that date back nearly that far. And in Peru they've found tools going back eighteen thousand years. It's a better fit."

"And around here?"

He shrugged. "The oldest I know about is a cave in Idaho where tools date back about twelve thousand years. But that's to be expected, I guess. The ice sheets would have retreated much more slowly inland, especially from the high places. Hell, there are still glaciers left in the Rockies. Imagine having to cross those mountains on foot, mountains where the snow lasts year-round." He shook his head. "I'm not at all surprised the interior was settled later."

"Besides," Harriet said, "what would be the pressure to push inland? I imagine life on the coast was a lot easier, with a milder climate and plenty of fishing."

"Exactly." He gave her a smile that seemed to approve of her thoughts on the matter.

When, Harriet found herself wondering, had any man other than a client approved of her thinking? She was far more used to being lectured and told that she didn't know what she was talking about—which was probably true when the subject was marketing, advertising or Wall Street. Not that she'd ever allowed herself to be subdued by men who needed to believe they were experts on everything. Or had she? The thought made her uncomfortable, and she fixed her attention on the countryside again.

Her imagination began to take flight, wondering what it must have been like to be the first people ever to walk this land. They must have had a very different view of life, she thought. Look at how overwhelmed she had been by the wide-open spaces when she had first arrived here, how isolated she had felt. The first comers must have been inured to such things, finding companionship and security in their small bands. They must have reveled in the blessings of lands that teemed with wildlife and vegetation.

This new land held many dangers for them, though. Perhaps they had simply learned to live side by side with fears that she could barely imagine. In a time when a broken leg could end a life, people must have had a very different view of the dangers of the world.

Being hunter-gatherers, they must have seen this place as a paradise, not as the desolate, empty space she had first perceived. Perhaps in crossing those western mountains they had left the worst of their fears behind.

Or maybe not. She sighed and glanced up at the mountains, wondering if life had really changed all that much, or if human beings had merely changed one set of problems for another.

She almost smiled as she imagined some skin-clad caveman telling his wife she didn't know what she was talking about when she suggested there had to be a better way to kill a woolly mammoth than running the entire herd over a cliff edge when the village couldn't eat more than a half dozen of them. Some things probably never changed.

By noon, Harriet and Jeff had risen above the prairie onto a plateau at the foot of the mountains. Ahead of them she could see the signs of an encampment: tents, cars and long folding tables.

"They're probably down in the gorge," Jeff remarked, explaining the absence of people. "In addition to digging downward from the top, they're digging in from the side. That's where I first spotted the signs of the fire pits."

"Hey," Harriet asked, just to be difficult. "How come they get to come out here in cars but we had to ride?"

Jeff flashed her a grin. "I suppose I could have driven the long way around with the horse trailer, but it would have been the *long* way. It would have taken us nearly the same time to get here."

"So we came as the crow flies?"

"Basically."

"I'll remember that tonight when I'm too sore to walk."

He laughed.

They tethered their horses to a wind-twisted tree that shaded some of the tables and walked over to the edge of the gorge. Harriet noted that large squares of ground were staked out and marked by twine strung between the stakes, each section identified by a number tacked to the stakes. They worked their way around them until they reached the edge.

Considering they were working with little more than trowels and dental tools, Harriet thought, this group of a half-dozen people had moved a lot of dirt. What clearly had once been a sheer drop was now terraced steeply in layers that reached almost down to the riverbed. The stream was little more than a trickle now, but judging by the depth of the gorge, it was often a swollen torrent.

"Jeff!" A dark-haired woman in dusty denim shorts and a faded pink T-shirt waved from below. "You've got to come down and see this! I think we're going to push the time line back with this find."

"We'll be right down, Freda."

Harriet looked around. "Uh...how do we do that?"

He flashed her a smile. "Follow me."

The path down the side of the gorge was narrow and steep, better suited to mountain goats than people, but Jeff assured her it was a lot easier to come back up. Harriet reserved judgment.

When they reached the bottom, they crunched their way across gravel and rocks to where Freda was waiting with three other women and two men who all appeared young enough to be students. Freda herself looked a pleasant forty, with lines carved by the sun and good humor around her hazel eyes.

"This is great," she was saying excitedly before they even reached her. "We were just about to give up going any deeper. We haven't found anything in several layers now." As they walked up to her, she made a sweeping wave of her arm toward the terraces and the plainly visible layers that climbed the gorge walls.

Harriet glanced up, in the direction of Freda's gesture. "Is that really sedimentary?"

She apparently couldn't have asked a better question. Freda was off and running, explaining that this area had once been a lake as the glaciers melted away. "There's glacial moraine of course, and sediments from the lake, but on the higher layers we see sediment from this little river here. When it started out, the land was a lot lower. Each time it flooded its banks, it deposited another layer of sediment from the mountains. So we have two processes here. The river is cutting an ever deeper gorge, while at the same time building the walls higher when it floods. Fascinating geology."

Harriet nodded her understanding.

"Flooding was more common in the past, though, when the gorge wasn't so deep," Freda told them. "And that's where the fun comes in. Come over here."

They followed her over to the lowest terrace and stood looking at it from both above and the side.

"We found nothing at all in the layers above," Freda continued, her voice containing excitement. "We figured we were going to date the oldest finds around eight to nine thousand years ago. And then we found this, well below the last evidence of human occupation."

She pointed triumphantly with a trowel. Leaning forward, Harriet could barely make out what appeared to be a smooth piece of dirt.

"It's a pot," Freda said. "A clay pot! Way below anything else."

"It wasn't buried, perhaps?" Jeff asked.

Freda shook her head and leaned forward, using her trowel to touch the black dirt just below the pot. "See? Charcoal. This pot was sitting in a fire pit when the river flooded. I won't know for sure until we carbon-date the charcoal, but I'm guessing this pushes us back to at least ten thousand years."

Harriet stared at that little piece of clay visible in the side of the lowest terrace and felt awe steal through her. Ancient hands, work-roughened hands, had formed that piece of clay and used it for cooking or other tasks before abandoning it in a fire pit. Why had they left it? Perhaps the river had risen suddenly and driven the people away. Perhaps some other danger had caused them to move. Or maybe they were simply following the seasons and the herds and had left that pot behind because they no longer wanted it.

"I can hardly wait to see if there's anything in it," Freda was saying enthusiastically. "Listen, I hope you don't mind, but I'm not going to pack up next week the way I planned. This is too exciting to take a chance that flooding will wipe this out before we get back next spring. I want to keep working until the last possible moment."

"That's fine by me," Jeff said. "You've probably got another four weeks or so before it gets too cold at night."

Freda waved a hand. "I'll get some portable kerosene heaters to use at night. I can't risk having this washed away until I'm sure there's nothing else here." She stood with her hand on her hip, admiring that nondescript little potsherd.

"I wish I could stay and help," Jeff said. "Do you need more people? Maybe I can find some locally."

"Let me think about that," Freda replied. "If this is all we find, more people would be a waste. But if there's additional fragments around the pot, extra hands would be helpful. I'll let you know.''

"Speaking of people," Jeff continued, "have you folks seen any strangers hereabouts in the last few weeks? Or anytime over the summer?''

"No…'' Freda shook her head. "Actually, we haven't seen anybody but you all summer, and some of your hired hands.''

"When did you see them?''

She cocked her head thoughtfully. "Damn, I don't know. Hal, do you remember when it was we saw those guys driving the herd? I was so worried they were going to bring them into the gorge to drink.''

Hal, who was busy using a paintbrush to sweep soil off one of the higher levels, glanced down at her. "Oh, that was a long time ago," he said. "Gee, it must have been a couple of weeks after we got here. Maybe the first of July?''

"July?'' To Harriet it seemed that Jeff stiffened a little. "Which direction were they headed?''

Freda pointed east. "Back to your ranch, of course.''

Jeff's face, usually expressive, grew wooden. "Thanks. Well, I'd love to stay and help you guys dig, but Harriet and I are on business, and we've got to move along. I'll try and get back out here in a few days to see if you need anything.''

Freda shook her head. "If I need anything, I'll just drive down to the ranch and ask. You know that.''

The climb back up the side of the gorge *was* easier than coming down. The horses were contentedly cropping the grass beneath the tree, although to Harriet it looked rather yellow and untasty.

"The horses must be thirsty by now," Harriet remarked. Maggie actually looked quite contented, but Jeff's mount, a tall chestnut gelding, didn't seem as happy.

"We'll run into the creek a little farther up. They can drink then. We'll eat lunch there, too, if you don't mind. Freda looks as if she's not going to stop digging for anything.''

"Okay.''

In the short time she had been out of the saddle, her thighs had begun to stiffen, but not too much to mount Maggie again. Harriet hated to think how she would feel come morning.

"We weren't moving any cattle in July," Jeff remarked. "And certainly not in that direction."

Harriet looked over at him and found his expression grim. "The rustlers?"

"I don't know who else it could be. We took the herds up to the high pastures in late May and early June. And as far as I know, nobody moved any of them until last week."

"So it's bad."

"Very bad." He reigned his mount suddenly. "I'm wasting my time. If they moved the herd toward the ranch, I'm not going to find anything up in the pasture."

"But you can't be sure without looking," Harriet said tentatively. "I mean, maybe Freda got mixed up."

Jeff shook his head. "I seriously doubt it. That woman could find her way across the Sahara with nothing but the stars and sun to guide her."

Harriet, who couldn't find her way across town without remembering which direction the streets were numbered, felt envious. She had to admit it seemed unlikely that Freda was mistaken.

After a few moments, Jeff kneed his horse forward again. "Okay, we'll look. It's the only way I have right now of guessing how many cattle they took back in July."

"I'm surprised nobody else caught wind of this," Harriet commented. "I mean, don't you have people check on the cows from time to time?"

"Supposedly. I certainly pay them to do it."

"So somebody should have reported it if whole bunches of cows were missing, right?"

"Theoretically." Jeff had to repress a grin. He wasn't used to thinking of cows in terms of "bunches." Even with his present worries, the humor of it struck him.

* * *

By four that afternoon, Jeff knew the worst. He looked out over a huge mountain meadow and saw no sign of either cattle or recent grazing. "They're gone."

"Maybe they wandered off?" Harriet said.

He shook his head. "The reason I can leave them here pretty much unattended for the summer is because this bowl is about the only place they can graze. Some of them might have wandered a little distance, but not all of them. And they would have wandered back for the grass and water. Nor could they have gone very far, anyway." He pointed at the fence line that vanished into the trees farther up. "They could come down, but they couldn't go very far up. And if they'd come down, we would have seen them." There was a burning flame in the pit of his stomach as he faced the likelihood that rustlers had been ripping him off all summer.

"How many?" Harriet asked.

"We put maybe fifty head in this meadow."

"And the other meadows?"

"I don't need to look." He shook his head, his hands tightening on the reins. "I can wait until the roundup is finished. I just wanted to know if it was more than that one incident."

She nodded, giving him a sympathetic look. "I know how you feel. I felt that way when I was mugged and my purse was stolen. Do you suppose these were the cattle taken to market last month?"

"Probably. All nice and fat from the thick grass up here. Hell."

He scanned the meadow and shook his head again. "I bet all the high pastures are empty."

Harriet didn't answer.

"Well," Jeff said a couple of minutes later, "we might as well make camp here along the stream bank."

The sun had disappeared behind Thunder Mountain, leaving the world in the eerie mountain twilight with blue sky directly above. Thunderheads were building around the high western peak, though, and the wind was developing a chilly bite.

"It's going to rain soon," Jeff said. "Let's pitch the tent."

Eleven

The rain started after dinner. Harriet and Jeff lay side by side in the tent on their sleeping bags, looking out the screened door and watching the torrents fall. Thunder boomed hollowly, loud enough at times to be almost deafening.

"I feel like I'm right up inside the storm," Harriet remarked.

"You almost are. It gets even better higher up. Of course, it's more comfortable if you're inside a building. I was outside. Scared me half to death."

"What were you doing?"

He rolled onto his side and propped his cheek on his hand. "When I was about twelve, I went through what I think of as my Native American stage." He gave her a smile that was visible in the flicker of lightning. "I decided to do a vision quest, all by myself."

"And your parents let you?"

"Well, my mother wasn't terribly involved in anything I did. George was the apple of her eye. And my dad...well, my dad had hardly been more than a boy when his father died and he had to take over the running of the ranch. He was of the opinion that twelve-year-old boys were nearly men. And maybe I was, in some respects. I was already hunting and fishing and doing a lot of chores around the ranch. A man's jobs, limited only by my school hours."

"So you had a lot of responsibility from an early age?" She thought that might be the key to Jeff Cumberland's character.

"I guess. Probably no more than other ranch boys my age."

"Maybe."

"Anyway, he didn't seem to mind too much when I told him I was going up to the mountains for a couple of days."

"Did you tell him why?"

"Hell, no." His tone was almost wry. "My dad's dad had helped take this land away from the Indians. His opinion was that they were nothing but savages. My father didn't understand my fascination, so I stopped talking about it."

Harriet nodded her understanding. "I got that way about some things, too. My parents wanted me to be serious like my older brothers and sisters, but I was always taking off on flights of imagination."

"You're creative. Of course you did."

His assessment warmed her. "So what happened with the vision quest?"

"It didn't work. Probably a good thing it didn't, because I'd forgotten some crucial things."

"Such as?"

"If you go hungry and thirsty long enough to start hallucinating, you'd better have somebody around to rescue you. I didn't have the kind of preparation Native American youths had. I just had some cockamamy notion about fasting until I had a vision. Dangerous, if you don't know what you're doing, especially all alone on the side of a mountain."

"I guess so."

"Anyway, I hardly got off the ground, as it were. I went without eating or drinking all day, sitting on a boulder that gave me a view of treetops and the mountain. By nightfall, I was miserable. Then the storm hit."

Jeff shook his head, pointing out the screen. "Imagine sitting all night in a storm like this without any shelter. Only I was higher up, and it seemed like the thunder and the lightning were all around me, as if I could fall right into the clouds and be swallowed forever if I took a single misstep. It was wild and beautiful and as terrifying as anything I've ever done."

"Maybe that storm was your vision."

"How so?"

She shrugged, forgetting he probably couldn't see her. "I don't know. What did you take from it?"

"A very strong feeling that thunder is the voice of the heavens. And the realization that at twelve, I was nowhere near as mature as I thought I was."

Harriet laughed softly. "I take it you won't let your son come up here all alone at that age."

"No, I'd insist on bringing him myself."

And he probably would, thought Harriet. He'd put everything aside to do something like that with his son. She supposed the world was full of men like that, but she'd never dated any. Hell, the men she'd dated wouldn't put anything on hold for *her,* even during the first flush of the relationship. Which was another indicator of how lousy her taste in men was. Somehow her courtships, if you could call them that, had all seemed to start somewhere in the middle of the relationship.

"What about George?" she heard herself saying.

"What about him?"

"He was the apple of your mother's eye. That would seem to indicate he didn't get treated the same by her."

"He didn't." Jeff fell silent a moment. "I try to tell myself I'm misremembering, but I honestly don't think I am. George never had any real chores to do all the time he was growing up. Mom was determined that he should have a childhood, that he should have time for a social life, parties and games and hanging out."

"And you?"

"She said I was my father's son. I guess I was. Besides, someone had to help out. My dad wasn't making a lot of money, and he couldn't afford to hire enough hands."

"So you filled in. You must have resented that."

"At times."

"I take it George is still having fun going to parties and playing games and hanging out."

A snort escaped him. "Sometimes it sure looks that way."

"I guess my childhood was a lot like George's. Being the youngest, I had a lot of rope and a lot of freedom, and plenty of older siblings to make my way easier."

"But you didn't turn out like George," he said. "You've got a career, and from what I can tell, you've got a fire under you to be successful."

"Well, yes. I may not be a doctor or a lawyer, but I'll admit to a very strong need to make my mark so I don't spend the rest of my life feeling like an also-ran."

"You could never be that," he said. "Never."

This man, Harriet thought, sure knew how to make a girl feel good. She had just started to smile when lightning struck a tree nearby. For several seconds her heart seemed to stop beating as thunder cracked deafeningly and the ground beneath her shook as if the world were falling apart.

Jeff's arm closed around her shoulders, and from what seemed like a long distance away, he said, "Look!"

The solitary pine stood aloof in the meadow, away from the surrounding forest, like a scout seeking out new territory. The lightning had blasted it, and as they watched, it burned brightly for a few minutes before being extinguished by the downpour.

"Thank God for the rain," Jeff said. "I wouldn't want to be trying to race ahead of a forest fire tonight."

"The poor horses! They must be terrified."

"They've been through this before," Jeff said reassuringly. "They're probably hunkered under some trees." He had hobbled them earlier, giving them the freedom to graze the meadow but preventing them from running. "Very little gets to Maggie. She's probably keeping the other two calm."

"I'm beginning to think Maggie is a remarkable horse." She was also becoming acutely aware of Jeff's arm around her shoulders. It was a heavy, warm weight, at once soothing and exciting. Her breath caught and her heart stuttered a few rapid beats. All she had to do was turn her head a little bit and...

It was as if a whirlpool suddenly sprang up deep inside her, drawing her awareness downward to her most private places. The world became a throbbing ache and nothing else—not even the wild storm that slapped against the tent walls— seemed to matter.

If she just turned her head a little bit...

His mouth was so near. Just a few inches and her lips would meet his. Just a little twist of her body and she would be pressed intimately to him. Just the slightest of moves...

Her heart stilled, replaced by the throbbing between her legs. Her breath locked in her throat and her mouth went dry with yearning.

No, she begged herself. Don't move. Not a muscle. One- night stands were not her style, and this couldn't possibly be anything else. They lived in different worlds, and neither of them was going to pack up and move.

Besides, said a little voice of sanity, nobody wants you, Harriet. Not really. Men *used* her because they sensed she was usable. They sensed her insecurity and used it as a tool to get her to do what they wanted until finally she grew difficult and resisted. Then they blamed her and left—or threw her out.

They always acted as if they had tried to make a silk purse out of a sow's ear and she had failed to live up to their ex- pectations. But the truth, painfully realized at last in these moments as she lay paralyzed by want and fear, was that she was already a silk purse, just not their type.

She wore men's clothes and kept her nails and hair short because she was trying to hide the beauty that turned her into an object. The men she had dated had seen what she was hiding and had tried to bring it out, but they had never un- derstood *why* she was hiding it. Nor had they wanted to.

Jeff seemed different, but that didn't mean he was. Hadn't she learned she couldn't trust her judgment in these matters?

But her body wasn't listening, and just as she was about to

force herself away, Jeff moved, turning her face gently toward him with the pressure of his fingers. His lips hovered only an inch from hers while lightning flashed wildly and thunder rolled.

"We don't want to do this," he said huskily.

"No." The word almost refused to pass her lips. Fire seemed to leap in his eyes, just as it was leaping inside of her.

"You're leaving," he said.

"That's right."

"You won't stay."

"No, I won't."

"That's what I thought." But his face moved a fraction closer. "One kiss wouldn't be…so bad."

"Just one," she heard herself agree in a throaty voice she almost didn't recognize.

She was playing with fire and she knew it, but she didn't care. Need consumed her past the point of reason. If she couldn't stop there, too bad. There'd be time enough later to become sane.

His lips touched hers, a gentle, questing pressure as if he were testing the waters. Everything inside Harriet turned soft with longing. The racing of her heart quieted for one blissful moment, just enough time for her to wonder why no one had ever made her feel this way before, as if she were floating and melting at the same time.

The kiss deepened, the pressure of their mouths becoming firmer and more mobile. Harriet felt herself turning, twisting toward him, needing more closeness than the touch of their mouths.

A delighted shock rippled through her as she felt his hard, narrow hips press against hers, as she felt his arms close around her back and flatten her breasts against his chest. What could be more exquisite?

It felt like a lifetime since she had last had arms wrapped snugly around her, arms that wanted to hold her tightly. It felt so good that for a little while she hardly noticed the tenderness of the kiss he was giving her. It was enough to be held.

Daring, she slipped her arm around his back and felt the firm play of muscles beneath his sweater. Jeff Cumberland was a man who worked hard for a living, and his body reflected that. There was none of the softness she was accustomed to in the past, and none of the showy built-in-a-gym muscles. What she felt beneath her hands was flat layers of steely strength that could be depended upon.

All those hard, sculpted contours made her hands itch to explore further. But before she could do so, a sudden flood of emotion swamped her, carrying her to a place she had never been before.

She felt *safe,* she realized with amazement. Utterly and completely safe. She had never felt that way with a man, had never been so sure that whatever followed would not leave her feeling disillusioned or hurt or vulnerable.

Jeff had never done anything to make her feel vulnerable, not even the night he had picked her up on the road. Instead he had always made her feel cared for. Sheltered. As if he would protect her from anything.

And the yearning, oh, heavens, the yearning. This was no mere sexual arousal. This was a heart-deep, soul-deep longing for something that transcended mere mating urges. Somehow she must have poured those feelings into her kiss, because he drew her even closer and expanded the caress, running his tongue teasingly along the seam of her lips, asking for more than she had thought she would give—asking for more, she suspected, than he anticipated wanting.

Just one kiss, they had said, but this kiss wouldn't end. Neither of them seemed to want to let go of these ecstatic moments.

Harriet parted her lips, understanding how a parched flower must feel when it was kissed by raindrops. The thunder and lightning outside the tent seemed to come inside her, to fill her with the wildness of nature and the power of the storm.

Her hand no longer stayed on his back. It wandered down his side, to his denim-clad hips, feeling their narrowness and hardness. His tongued teased hers, carrying her high on a wind of passion, and as her hand began to wander, his began to explore.

Down her back ran his palm, causing a shiver of delight to race through her. Down to her softly rounded hip in its un-accustomed covering of jeans. Around to cradle her soft rump and pull her into him.

Against him. The sheer magic of the feeling sent another bolt of lightning streaking to her center, caused an earthquake inside her that made her hips rock with need. She needed him in ways she had barely imagined, and she needed him now.

She almost cried out with disappointment when he broke the kiss. In the flicker of lightning she saw the sparkle of his eyes.

"One more," he said hoarsely. "Just one more..."

"Yes..." She sighed her consent and gave him her mouth once more, feeling as reckless as the storm outside.

This time his tongue plunged confidently into her mouth, and she met him in a mating dance as old as the human race. This time his hand trespassed in new territory, stunning her with the sharp, aching response of her body when his palm slid up beneath her sweater and shirt and found the warm skin of her midriff.

His hands were work-roughened, and the sensation was a surprising aphrodisiac. Not the smooth, carefully manicured hands of the men in her past, but the hands of a working man, hard, strong and sure. In that instant those other men—those very few other men—vanished from her memory as if they were merely bad dreams.

This was what she had been waiting for, like a butterfly in a chrysalis. She could feel her wings stirring for the first time as the heat he awakened in her brought her near the brink of emergence.

His fingers stroked gently back and forth on tender skin,

mimicking the rhythms of his tongue. Higher and higher she seemed to rise, reaching for a barely discernible light.

Thunder roared, shaking the ground. Lightning flashed, brilliant even through her eyelids, and then, in a moment of utter stillness and silence, his hand slid upward and cupped her breast through the simple tricot of her bra.

She caught her breath, holding it in anticipation, fluttering on the wings of hot desire. Yes, her mind cried out. Yes, her heart called. Oh, yes, please…

He squeezed her gently, and his thumb brushed over her hardening nipple, a sensation more astonishingly exquisite than the mere brush of flesh on flesh. She arched sharply, a helpless moan escaping her, and she pressed herself more tightly to him, seeking the answers he offered to the needs of her womanhood.

She thought she heard him moan, but the sound was nearly lost in the thunder. Then his leg lifted and fell over hers, drawing her deeper into the cradle of his thighs so that she could not mistake his rising heat.

And suddenly she didn't care that this could go nowhere, that by virtue of their separate lives this could never be more than a fleeting memory she would carry with her down the uncertain and lonely corridors of her future. The only thing she wouldn't be able to bear was not having this memory to take with her.

The words "Don't stop" were rising in her throat, ready to be spoken, when Jeff suddenly went rigid and tore his mouth from hers.

"What was that?" he asked.

"What?" Startled, almost confused by the sudden change, Harriet looked up at him. Lightning flickered, revealing his face, but she couldn't read his expression.

"I heard something," he said after a moment. "It sounded like one of the horses."

He started to pull back from her, but she caught his shoulder. "Jeff, you don't want to go out there! The lightning is dangerous."

"I've got to see if one of the horses is hurt."

Gently, he disentangled himself and sat up, reaching for the yellow poncho in the corner. "Besides, Harriet, we really can't go any further. You'd never forgive me."

He pulled the poncho over his head, and she wanted to cry. Then he unzipped the door of the tent and stooped as he stepped out.

Rolling onto her stomach, Harriet watched as he strode across the clearing to the trees where he had left the horses. By now they could be almost anywhere, she thought. How could he hope to find them in the dark, with the lightning and thunder probably keeping them on a constant move?

It was just like him, she thought miserably, to be more concerned about the horses than his own safety. His sense of responsibility extended to everything that came into his care, from horses to her.

It didn't escape her that the computer system he'd bought was almost identical to the one she would have purchased herself, if she'd had the money. Nor did it escape her that after he had helped her assemble it, he'd displayed no interest in playing on it.

It made her feel a little uncomfortable, but she had the strong suspicion he felt responsible for her being trapped in Conard County and he was trying his damnedest to make up for it, even if it meant spending a ridiculous sum on a computer system he didn't need just so she could work.

A sigh escaped her but was lost in the steady roar of the downpour outside and the hammering of millions of raindrops on the tent roof.

It would be easy to fall in love with Jeff Cumberland, she thought miserably. Too easy. If she had a brain in her head, she had to make sure that didn't happen. Breaking off a lousy relationship was painful enough. Losing Jeff could conceivably tear her heart out by the roots.

After a few minutes she realized that the storm sounded as if it were moving away. The lightning and the thunder were no longer so close together, and the thunder had begun to take on the rolling growl that meant it was coming from a distance. Relief poured through her as she realized that the worst of the danger was past.

Even the deluge seemed to be letting up a bit. Crawling closer to the tent door, she looked out and saw that the rain was indeed lessening. The trench that Jeff had dug around the tent to direct the downpour around them was still full of rushing water, but the steady roar of raindrops on canvas had become a quiet drone.

A flicker of lightning in the clouds revealed Jeff's tall frame as he strode back toward her from the woods. When he reached the tent door, he pulled the poncho over his head and held it so he wouldn't drip all over her and the sleeping bags when he stepped inside.

"The horses?" she asked, moving aside for him.

"They're all right. Something must have scared them, but they seem calm enough now."

And maybe he hadn't heard anything at all, she thought. Maybe he had just used that as an excuse to cut off their lovemaking before it got out of hand. She imagined a brisk walk in the rainy woods had thoroughly dampened his ardor.

Hers had certainly calmed down. It rested now like a soft ache between her thighs, a memory of what might have been.

Jeff sat on his sleeping bag and pulled off his boots.

"Maybe we'd better get some sleep while we can," he said. "If we get any more storms like that one, it's apt to be a rough night."

Harriet had hardly noticed before, but now she felt how chilly the night air had become. Shivering, she crawled into her sleeping bag and pulled it up to her chin.

"You'd be warmer if you took off your pants," Jeff remarked. As he spoke, he rose to a crouch and began to pull off his own jeans.

Harriet's breath locked in her throat and she closed her eyes tightly before she could see anything tempting. "I'll be fine," she managed to say hoarsely.

"Suit yourself."

She heard him crawl into the bag only a few inches from her own. Her heart was hammering so loudly she couldn't believe he didn't hear it.

"Good night, Harriet."

Just like that, she thought miserably. Just like that he had rejected her. Had she done something wrong? Had *she* turned him off, or was he struggling to exercise self-control? There was no way to know. All she knew was that the warmth she had felt with him earlier was gone as surely as if someone had flipped a switch.

Turning onto her side away from him, she grabbed the bag containing her spare clothes and tucked it under her cheek, trying to use it for a pillow. Feelings of hurt and anger warred within her, and she tried to battle them down. What was the point?

Then, stunning her, she felt the butterfly brush of lips on her cheek.

"I'm sorry, Harriet," he said softly. "Good night."

She lay awake for a long time, watching the patterns the dying lightning made on the tent wall, and wished to God she had never come to Wyoming.

Twelve

Morning dawned with a clarity of light that was almost painful. The storm had apparently been the leading edge of a cold front, Jeff thought as he stood in front of the tent and looked around. It was *cold* out here this morning.

He'd been thinking about saddling up and getting the hell out of there, waiting for breakfast until later, but as cold as it was, he didn't have the heart to wake Harriet and ask her to move without warm food in her belly.

He brought the horses to water, then left them grazing happily in the middle of the meadow. It was easy to gather dead wood for a fire, but it wasn't going to be so easy to start one. Everything was soaked and hadn't dried out much overnight.

In the underside of an ancient, fallen tree, he found enough splintery dry wood to give him hope. Under another fallen tree he found several handfuls of reasonably dry pine needles and bark. Breaking off the lower limbs of several dead trees gave him some wood that had been reasonably well protected by bark. He ought to be able to get a fire going with that.

The fire pit they had cooked in last night was sodden, so he dug out a new one a few feet away. It took him a few minutes longer than usual, but he got a small fire going and spread some additional wood around it to dry.

Then he put on the all-essential pot of coffee. To his mind, a day in the outdoors didn't really begin until he'd swallowed a few cups of thick black brew. He half expected that Harriet wouldn't like it—she was probably used to drinking the drip brew like Sylvia made at home, not the muddy brew made in a tin pot over a campfire. But there was no way he could plug in a drip coffeemaker up here.

He smiled a little as he nursed the fire, then set the pot on it. He wondered if she would turn up her little New York nose at the stuff. The thought tickled him rather than offended him. Since he'd first set eyes on Harriet, she'd struck him as being determined to hate Wyoming. Unfortunately for her, he could see she was coming to like the place.

The fire continued to burn as the sun crept higher, but it was the only warmth in a world that had decided winter must be just around the corner. Jeff moved the coffeepot to one side, put on some of the wood he'd dried and watched with satisfaction as it caught.

It just might be a decent day after all. If he didn't count all his missing cattle. And assuming Harriet wasn't still mad at him about last night. The memory drew a sigh from him as he rummaged around in the saddlebags for his frying pan, a can of Spam and small jug of sourdough starter he'd packed. With the addition of some water and flour, it would make the best flapjacks this side of heaven. He'd even brought a tin of sugar and a small plastic bottle of maple syrup for the occasion.

He mixed the pancake mixture in an aluminum pot, adding a little powdered milk for flavor. All the time he was trying to decide whether he wanted to be angry about the theft of his cattle this morning or worried about how Harriet might feel about last night. Either way, he was going to make himself miserable.

She had a right to be angry. The way he had ended their embrace last night had been abrupt, but he really *had* thought he'd heard one of the horses scream. It had turned out for the best, of course. If he hadn't gone to investigate, they would have wound up making love, and then she'd really have a reason to be angry with him.

What had gotten into him, anyway? At his age, he'd long since learned to control his sexual impulses. He'd been wanting to kiss Harriet for days, but so what? Wanting things he couldn't have wasn't so unusual. He should have been able to control the impulse. Hell, he had a lifetime of experience in denying himself.

So why had he blown it last night? Isolation, the threat of a serious rainstorm and their close proximity shouldn't have been enough to overcome his usual scruples and self-discipline. Nor should the heady scent of her in that small tent have been an impossible temptation.

But Harriet, he admitted reluctantly, *was* an impossible temptation. He'd been infatuated before—hell, once or twice he'd even believed himself to be in love—but he'd never had a woman prey on his mind and senses the way Harriet did. At least not since he was in high school and dealing with the raging hormones of adolescence.

But he had no raging hormones now, and Harriet was working her way into his every waking thought and even into his dreams. Last night he'd dreamed of her naked and writhing with pleasure in his arms, and he'd awakened in the pitch dark, swollen and aching. He hadn't done anything like that since…well, it had been a hell of a long time.

But he judged Harriet to be more vulnerable than the women he was usually attracted to. Something about her made him believe that she could be very easily hurt. Last night had probably hurt her, but not nearly as much as their lovemaking would have. He knew *that* as sure as he was sitting here stirring pancake batter while the fire crackled and the coffee perked.

And maybe that was part of what was attracting him to her. He didn't think she was sexually inexperienced, but he strongly suspected that she didn't give herself casually, unlike the women he had had affairs with before. She just didn't have that edge of confidence to her.

So if she gave herself to a man, she had to care, had to expect something more than a collision of bodies in the night. He wasn't averse to offering more, but the woman was heading back to New York in a few days, hardly enough time to do anything more than give them both something to regret.

He was glad the horse had screamed last night. Or that the wind had howled in a way that had sounded like a scream. He only hoped Harriet would be grateful, too.

The sun was higher now, taking the edge off the chill, although the air remained brisk. He went to wake Harriet and found her sitting in the doorway of the tent, her hair tousled and her eyes still puffy from sleep. In her hands she held the camera she never went anywhere without.

She barely glanced at him. "Look," she whispered. "Over there by the trees."

He looked and caught his breath. Two gray wolves stood about a hundred feet away, staring at the humans from tawny eyes that seemed to hold as much curiosity as apprehension. Neither wolf moved so much as a hair, both standing so still they might have been carved out of one of the trees beside them.

"They've been watching us for at least the last five minutes," Harriet said.

Moving slowly, Jeff squatted. Down low he was less likely to intimidate the creatures.

"God, they're beautiful," Harriet murmured.

"They sure are."

The wolves stared at them for a few more minutes, while Harriet cautiously snapped some photos, then with a liquid movement of muscle, they vanished back into the woods.

Harriet turned to Jeff, her expression one of sheer delight. He searched for shadows that might have lingered from the night before but saw none.

"That," she said quietly, "just made this whole trip worthwhile."

He nodded agreement, pierced by the sudden wish that *he* could have been enough to make this trip worthwhile for her. Ridiculous, dangerous thought, he warned himself. Thoughts like that could only lead to some kind of disaster.

"Coffee's ready," he said, clutching at normalcy. "Pancakes and Spam in a couple of minutes."

Her smile slipped a little and she looked rueful. "Um...I'm not sure I can move."

He stared at her blankly for a second, while his morning-sluggish brain made the connections. When it did, a slow smile spread across his face. "Saddle sore?"

"You could call it that, I suppose. I feel like somebody beat me with a baseball bat."

"Well, I'd offer to carry you over to the fire, but that won't help you much."

"What will?"

He made a face. "I hate to tell you. You need to move around until the stiffness loosens up."

She groaned. "I was afraid you were going to say that."

"Let me help you up." Reaching down, he grabbed her hands and pulled her to her feet.

Harriet grimaced and stood bent over, as if straightening up were too much to ask.

"Need any help?"

She looked at him, her blue eyes rueful. "I'll just shuffle my way over to the fire."

"Okay. I'll start the flapjacks, then." He moved away from her reluctantly, surprised by his own unwillingness to put any distance between them. When he glanced back, he saw Harriet was doing exactly what she had said, shuffling in the direction of the fire.

Hiding a sympathetic smile, he squatted by the fire and put the frying pan on the hot coals to heat. When a couple of drops of water flicked onto its surface bounced and danced, he judged it was ready. He poured batter into the pan, making a large, round flapjack. While he waited for it to cook, he dug out a knife from his pack.

He cut thin slices of Spam on one of the plates, planning to fry them after he was through making flapjacks. By the time he finished slicing the canned meat, Harriet had managed to make it to the fireside. He looked up at her. "Loosening up any?"

"I think so." She screwed up her face and rubbed one hip. "I really didn't think the ride yesterday was hard enough or long enough to cause all this soreness."

"It'll mostly wear off in a few minutes. Just walk around."

She took his advice while he cooked a stack of flapjacks, then fried the meat. She ate standing up, remarking that she'd never had Spam before.

"It's not bad," Jeff remarked. "And it sure is handy on the trail."

"Well, I'll eat it again," she said with a smile. "And these pancakes are heavenly."

"The sourdough starter I used has been in my family for three or four generations. Pretty good stuff."

"I'll say."

Her appetite was huge this morning, and she ate nearly as much as Jeff did, which he took as a compliment. After they washed up, he packed the camp with Harriet's assistance and saddled the horses.

As he anticipated, Harriet couldn't get herself into the saddle, hard as she tried. Her muscles refused to go that last little bit necessary, so he gave her the boost she needed. It kind of tickled him, how startled she looked when he lifted her so easily.

"Okay?" he asked, looking up at her.

"No worse than a toothache," she replied, indicating her bottom. "I can make it."

"There's a nice hot bath waiting for you at home," he promised with a smile.

"Just keep reminding me."

The night's rain had washed the countryside clean again, settling all the dust and making the air so clear that Jeff felt he could see all the way to the ends of the earth. Even though Maggie was feeling frisky again, he kept the horses to a sedate pace out of consideration for Harriet's aching muscles.

They returned home by a different route, bypassing the archaeological dig. Harriet stopped Maggie from time to time to take pictures of the spectacular view unfolding below them as they descended from the mountains. A couple of times she even turned to look over her shoulder at the craggy peak of Thunder Mountain.

"Don't you worry about those wolves being so close to your cattle?" she asked Jeff as they reached the foot of the slope and moved onto flatter ground.

"I used to. But the simple fact is, wolves generally only bring down the sick and the weak from the herd. So far I haven't had one kill I could attribute to them. Rustlers are more of a problem."

A whole lot more of a problem. If those five hundred head that Nate had mentioned going to market were his, no wolf pack could ever compare.

Harriet spoke. "I've long thought we humans are our own worst enemies."

"You won't get any argument from me on that score. Over the years I've had some trouble with predators, but nothing that was worse than a nick. Oh, I get concerned anytime I lose an animal, but some losses are inevitable."

"I guess so."

"I was worried when I first heard there was a wolf pack up on Thunder Mountain, but then I read up on the subject and realized it wasn't going to be a problem. As long as there's plenty of wildlife up in those mountains, they're not likely to venture near my stock."

"I'm surprised we even got to see them."

"So am I. There's a fellow named Gray Cloud who spends his summers up on the mountain with his family. His wife is a college professor who studies the wolves. Maybe these wolves have grown used to people."

"That could be a good thing or a bad thing."

He chuckled. "It depends on how you look at it."

He was more relieved than he could say that no shadow of

last night seemed to linger in Harriet's gaze or attitude. If she *had* been mad at him, she had apparently put away her anger.

Maybe, thought Jeff, it was going to be a *good* day after all.

He changed his mind about that shortly after lunch when they found the body. They had stopped to eat some jerky and water the horses at one of the streams that ran through his ranch, then had continued their ride along the streambed. Half a mile from where they had taken their break, they came upon a four-wheel-drive vehicle hidden behind a bend in the creek. Sitting at the wheel was the slumped figure of a man.

Or, more accurately, the slumped remains of what had been a man. Harriet took one look and turned her head away, fighting an overwhelming urge to vomit.

"Damn it all to hell!" Jeff said savagely.

Harriet drew a deep breath, trying to control her gagging, but before she could do anything else, Jeff caught the reins of her horse and led her away from the car and out of the creek bed.

This time he didn't take pity on Harriet's stiff muscles, nor did she want him to. He kept the horses at a trot and didn't say another word all the way back to the ranch. Once there, he stopped just long enough to help her down and turn the horses over to one of his hired hands.

Harriet hesitated, feeling oddly displaced, as if she had somehow slipped into another reality. Nothing looked right. Nothing felt right.

Finally, gaining control of her still-aching muscles, she followed Jeff into the kitchen. He was on the phone with the sheriff.

"I can tell them exactly where to find the body," he was saying tightly. "I want it gone."

Sylvia tossed Harriet a concerned look as Harriet made her way to the island and sat on one of the stools. "Are you okay, honey?"

Harriet managed a nod. "Sore, tired and sick to my stomach, but I'll be okay."

"Why don't you go up and draw a nice hot bath?"

Harriet shook her head. "I don't want to be alone just yet."

"I can understand that." The older woman went to the refrigerator and pulled out a chilled bottle of club soda. "Here, this is good for nausea."

Harriet poured the sparkling water into a glass and sipped it gratefully. It tasted clean, fresh. It washed away the smell of what they had found.

Jeff hung up the phone and turned to look at Harriet. "I'm sorry."

"For what?" She managed a weak smile. "It's not as if you were killing these people yourself."

"I wanted you to like it here," he said tautly. "Instead you're going to go home hating this place and thinking this county is populated by a bunch of murderous barbarians."

"But…"

He turned and walked out of the kitchen, not giving her an opportunity to reassure him that she really *was* coming to like this place. At the other end of the house she heard his study door close with finality.

"Oops," said Sylvia.

Harriet looked at her.

"I think he's angry about the murders as well as his cattle," Sylvia said. "It'd be kind of hard to miss the feeling that somebody hates him."

"Hates him? They don't give a damn about him. If they did, they wouldn't be stealing his cattle."

The housekeeper shook her head. "Don't you see? He feels that these people are being killed on his property to make him look bad."

Harriet hadn't thought of that. But of course, someone might get the idea that Jeff was taking the law into his own hands and killing people he thought were rustlers—or just trespassers. After all, two of the three bodies had been found on the Bar C.

"Nobody could seriously believe that," Harriet said, looking at the doorway through which Jeff had disappeared.

"Nobody who knows him," Sylvia agreed. "But there are a lot of people who don't know him, people who might resent his wealth and success. They'd be inclined to believe rumors that made him look bad."

Harriet suddenly felt she couldn't take any more. Excusing herself, she limped upstairs to draw that hot bath Jeff had promised and to think over all the things that had been happening.

Jeff wasn't a murderer. The thought was too ludicrous to contemplate. But who could hate him so much that they'd not only steal his cattle but try to make him look responsible for murder?

She heard the police cars pull up. Leaning over, she peeked under the curtains of the window beside the claw-footed tub and saw the men gathering in the yard as they had gathered when the last body was found. Jeff was out there talking to the sheriff, then all of the police officers and then they climbed back into their four-wheel-drive vehicles and set out across the open ground.

Harriet sank back into the tub and blew a long, cooling breath up over her flushed face. The hot water was easing the muscular stiffness that had plagued her all day, but she hardly noticed.

Fact was, she was feeling responsible for this latest disaster. If she hadn't so foolishly disregarded Nate Tate's warning not to take any pictures without the permission of the ranchers, she never would have stopped alongside the road and photographed the rustlers. And if she hadn't photographed the three men, they wouldn't now be dead. It was all her fault this latest catastrophe had landed on Jeff's doorstep.

She only wished there was some way she could make things better.

After she climbed out of the tub and dressed, she went downstairs again, this time to the living room, where she picked up a phone and used her credit card to call her agent at home.

"Harry! My God, I'd begun to think you'd fallen off the planet. Where have you been? I tried that fleabag motel you were at and they said you'd checked out days ago!"

"Sorry, Marcie. Things got a little complicated."

"Complicated how?"

"Rustlers started turning up dead, and the sheriff thinks I may be a potential target."

"Then get your butt home right now! Are you crazy, staying out there if somebody wants to kill you? I'll think of something to tell the client, don't you worry."

"Actually, I think I've got most of what I need. I've been working on the enhancements and retouch even."

"Really?" Marcie sounded intrigued. "Where did you find the equipment to do that?"

"Well, Jeff Cumberland has—"

Marcie interrupted, saying, "Oh, Jeff Cumberland..." in a tone that was far too knowing.

"Don't make anything of it, Marcie. He's just trying to help me out of a rough spot. He feels responsible for me getting attacked by the rustlers."

"Responsible how? Did he hire somebody to steal his own cows?"

The absurd suggestion should have made Harriet laugh. She knew Marcie meant it to be sarcastic, but she found herself jumping to Jeff's defense. "He did no such thing, Marcie! He's a good and decent man, and all of this is really cutting him up!"

Marcie maintained a diplomatic silence. Harriet could sense that she was feeling her way to a cautious reply.

"I'm sure he's a very nice man," Marcie said finally, her voice almost soothing.

"Yes, he is!"

"I just meant he couldn't really be responsible for you getting hurt."

"Of course he couldn't! But I feel responsible for this latest mess."

"You?" Marcie sounded surprised. "How could *you* be responsible? What have you been doing?" Her tone implied that she could imagine Harriet doing almost anything, most of it unwise.

"It's my damn jinx again," Harriet said glumly. "And this time it's all my fault."

"Harriet," Marcie said in her sternest this-is-your-agent-speaking voice, a voice reminiscent of her mother's, Harriet sometimes thought, "jinxes aren't real. Nobody gets hexed. Sometimes we all just have a run of bad luck."

"Mine's been going on forever."

"No, it hasn't," Marcie said firmly. "We joke about the weird things that happen to you sometimes, but trust me, those weird things happen to everyone. If they're all you pay attention to, you can start to feel jinxed. But when I say you're jinxed, I'm just kidding. Hell, I represent photographers and actors and musicians all over the place. Any one of 'em could appear jinxed if they wanted to look at it that way. It's the nature of your job that you get into situations where strange things can happen. But it's not some kind of curse on your head. Good heavens, Harriet, if you seriously believe you're cursed, how can you explain how well your career has been going? Demand for your services has been growing steadily. You're commanding the kind of sums most freelancers only dream of."

"I know," Harriet said miserably.

"So you're hardly jinxed. Get a grip."

"But this *is* my fault."

Marcie sighed. "Right. *You* hired the rustlers."

"No, of course not."

"Then how is it possible you could be responsible for anything they do? Get real, sweetie. Now, when the hell are you getting your butt back here where it's safe?''

"Well…the sheriff thinks I might not be safe back there.''

Shock silenced Marcie for all of ten seconds. "While I'm inclined to agree that the streets of New York may not be the safest place on the planet, particularly for pedestrians, I fail to see how they could be less safe than hanging around where somebody wants to kill you.''

"The sheriff think these guys could follow me home.''

"Are we talking about the Mafia here?''

"No, of course not.''

"Then we're talking about small peanuts. Why would they even bother?''

"Why would they bother to kill people merely because I happened to see them?''

Marcie thought about that. "But you're right there where they can get to you without even buying a plane ticket.''

"Almost no one knows I'm here, Marcie. It's been put around that I went home, and I haven't left this ranch since then.''

"This ranch? Which ranch is this ranch?''

"I'm staying at the Cumberland place.''

"Oh.'' Marcie mulled that over. "Well, that's probably worth the risk, then.''

"Just what do you mean by that?''

"Not a thing, Harry. Not a thing. Just do me a favor and call every twenty-four hours so that I know I don't need to make funeral arrangements, okay?''

Jeff didn't return to the house until nearly nine-thirty that night. After a solitary dinner, Harriet had gone upstairs to work on the new computer. She spent more time than was probably necessary working on a photograph she had already enhanced and retouched, bringing out certain details and minimizing others. Then she went to work on a new photo, this one of a cowboy cutting a steer from the herd.

She could get used to this, she found herself thinking. She could get used to having an entire room for an office instead of just a corner of her living room. She could get used to a laid-back life-style where someone else did the cooking and cleaning. She could get used to riding on horseback over open prairie and up the side of Thunder Mountain to see the wolves.

She could get used to opening herself to the experience of weather and wildflowers and wild animals and the daily rhythms of ranch life, instead of closing herself inside her own head to keep out all the inconveniences of modern life the way she had to do too often in the city. She could get used to not having to face crowds or sit in traffic jams or stand on subways or buses to get anywhere. She could get used to the incredible silence of the night outside her window, and a quiet so intense that the singing of birds at dawn sounded like a full-throated rendition of the Hallelujah Chorus.

But there was no point in getting used to it, she reminded herself with a sigh, because she was going home just as soon as this mess was cleaned up—and that could happen at any minute.

She heard the sound of Jeff's booted feet climbing the stairs, and her heart leaped with happy anticipation. No, oh, no, said her brain. You don't want to feel this way. Yes, oh, yes, said her heart, and leaped again.

"Hi." Jeff spoke from behind her. She turned and found him standing in the doorway, looking weary and worn.

"Hi," she said, feeling inexplicably shy. "You look beat."

"I am. Is everything okay?"

"Sylvia makes a good mother. I couldn't ask for better care."

He managed a tired smile. "Great. I think I'll go take a shower."

"Is everything okay?"

"Depends on what you mean by okay." But he didn't elucidate, simply gave her a nod and vanished up the hallway to his bedroom. A few minutes later she heard the water pipes clank as he turned on the shower.

Something inside her seemed to shrink with disappointment, as if some bright promise had been left unfulfilled.

Don't be ridiculous, she told herself angrily. *He's just a casual acquaintance.* But her heart didn't feel that way anymore.

And that knowledge terrified her even more than the thought that someone might want to kill her.

Thirteen

An hour later, freshly showered and shaved and dressed in a clean T-shirt and jeans, Jeff reappeared in the doorway of the computer room.

"Still up?" he asked.

"For some reason I don't feel very sleepy."

"At home for you it's past midnight."

"I guess I'm adjusting."

He nodded. "I don't feel sleepy, either. Want to join me for a drink?"

"Alcohol doesn't help you sleep."

"I wasn't thinking of alcohol. I was thinking of a glass of milk. And maybe some cookies."

Harriet smiled. "I can't pass that up."

She followed him downstairs and into the kitchen. At this hour of night, after sitting in the dimly lit computer room upstairs, the overhead fluorescent lighting seemed harsh. Jeff turned on the lights over the stove and sink and switched off the overheads.

"That's better," he said. "Chocolate milk?"

"Sure."

He filled two glasses with milk and stirred in chocolate syrup until they were dark. He passed one to Harriet and joined her at the island. Sylvia kept the cookie jar there except when she was using the island for cooking. It was a huge clay crock, bigger than any cookie jar Harriet could ever remember seeing. When Jeff opened it, it was full to the brim with chocolate chip and sugar cookies.

Harriet helped herself to chocolate chip. Jeff took one of each.

"How did it go?" she asked finally.

He shrugged. "How do things like that go? I don't know. It's not like I'm in the habit of finding bodies on the ranch—recent evidence notwithstanding."

"Does the sheriff have any idea what happened?" Though she couldn't imagine how you could tell anything about a corpse in that state of decay.

"He was shot."

"Damn."

"Nate thinks it was the other rustler. I mean, there's no way to be sure now, but it's too coincidental."

"I guess so."

"Nate also thinks it might be safe for you to go home."

Harriet felt her heart sink and her stomach along with it. She should have been relieved at this news, but instead she felt crushed. *Girl, you are losing your mind.*

"The guy was killed a couple of days ago. Nate thinks that considering no attempt has been made to find you, they might think the danger is over now that they've killed everyone you saw."

"If that guy we found today was one of them."

"Well, there is that question," he agreed.

"But how can Nate be sure no one's looked for me?"

"Because no one's asked for you at the motel—other than some harried woman who keeps calling from New York and getting more insistent about where you are."

"That would be my agent."

"Probably. But no one else has asked any questions, so Nate figures they think you've gone back to New York. He asked the NYPD to check on your apartment. Nobody's tried to break in, and your building super says nobody's even asked about you."

"So it's over?" That seemed difficult to grasp.

"Most likely." He finished the sugar cookie and took a

deep drink of milk. He didn't look any happier about this turn of affairs than she felt. But he was probably just tired, she decided. He *had* to be glad to get his house and his life back to himself.

"Anyway," he continued, "Nate says you're probably safe and he can't keep you any longer—but he wishes you'd hang around a few more days just to be sure."

Harriet felt a burst of hope but restrained her excitement. "I couldn't possibly impose on you any longer."

Jeff looked at her. "Trust me, you're not imposing. And to be honest, I'd like it if you stayed awhile longer. It would give me a chance to show you it really isn't so bad around here."

She looked into his eyes and felt herself grow heavy and weak. Her heart thudded. How could he keep doing this to her with no more than a look?

"Of course," he said, "you might have other commitments."

"I don't have any commitments other than my photo deadline. And I've got time for that." Was that really her, sounding so husky and breathless?

"Well, you're welcome to stay as long as you like. I've kind of gotten used to having you around."

Used to having her around? It wasn't what she had hoped for, but neither was she so proud she wouldn't gladly take the offered excuse. "I've kind of gotten used to being here."

"So you don't hate it here?" he asked almost hopefully.

She shook her head. "It's actually growing on me."

He smiled then. Rising, he came around the island to her. She twisted on the stool so that she faced him, and caught her breath when he leaned forward, putting his arms on either side of her and bracing himself. His face was only a few inches away from hers.

"You're kind of growing on *me*," he said huskily.

Her heart hammered loudly in her ears. "But…" she trailed off, unable to make the cogent argument.

"I know," he said. "You're leaving. We really shouldn't

get attached because you can't stay. I know all the arguments, Harriet. I've been reciting them to myself for days. It's dangerous. Somebody could get hurt. But you know what? I'll take the risk, because I sure as hell don't want to miss the chance.''

Panic flickered in her, quieting her growing desire. She couldn't do this! It would be a major league mistake! Her heart had already taken enough beatings without volunteering for another one. And she knew herself too well. Much as she had tried to adopt a modern attitude toward sex, the bottom line was, if she made love with a man, she always wound up becoming emotionally involved. That's what had led to her lousy relationships.

And this time she was even more at risk. She could feel her heart already teetering on the brink of something bigger and scarier than she had ever felt before. She couldn't allow it.

So she tried for lightness. "Like skydiving, hmm? The thrill is worth the risk?''

He frowned and drew back a little. "I'm not looking for thrills, Harriet.''

"No?" She tried to smile but had the feeling that she was failing miserably, probably because her lower lip was quivering.

"No," he said. "I stopped wanting sexual thrills by the time I was twenty. It was cheap.''

"And this isn't?''

He shook his head slowly, never taking his eyes from hers. "No," he said quietly. "This is going to be very expensive.''

She slid off the stool and backed up, reaching for the last threads of her sanity and clutching them desperately. "That's the problem, isn't it? You go your way and I go mine. Except that I don't want to leave little bits and pieces of myself here in Wyoming.''

He stayed where he was, watching her, and something in his gaze seemed infinitely sad. "You're right," he said finally.

"Nobody in her right mind would want to leave pieces of herself in Wyoming."

Now, what the hell did he mean by that? Harriet wondered. She had the distinct feeling that he was speaking of something much larger than their attraction to each other.

"So," Jeff said after a moment, "I've never showed you my artifact collection, have I?"

"You mean the stuff in the cases in the living room?"

He nodded.

"I've kind of glanced at it and wondered about it."

"Let me tell you a little about it. You might as well know the full extent of my madness."

"Madness?" She found herself following him to the living room, wondering how the husky spell of passion had been so quickly defused.

"Well, it's really a hobby," he said, turning on the lights. "A ridiculous hobby, I guess, since it'll never amount to anything. Most people would call it a waste of time and money."

"Not if it gives you pleasure."

His eyes seized hers for a moment, and she felt the lick of flame. She looked quickly away.

"The arrowheads," he said, pointing to one glass case, "were found around the ranch over the years while I was working. They've been dated as accurately as possible by the type and workmanship, but they're actually useless as archaeological artifacts because they weren't found in situ. Which basically means they don't have any kind of story to tell. They rose to the surface of the land, probably through the action of water."

"Oh." She wondered why he was putting them down.

"They fascinate me anyway," Jeff said, leaning over the case. "I spent a lot of time one summer with flint and bone trying to copy them. It takes real skill to make one of these. And the edges can be sharper than a diamond." He held out one hand for her inspection. "See all those little scars? I kept cutting myself." A quiet laugh escaped him.

"So how *do* you make one of these?"

"You have to chip the flint with bone or a rock. And you have to chip it at exactly the right angle to make flakes come off. I'll show you sometime, if you want."

As if they had a lot of "sometimes" to look forward to. Harriet stifled a sigh and absolutely refused to consider the question of whether she had to go back to New York. Of course she did. Her life was there.

But it was also too easy to imagine Jeff as a youth, trying with infinite patience to learn to make his own flint arrowheads and knives. And she had a sudden, unwelcome vision of him trying to teach the skill to his own son someday.

"Over here," Jeff was saying as he led the way to the next case, "are gifts that were given to me by Native American friends."

"It's so beautiful," Harriet said as she looked into a case containing an intricately beaded buckskin shirt. She had admired it before. Turquoise and coral beads combined with porcupine quills in swirling circular patterns.

"Nina Ziegler made it for me."

"It must have taken an incredible amount of work."

"It did." He stood over it, looking almost sad. "Her husband worked for me before he died. Nina was a Shawnee. Their home got wiped out in a flood one spring. All I did was help out like any neighbor ought to, but Nina insisted on giving me that shirt."

He had probably done more than help out just a little, Harriet thought, knowing Jeff as she did. And Nina wouldn't have devoted all those hours to making that shirt to say thank-you for a few bags of groceries.

He moved on to other cases, showing her tobacco pouches, shields, baskets and pottery. Some he had purchased on his travels around the West, but a surprising number of pieces had been given to him. The ones that had been gifts had little stories of friendship attached. Harriet realized his interest in Native Americans extended far beyond reading about them.

Jeff, she found herself thinking, would have made a wonderful scholar. He was able to tell her about each item, how it had been made and what meaning it had, if any.

They came at last to the final case, one filled with fossils.

"This is my paleontological exhibit," he told her almost ruefully. "Again, these are fossils I found around here, but they don't really have any scientific usefulness. There's nothing rare, in terms of the fossil record. Just things I found interesting."

Things he had probably been thrilled to find, she thought, again imagining the young man who had bothered to look for such things. She admired the fossilized fern imprint, the piece of woolly mammoth tusk and the small footprints of mesohippus, the ancestor of the modern horse.

"Now, that has an interesting story," Jeff told her. "It appears the ancestors of the horse evolved in North America, but then they vanished, only to return with the Spanish conquistadores five hundred years ago."

"Really? There were no horses here before the conquest?"

"Not a one. It's intriguing, isn't it?"

It was, she thought, looking down at the footprints of a creature that couldn't have been much bigger than a dog. "I think it's wonderful that you've done all of this," she told him. "Don't put it down. Renaissance men are hard to find."

"Renaissance men?"

"People who have broad interests and pursue them as time permits." She looked up at him. "Too many people are one-trick ponies."

He smiled at that, and for an instant, just an instant, she thought he was going to kiss her. Every nerve cell in her body seemed to reach toward him.

But then he glanced at his watch. "Look at the time," he said. "I have to be up early. I'll walk you upstairs."

They said good-night at her bedroom door and she watched him walk down the hall and disappear into his room. Why did she have the feeling that she was making a big mistake by staying longer?

Harriet couldn't sleep. She felt hot, even though it was cool in the room, and she tossed and turned, kicking the blankets off, then pulling them back on again a few minutes later.

And all she could think of was Jeff Cumberland only a few feet down the hall from her. All she had to do was walk down that hall and into his room. Regardless of his early morning, she had the feeling she would be welcomed.

But the cost! she reminded herself. The cost would be insupportable. She was already becoming too fond of him, but as long as they didn't cross the line, they could part as friends, with no more emotional investment than that. And part they would.

She looked at the phone beside her bed and thought about waking up Marcie. Marcie would talk sense to her. Or one of her other friends. *Any* of her friends would think she was in danger of losing her mind.

They might be right. But she didn't want to lay the responsibility on one of her friends. This was her problem, not theirs, and whatever she did or didn't do, she didn't want to find herself blaming anyone else for it. She had to make her own decision.

The bed felt as if it were full of hard lumps, and finally, weary of fighting for a comfortable position, she got up and padded across the hardwood floor and the throw rugs to the window, shivering a little in her thin cotton sleep shirt.

There were no clouds tonight, and the moon shone bright and cold over the hulking mountains. Those mountains drew her. It was not the first time since she had arrived here that she had found herself staring at them, watching their changing moods, thinking that she had never seen anything more beautiful.

They dwarfed the tallest skyscrapers. Towering over the plains below, they created their own weather, and like chameleons, they changed color with each hour of the passing days. Sometimes she felt as if she could look at them forever.

But tonight they were not enough to distract her from the aching needs of her body and heart. *You're already in trouble,* said the quiet observer in her mind. *How much worse could it get?*

A lot worse, she argued. A whole lot worse. Lovemaking was not a simple game of cards or tennis. It was not merely a pastime. It tended to carry her feelings to new levels, to open doors that led to her most vulnerable places.

Or perhaps, argued the quiet observer, *it merely expresses what you already feel.*

The thought drew her up short, making her reconsider. Maybe that was true. Maybe she only made love when she was already involved, and all the act did was bring her feelings to the fore. Maybe it didn't really get her in more deeply than she already was.

For certain, she was in deep with Jeff. She could feel the icy waters of impending loss lapping at the edges of her heart. She didn't love him. Not yet. But she cared enough that leaving him behind was going to hurt, even if she left right now, right this instant.

Maybe, instead of running in fright from her feelings, she ought to acknowledge them. Maybe she ought to seize every sweet little bit that life offered her rather than regretting later what she had missed and hurting anyway.

Her feet seemed to have developed a mind of their own. They turned her from the window and carried her across the cold floor to the bedroom door.

She shouldn't be doing this, but she was doing it anyway, because the simple fact was that not having Jeff was going to hurt every bit as much as having him and leaving. She had already reached the point where loss was inevitable.

Feeling as if she moved in a dream, she opened the door and stepped into the hallway. The house was silent, so very silent. The utter silence of the Wyoming night still astonished her. No honking horns, no roaring engines, no sirens, no voices shouting and laughing. Just the quiet of an entire world asleep. She could hear her own heartbeat and the whisper of cotton against her thighs.

There was light coming from under his door. The sight froze her with trepidation. He couldn't sleep, either. What if he had insisted on going to bed only because he wanted to get away from her? It wouldn't be the first time a man had claimed fatigue to escape her.

Her heart climbed to her throat, making breathing difficult. She should go back to her room right now. Just turn around and get out of here before she learned something that would hurt her more than going back to bed.

But her feet carried her forward anyway, overriding all the frantic warnings of her mind. *You'll never know if you don't try.*

At his door she froze again, unable to knock or call out. She couldn't do this. She simply could not do this. She had never made the first move with a man in her life. What had come over her?

But then, almost as if he had ESP, Jeff opened the door. He was still wearing jeans, so he hadn't gone to bed, but he had shed his shirt, and for the first time she got a look at a broad, bronzed chest. A powerful chest that begged to be touched.

"Harriet?" Surprised, he halted and looked at her.

She licked her lips but couldn't answer.

"Harriet? What's wrong?"

She shook her head and tried to turn, to flee, but her feet kept her rooted as surely as if they were planted in cement.

"Are you having trouble sleeping?"

To that she managed a nod.

"Me, too," he said ruefully, and ran his fingers through his mussed hair. "I was just going down to get another glass of milk—this time one without the chocolate. Want me to bring you some?"

Milk? He was asking if she wanted *milk?* The first waves

of humiliation began to lick at her aching heart. Just tell him you want the milk, Harriet. That's all you have to do and you'll be safe again.

But the words that passed her lips in a broken jumble had nothing to do with milk. "I realized…I'm going to…leave bits…bits and pieces of me here, anyway."

For an instant he looked confused, then understanding dawned. His whole face softened. "You're going to take bits and pieces of me away with you," he said gently. "Large bits and pieces."

Then, without another word, he reached for her, scooping her up into his arms. He turned, kicking the door shut with one foot, and carried her to his bed.

She could feel the heavy thud of his heart against her breast as he carried her. Beneath her knees she felt the warm skin of his forearm. This was real, not some fevered dream that she was going to wake from all achy and sad. This was really happening.

Jeff paused before he laid her down among the rumpled sheets. He looked deeply into her eyes, searching for something. "Are you sure?" he asked finally.

She nodded mutely. The ability to speak had deserted her. It was all she could do to continue drawing the deep gulps of air that she suddenly seemed to need.

He lowered her carefully, placing her gently among the sheets. Then, standing over her, he reached for the snap on his jeans.

Oh, God, Harriet thought, I'm not ready for this. She ought to close her eyes, turn her head modestly away, anything but watch avidly as he stripped off his jeans and revealed the full glory of his manhood.

She drew a sharp breath, thinking she had surely never seen a man so beautiful. He could have modeled for Michelangelo, she thought dizzily. The hair of his head was brown, but his body hair was a honey color, much lighter and soft-looking.

His shoulders were broad and tapered down to narrow hips and powerful thighs. She simply could not look away.

But he gave her only a moment to admire him. In fact, he seemed unaware that she was admiring him. He stretched out beside her and drew her into the cradle of his arms, tucking her into him as easily as if he had done it a hundred times before.

"I've been going crazy with wanting you," he said huskily, then bent his head and stole the last of her breath in a kiss that seared her soul.

Whatever remaining qualms she had vanished as he claimed her. *This* was what she wanted, this and only this. Tomorrow and all its problems could go hang. He was going to break her heart, but at least she could take the memory of this night with her.

His tongue plunged playfully into her mouth, setting up an evocative rhythm that seemed to pass through her entire body. When his palm found the smooth skin of her thigh and began to stroke gently, she felt as if he were painting her with fire.

Over and over he ran his hand from her hip to her knee. Each time it began its upward journey, anticipation filled her. Surely this time he had to go further, to find her breasts and her aching center.

But he didn't. He seemed determined to take his time and draw every moment out to its fullest. He hadn't even taken off her sleep shirt yet, so that the layer of cotton lay between them, keeping her secrets awhile longer.

A steady throbbing grew between her legs, filling her with languor and making her at once more eager and more patient. So delicious. So...teasing....

His hand rose a little higher this time, and she caught her breath with excitement. She broke the kiss and looked into his eyes, finding a slumberous smile reflected there. He knew exactly what he was doing to her, and he was enjoying it fully. For the first time in her life, she was glad the lights were on when she made love, because even though the light seemed too bright for her eyes, she wouldn't have wanted to miss a single nuance of the expressions that flitted across Jeff's face.

But then he moved so that he was kissing the side of her neck, just behind her ear. When had that become an erogenous zone? she wondered hazily. When had the nerve endings there become attached to her—

Oh! Her eyes flew wide open as an electric thrill shot through her, straight to her center. His teeth nipped gently at the cords in her throat, a sensation so erotic it nearly stunned her. A moan escaped her and she felt her entire body arch toward him, seeking and needing more, so much more.

A throaty chuckle escaped him and he lifted his head, looking down into her wide blue eyes. "Damn, you're sexy," he said huskily. "So responsive..."

"I can't help it...." Of course she couldn't. No one had ever made her feel anything approaching what Jeff was making her feel, and they still hadn't done one thing they couldn't have done in broad daylight in public.

"Don't apologize. Don't ever apologize." His lips trailed along her throat to the hollow where her pulse beat a rapid rhythm. "I love it."

"I wasn't—wasn't apol—apologizing...." She hardly had enough breath left to squeeze out the words, and they trailed away into a deep groan as his mouth moved lower and found one of her nipples through the layer of T-shirt that separated them.

It was as if he unleashed a lightning storm within her, and every one of the bolts zapped straight to her throbbing, aching core. With gentle nips of his teeth and the firm pressure of his tongue, he built the pounding pulse in her blood, filling her with pagan rhythms that were driving out all coherent thought.

She wanted him, she ached for him with a deeper yearning than any she had ever known. And he was taking his damn time about it, teasing her, tormenting her, nearly taunting her with the promises of his mouth and hands.

It was as if desire unleashed something locked deep inside

her. Where she was usually passive, she became aggressive, pushing him back and sitting up. With a single impatient movement, she yanked the sleep shirt over her head.

Jeff drew a sharp breath. She looked at him and found he was studying her with blatant approval.

"You're gorgeous," he said. "You are absolutely gorgeous."

"So are you," she replied, and laughed, all of a sudden feeling as if some shackle from her past had broken free. She didn't mind his admiration. He wasn't telling her to make herself over. He liked exactly what he saw. He wasn't complaining that her hair was too short or that she ought to consider getting breast implants, or muttering because she kept her nails trimmed. He was simply approving of her exactly the way she was.

She returned his admiring look, letting him know that she very much approved of what she saw. Then, with a boldness that was utterly new to her, she straddled his hips and bent over him, taking the chance that she would disappoint him with her attempts to please him.

It was a risk. She knew she wasn't the world's best lover. She'd heard it often enough to be convinced that she was lacking some essential understanding of what pleased a man. But she was willing to take the risk, because she so desperately needed Jeff to make this journey with her, because she so very much wanted to give him back all the things he was giving her. And because she trusted him.

"Tell me…tell me if I do anything you don't like," she said, plagued by a moment of uncertainty.

The smile he gave her was lazy and seemed to hold some secret knowledge. "Sweetheart, anything you do will please me."

He couldn't know that for sure, but she let it pass. She was discovering something about herself and about her feelings for this man, and she was willing to take the risk. She *needed* to take the risk.

Propping herself on her hands above him, she bent down to trail kisses across his throat. She could feel the prickly stubble of a day's growth of beard, and she liked the sensation. It was one of those things that made men and women different, and she had always loved it. She had girlfriends who didn't feel the same, but she couldn't understand why not. This was part of being a man, to have stubble at three in the morning.

Her kisses trailed lower and she felt him catch his breath as her mouth neared one of his nipples. Really? Understanding dawned and she hesitated only a moment before gently taking a small nub into her mouth and teasing it with her tongue.

Much to her delight, he groaned and arched up toward her, creating the most delicious pressure between her legs, right where she needed it. Encouraged, she licked him again and heard another soft groan.

So they were alike in this way. A heady sense of power filled her and she began to tease him as he had teased her. He endured the torment for several minutes, rewarding her with his moans and the writhing of his body, but then he turned the tables on her.

Suddenly, without warning, one of his hands found her breast and the other one found the cleft between her legs. She gasped, caught on an arch of excruciating pleasure that seemed to fill her entire body. He squeezed her nipple between two fingers, creating an unbelievable pain-pleasure sensation. Then, at the same time, he slipped his finger between her moist folds and stroked her.

Her body seemed to shatter into a million glowing pieces. Some small corner of her mind wanted him to stop so she could regain control. Loss of control terrified her. But he was merciless, his fingers pressing and stroking in a rapidly building rhythm that held her helpless on the cusp of a journey toward a culmination she had never before reached.

She was in thrall to the sensations he was evoking in her, to the pounding, rhythmic drive of her body toward completion. And then, in an instant, she was frozen by an incredible sense of disappointment as his finger ceased its motion.

No, oh, no, don't stop, she thought wildly, on the edge of tears.

But he stopped only long enough to lift her a little so he could enter her. She felt his shaft glide into her, stretching her, filling her, and the most delicious throb of pleasure streaked through her when he was fully sheathed. And now that he was, her hips were pressed perfectly to his, intimately to his. If she rocked just a little...

Jeff's hand found her breast again, and his other hand found her moist folds, resuming their pleasurable torture. It was almost too much, and Harriet wondered if she could bear it all, but the question became moot as she rose higher and higher, carried to dizzying heights by the strength of him within her and the touch of his hands.

She had never known it could be like this, and now that she did, she had a fleeting fear about how she was going to live without this, but spiraling pleasure drove everything from her mind, holding her hostage to the whims of her body.

"Yes...." She heard herself whisper the word as her body took over, setting the pace she needed, carrying her to unexplored lands. She was helpless and she loved being helpless. In a heartbeat she surrendered to the moment.

And shattered into a million ecstatic pieces.

Moments later, before she even caught her breath, she felt Jeff join her. His hips rose upward, meeting hers and stirring the embers of her passion anew. She gasped as yet another, even stronger explosion ripped through her.

And then, with a groan, he arched one last time and jetted into her.

With a tenderness that made her throat ache, he drew her down onto his sweat-drenched body and cradled her gently in his arms.

Fourteen

They dozed for a little while, but eventually the chill woke them both up. They looked into each other's eyes and smiled.

"May I suggest," Jeff said after a moment, "that since it's three in the morning, we might as well cancel sleep?"

"I thought you had to be up early."

"I do. But at this point I'm apt to be worse off if I go to sleep. A couple of hours just won't hack it. So why don't we take a shower, raid the refrigerator, bring a repast up here and act like a couple of irresponsible kids until the sun comes up?"

"Sounds like a wonderful agenda."

His bathroom was right off his bedroom, so he went to turn on the water and get it warm while Harriet snuggled under the blankets.

"Do you need me to get anything from your bathroom?"

She opened her eyes and looked up at Jeff. He was standing beside the bed, hands on his hips, looking as pleased as if he had just conquered Mount Everest. "Shampoo?"

"Do you use some special kind? I just use baby shampoo."

She sat up. "Me, too."

"Well then, what are we waiting for?" Grinning, he reached for her hand and tugged her to her feet. "I get to wash you," he said in her ear, sending a pleasant shiver running all the way to the soles of her feet.

"And I get to wash you," she countered.

"Well, of course. There's no point in taking a group shower otherwise, is there?"

His bathroom was large, and his shower made her smile

with delight. It was definitely big enough for two people, a beautifully tiled walk-in shower with two showerheads, both of which were spewing hot water and steam, and even a bench to sit on.

"Can I have this bathroom?" she asked.

"It comes with the owner of this place," he replied. "You can't have one without the other."

She stepped in and sighed as the water beat on her skin, warming her. "This isn't what I expected."

"Well, I had dreams once."

She opened her eyes and turned to look at him. "You've had a lot of dreams, Jeff. Have any of them ever worked out?"

He gave her a rueful smile. "I put this shower in when I was crazy about a lady in Chicago. She never came to visit— I should have gotten the hint. So be honored, sweetheart, you're the first woman to ever share this shower with me."

I'd like to be the last. The thought wafted up from the depths of Harriet's mind and she flicked it impatiently away. This was not the time to get all emotional. She had to savor every moment of the present and let tomorrow take care of itself.

"I was kind of afraid," he said, reaching for soap, "that the other showerhead might not work. I don't think I've used it more than once or twice."

He held out two bars of soap, each a different brand. "This pumice soap would probably be too rough for your skin."

"Probably." Another delightful shiver ran through her. "Is that a loofah?"

"It sure is." He picked it up and rubbed soap into it. "Where do you want me to start?"

"Wherever you like." Good heavens, she couldn't really be feeling sexy again so soon, could she? But she was almost disappointed when he turned her around and began to gently scour her back with the sponge.

"We save the best for last," he said huskily in her ear.

Another shiver trickled through her. Somehow she didn't think they were going to make it downstairs to the refrigerator.

"You have dreams, too, don't you, Harriet?" he asked quietly.

"Oh, sure. Lots of them. I'd love to be successful enough as an artist that I only need to do really creative work. I'd like to make enough money that I can afford to do charity work."

"Really?" He sounded interested. The sponge was moving lower, to the small of her back. "What kind of charity?"

"Oh, I don't mean committee things. I'm not that kind of person. But when I really see someone hurting, I'd like to be able to help out. There are so many people in this world who have nothing at all, you know?"

"I know. There are quite a few in this county just barely scraping by. Single mothers and families who've lost their ranches, and kids whose parents don't take care of them. Unfortunately, no amount of charity is enough to take care of all the world's unfortunates."

"I know, but I'd still like to be able to do something significant from time to time. I don't need to be able to help hundreds of people, but it just doesn't feel enough to donate canned goods and a couple of toys at Christmastime."

"I hear you."

"That's why I'd like to make some decent money. *I* have enough, but so many people don't."

"Amen." He bent down, scrubbing the backs of her legs. "What else. Kids? A family?"

"Oh, of course. I love children. And who knows, maybe I'll manage to have one or two before I get to be too old."

"The old biological clock is ticking?" he teased gently.

"It sure is. And it keeps getting louder with each passing year."

"I'm hearing it, too," he admitted. "One of these days I'll be so old I won't feel like it would be fair to bring a kid into this world."

"Not for a long time yet, Jeff. You're a long way from too old."

He turned her and began soaping the fronts of her legs. He was indeed saving the best for last. "I'd think it would be hard to bring up kids in New York City."

She shrugged. "Harder, maybe. I don't know. You have to watch over them more, I guess, than you would here. Or maybe not. I mean, a kid could get hurt out here, too, couldn't he? There must be all kinds of dangers that wouldn't even occur to me."

"Of course. But on the ranch there's always someone around to keep an eye out. It would make it easier. And of course, we don't have to worry too much about strangers running around on a regular basis."

"Except for the occasional rustler."

His hand paused just as he was about to reach the tops of her thighs. He must have heard her breath catch, because a quiet chuckle escaped him.

"Except for rustlers," he agreed, straightening so that he looked down at her. He began to rub the loofah gently on her throat and shoulders, and Harriet felt a stab of disappointment. "Look, I'm really sorry about the rustlers." Bending, he kissed her eyelid where a faint tinge of green was still visible.

"Don't be sorry. They weren't your doing. You have to do something about your exaggerated sense of responsibility." The sponge drifted lower, approaching her breasts. All of a sudden she could hardly remember what they were talking about. But so what? She could now scarcely breathe.

"Why?" he asked. His voice had taken on an unmistakable soft, husky note.

"Why?" She repeated the question. It made no sense to her. Nothing made any sense except the sponge that was now brushing lightly over the tops of her breasts, a delicious abrasion that made her throb deep inside.

"Why," he repeated, his lips hovering near hers. Hot water splashed them both, helping to awaken and sensitize nerve endings. Harriet felt a hot drop on her lips, but her eyes were closed now, and she couldn't tell if it was simply a splash or if the drop had fallen from Jeff.

"Why," he repeated huskily as his hand moved lower and found the aching, sensitive peaks of her breasts.

Harriet gasped and felt her legs turn weak. One of Jeff's arms closed around her and steadied her as her head fell back in surrender.

The loofah made a downward plunge across her belly and then was suddenly, shockingly replaced with his slick, warm, soapy hand. This time she cried out as his fingers slipped into her moist folds and caressed her with teasing determination.

"This isn't safe," she heard herself say as if from a great distance.

"It's all right," he murmured. "I've got you." And then his mouth closed on hers, silencing every thought within her, silencing everything except the growing, pounding, pulsing, aching passion he had unleashed.

She felt as if she were falling. She clung desperately to his shoulders, seeking an anchor in the raging tide of desire. When he lifted her with his hands beneath her rump and entered her, she felt as if her entire universe had narrowed to the points where their bodies met. Rhythms older than time lifted and carried her away on waves of need that were sweeping her to distant, exotic shores she had only dreamed of.

Then, in one simultaneous cataclysm that shook the foundations of her world, they reached the crest and tumbled gently down the far side.

"Turkey sandwich?" Jeff asked.

Harriet, wrapped in his terry-cloth robe, her hair in a turbaned towel, sat at the island, watching with interest as Jeff showed her he knew his way around a kitchen. She'd never seen a man who looked more gorgeous in nothing but a pair of jeans.

"Harriet," Jeff said, a tremor of amusement in his voice, "stop mooning and tell me if you want a turkey sandwich."

She scowled at him. "I am *not* mooning."

"Sure you are. And if I hadn't promised you food, I'd be mooning, too."

She pretended annoyance. "A turkey sandwich would be great."

"Hot turkey, maybe? There's gravy here and I could heat it up in a jiff."

"Whatever you prefer."

"Okay."

He pulled out an electric frying pan, plugged it in and spooned congealed gravy into it. Then, with a wickedly gleaming knife, he cut thin slices of turkey and put them into the gravy.

Harriet smelled the warming gravy and felt her stomach start to rumble. "There wouldn't be any leftover stuffing, would there?"

"There certainly would." He brought out a large plastic bowl and put it into the microwave, punching the buttons expertly. The microwave came on with a hum and Harriet could see the bowl of stuffing turning slowly.

"Consider this breakfast," he suggested, reaching for a loaf of homemade whole wheat bread. "It's almost late enough to qualify."

"My mother would shake her head in horror. In her book, breakfast was a meal with breakfast foods. Bacon, eggs, pancakes, that kind of thing."

Jeff shook his head. "I'll eat steak for breakfast if Sylvia cooks it. Or cold pizza."

"I *love* cold pizza for breakfast."

He leaned over the island and touched her cheek lightly with one fingertip. "We have so much in common," he said.

"We sure do. Let's see. We both like cold pizza for breakfast. There you have it, the basis for an enduring relationship."

He laughed. "You forgot the baby shampoo."

"Okay, okay, put two marks in the pro column."

His smile faded a little. "Let's not get into the con column. Not today."

She nodded, fighting back a wave of sadness.

"I mean, we both know what they are, right?" he added.

"Right." She smothered a sigh and looked down at the butcher block countertop. "Don't worry, I'm not asking for more than I can have."

"Maybe," he said enigmatically, "it's time you started asking for what you *want*."

She looked at him, wondering what he meant, but he had already turned his attention to the bubbling gravy and turkey. And she didn't feel brave enough to just come out and ask.

Some questions, she thought, were better left unasked.

After they ate, she helped him clean up. They went upstairs again, but this time he left her at the door to her room. "I have to get dressed and get to work," he told her. He gave her a long, lingering kiss. "Sleep as late as you want, sweetheart. Nobody will bother you."

But she didn't sleep at all. Instead she sat in the rocking chair by her window and stared out into the darkness. Dawn was only a faint gray light to the east when she heard Jeff go to work.

"Why don't you come along, Harriet?" Jeff asked that afternoon.

"Come along where?"

"To my first skydiving lesson."

"You're kidding, right?"

"Why would I be kidding?"

"Because you didn't have any sleep last night!" As soon as she spoke, Harriet wished she could snatch the words back. She could feel Sylvia's curious eyes settle on her. Harriet had been helping Sylvia dust the living room when Jeff had come in.

"I had all I needed last night," Jeff said unrepentantly, not caring how Sylvia might construe his words. "And I've postponed this lesson enough times. I'm going, so you may as well come along. You can scrape me up off the pavement."

Harriet shuddered. "Don't even joke about it."

"I'm sorry." Jeff touched her shoulder as Sylvia considerately eased out of the room. "I really would like you to be there."

"Really?" She felt herself weakening.

"Really. What good is all the excitement if I can't share it?"

That struck her as a remarkably perceptive question. He was right. A joy of any kind was multiplied when you were able to share it with someone. "I'll go," she decided. It seemed the least she could do when he had given her so much. "Just don't go splat on me."

"I have no intention of it."

"Of course not. You wouldn't be talking about jumping out of a plane if you really thought that might happen."

"Jo is a great instructor. She jumps all the time herself. There's not going to be a problem."

Harriet wished that didn't sound so much like famous last words.

Conard County had a small airport capable of handling light planes as well as the county's emergency helicopter. Harriet stood on the pavement in a moderately strong breeze and shook hands with Jo Cameron, an attractive woman of about forty-five wearing a bright orange jumpsuit. Squinting into the sun had added attractive crow's-feet around Jo's eyes, and laugh lines livened her face.

She was shadowed by a black-and-white husky named Fred. "Fred wants to jump, too," Jo explained when the dog barked eagerly. "He hates to miss a jump."

Harriet looked down at the dog, who was eagerly wagging his tail and making sounds somewhere between barks and groans. "He's talking," she said, amazed. She'd never been able to have a dog, so she didn't know much about them, but it seemed to her that this one was talking.

"Sure he is," Jo said. "He talks all the time. Admittedly he can't actually say words, but you can tell what he means. And whenever I get back from a trip, the first thing he does is say hi."

Looking down at the dog, Harriet could believe it. He seemed to be following the conversation intelligently. Fred barked again and groaned.

"Yes, you're going, too," Jo said.

Fred woofed and immediately darted over to the small plane.

"Not until you get your chute on," Jo said.

Fred made another groan and settled down with a huff.

"How did Fred ever start jumping?" Harriet asked her. "I'd never even think of taking a dog up for a jump."

Jo shrugged. "He was always going nuts trying to get on the plane with me. Pete—that's my pilot—said he'd heard of dogs jumping, and why didn't I try it." She laughed. "That first jump was something else. I had him harnessed to my chest, and he clawed me all the way down. Ruined my damn jumpsuit."

Harriet found herself laughing as she imagined the picture.

"I figured that was it," Jo continued. "But damn if Fred didn't want to get on the plane for the next jump, and if I hadn't been holding on to him, he probably would have jumped all by himself without a chute. And that time he didn't claw me at all. Three or four more jumps and I decided to make him his own rig.

"Okay," she said, turning back to Jeff. "We've been over all the basics, right?"

"Right."

"You know what you have to do when you go out that door?"

"Right."

"Now, the first time, I'm going to hold on to you in case

you freeze and don't pull the rip cord. We'll stay together until you pull the cord.''

He nodded.

Jo looked at Harriet. ''You want to come, too?''

Harriet quickly shook her head. ''I'm a dyed-in-the-wool chicken. Watching is going to be hard enough.''

Jo laughed, but the look Jeff gave her expressed gentle understanding.

''You really have to do these things?'' Harriet asked when she had a private moment with him.

He nodded. ''It's either that or go nuts doing the same thing day in and day out.''

She grimaced. ''Maybe you need to think about a major revamp of your life-style. Maybe you need to spend less time raising cattle and more time doing other things.''

''Why? I'll get this out of my system after a few jumps.''

She hoped so.

She watched as Jo helped him into his parachute and checked all the harness fastenings. ''I packed this chute myself,'' she told him as she finished. ''It's done right.''

Then she put the dog in a smaller harness and parachute and donned one herself. A small man who looked as if he could be either forty or ninety emerged from a tiny steel building and asked if they were ready to go. He wore a baseball cap and aviator glasses, and his name was Pete. It turned out he had given Jeff his flying lessons.

''How's the dog going to pull his rip cord?'' Harriet asked as everyone moved toward the plane.

''He doesn't,'' Jo explained. ''I do it. The cord is attached to a long tether that I hang on to. He falls about twenty feet from the plane and the chute opens.''

''Oh.'' She felt stupid for wondering.

Heedless of onlookers, Jeff gave her a long, deep kiss before he boarded. Harriet watched the plane take off and wished her heart would get out of her throat and go back to its normal position. She told herself that Jo would hardly let her dog jump if it was *that* dangerous.

But headlines of past disasters kept coming back to her, most of them involving parachutes that didn't open. Why had she agreed to come?

Because it would have been worse waiting at home and wondering, she realized. At least while she was here she would know exactly what was going on. Instead of panicking for a couple of hours, she would only have to panic for the few minutes it took Jeff to get from the plane to the ground.

Right. Except that her panic had already begun.

The plane rose until it was barely a speck in the sky. Surely that was too high? And the wind. The wind was too strong. Jeff would be at its mercy and might blow miles away. Of course, that wouldn't necessarily be a problem. It wasn't as if there were an ocean around here or anything.

And Jo had probably taken the wind into account, she reminded herself. The woman must have done enough jumps to know how to adjust for such things.

She strained her eyes, trying to see the speck that was the plane. She couldn't see exactly when they jumped. The sky was too bright, and she was seeing little specks everywhere. But she saw when the parachutes opened.

First one orange bloom, probably the dog, she thought. Then nothing until her nerves were stretched so tight that she felt she was going to scream. Then another orange bloom, and moments later, yet another one. A huge sigh of relief escaped her. All the parachutes had opened.

The three chutes looked so peaceful as they drifted in the sky, approaching the airport. They seemed to be falling so slowly, but considering how fast they were growing larger, she decided that was an illusion.

Actually, she thought as her heart began once again to climb into her throat, they seemed to be falling too quickly. A new worry assailed her as she wondered if something was wrong with the parachutes.

Then, drifting right in front of her toward the large grassy field to the left, came Fred. The dog seemed to be grinning as he approached landing. He hit the ground and scrambled for a few feet as the wind caught the parachute and dragged him a little way, but then the chute collapsed and Fred settled down to lick his paws and wait to be released from the harness.

A couple of minutes later, Jeff glided in for a landing. A wonderful landing, Harriet thought as she watched him hit feetfirst, take a couple of quick steps and end up still standing, leaning backward against the drag of the parachute.

Jo was right behind, letting out a loud "yee-haw" as she landed.

Harriet nearly collapsed with relief.

Jeff apparently knew how to unfasten the harness, because he stepped out of it and began rolling it up with the drogue lines. Jo paused long enough to unhook Fred, who apparently decided he needed to share his moment, too, and came dashing over to Harriet and jumped up to try to lick her face.

"Hey," Jeff said, approaching with a grin, "are you letting that dog steal my kiss?"

Harriet couldn't even answer. She simply reached for Jeff and sighed with great relief when she felt his arms close tightly around her. Thank God, she thought. He was all right.

"I was going to jump again today," Jeff murmured in her ear. "But if it worries you so much, I won't."

Harriet almost asked him not to, but then she thought of the man who had put so many dreams on hold to deal with responsibilities that had fallen his way, and she just couldn't do it. It might terrify her, but it was something he needed to do. It was a way for him to have fun away from his responsibilities. How could she deny him that?

"No," she said, lifting her face and smiling up at him. "You go ahead and jump again. Jump as many times as you want."

He looked surprised. "Really?"

"Really."

"But if it scares you—"

"Lots of things scare me, Jeff. And some of them are things I do anyway." Like making love to you. "Go ahead. It looks like a lot of fun."

"It was great! It was super! Are you sure you don't want to try it?"

"It's not my kind of thrill. But I'll watch."

She watched three more jumps and found that with each one it grew easier for her. Fred didn't make any more jumps, but he sat beside Harriet and watched. Apparently the dog didn't need more than one death-defying thrill a day.

She wondered how many it would take to make Jeff happy.

After the fourth jump, however, he called a halt. He carried his parachute into the folding room and helped Jo spread it out on the long table, but when he offered to help fold it, she waved him away. "Maybe next time we'll get into that. As it is, I prefer to fold 'em myself, just to be sure."

As Jeff and Harriet started walking away, Jo called out, "Same time next week?"

Jeff turned and shook his head. "I don't think so, Jo. I got what I wanted. But thanks a lot for a great experience."

"If you change your mind, just give me a call."

When they got into the car and headed back toward town, Harriet turned to Jeff. "Why don't you want to jump again?"

"It's like I said. I just wanted to try it. To see if I could and what it would be like. Besides, it terrifies you."

Harriet shook her head. "Jeff, you don't owe me that. You don't owe me *anything*. But even if you did, I wouldn't want you to deny yourself something you wanted to do because of me."

He looked at her, his eyes gleaming darkly in the failing afternoon light. "I know you wouldn't," he said. "It's a choice I'm making myself."

"You have to stop making your choices based on what other people want. You've told me of all the things you haven't done because you had to run the ranch. You told me you didn't even really have a childhood. At some point you've got to say to hell with what other people want and start doing things for yourself!''

"I agree up to a point."

"What point?"

"Well, it seems to me if we all do whatever we feel like without regard to others, we'll have one miserable world."

"Of course. I'm not talking about being completely selfish here. But when you want to do something like this, why shouldn't you? Just because it's going to scare somebody else doesn't mean you should deny yourself."

"Well, that depends. If it scared Ben—"

"Ben?"

"My ranch foreman."

"Oh, that Ben." She'd met him a couple of times in passing.

"That Ben. If it scared him, I wouldn't worry too much about it. You're a different kettle of fish."

Harriet shook her head. "You can't give me that kind of power, Jeff. It isn't right."

They were driving down the main street of Conard City now and Harriet felt a tug of surprise as she realized how her reaction to the town had changed. It no longer looked impossibly small and rural. It simply looked charming. A sheriff's car passed them, and the deputy inside gave them a friendly wave.

Jeff turned and pulled into a parking slot in front of Maude's. "I figured we'd get something to eat before we go home," he said as he turned off the ignition. "I told Sylvia we wouldn't be back for supper."

"Oh. Is it okay for me to be seen?"

"I guess, from what Nate said. Your decision."

Harriet only needed to think about it for a second. "Sure, why not? Besides, what are they going to do in a crowded restaurant?"

He smiled and pulled the keys from the ignition.

But before she got out of the car, she wanted to finish their discussion. "About what I said. You can't give me that kind of power, Jeff."

He sighed and turned in his seat, facing her more directly. "I'm not giving you power, Harriet. I'm respecting your feelings. There's a difference. I did enough jumping to find out what I needed to know. Now, why would I want to keep on doing it when I know it bothers you? There's a difference between giving someone power and respecting their feelings."

Harriet thought about that. "I don't quite see it."

He shook his head. "That tells me a lot about you."

"What?"

"That you've let people you love control you too much. No wonder you're prickly sometimes."

"They don't control me for long."

"No, I can see that. But they shouldn't have been controlling you at all. Don't you see? If I were to express a legitimate concern about something you want to do, and you were to respect my wishes, that would be entirely different from me telling you what to do and you feeling obligated to do it just because I said so."

"We're splitting hairs here."

"But it's a very important hair, Harriet. It's the difference between doing something because you feel obligated and doing it because you care. Doing something because you feel somebody won't love you anymore if you don't do what they want is giving them power over you. It allows them to control you. Doing something out of respect for another person's feelings gives *you* the power. You retain the power to make choices, and you choose between what you want and what the other person wants."

Harriet saw what he was getting at, and in a burst of clarity she realized that was what had been wrong with her other relationships. She had always given her boyfriends power over her, and the more power she gave them, the more they demanded. And not one of them had ever appeared to feel the same about her. None of them had respected *her* feelings.

Which was why she had lately decided to leave men out of her life. Not just because they wanted to change her, but because they wanted to control her. And the control had not been reciprocal. In fact, their desire to change her had merely been an expression of control.

In the end, in the process of fighting off all the bonds of control they had wrapped her in, she had even quit respecting *their* feelings.

"I don't have a very good track record with relationships," she heard herself saying.

"So? Neither do I. That doesn't mean I won't get it right one of these days. Besides, I get the feeling we've both been in the business of picking the wrong people."

And we aren't now? she wondered, looking at him in the golden afternoon light. She had picked a man she couldn't possibly have a relationship with, and he had picked a woman who, like all the others, wasn't going to give up her life for him. But maybe he didn't feel as involved as she was beginning to. Why should he? Men didn't toss their hearts away as easily as women did.

And she probably wasn't as involved as she thought she was, she told herself. No, it was just this great sexual attraction, and it would wear off shortly.

After one of Maude's hearty steak dinners, they drove back to the ranch. The sun had disappeared behind the mountains by the time they arrived, and the long evening twilight had settled in.

Sylvia was sitting on the front porch when they drove up, and she greeted them with a smile. "Sheriff Tate stopped by," she said to Jeff. "He says he'll come back in the morning."

"I'll be here."

"You and Harriet want to take a walk out to the pond?"

"Right now?"

Sylvia's smile deepened. "Right now."

Jeff looked at Harriet. "Okay by you?"

"After that huge dinner, I'd *love* to take a walk."

They followed the dirt road past the barn, walking beneath tall cottonwoods, the evening star guiding them.

"It's so quiet out here," Harriet said. "I just can't get over it." All she could hear was the rustle of the wind in the trees and the chirp of crickets. As if from a great distance, she caught occasional snatches of a TV program from the foreman's house, but even that was almost inaudible beneath the murmur of the wind and the cheerful sound of the crickets.

"It's God's country," Jeff said. He reached out and took her hand, holding it. "For all I've dreamed of doing other things, I'd never be able to leave the ranch. I'd miss the connection to nature, to the flow of the seasons and all the growing things."

Was that a warning? She couldn't tell, but she decided to take it as one—not that she needed it.

"I'm firmly rooted here," he continued. "When I go to the city, after a while I start to feel cut off. Drained. I need to hear the wind in the trees and see all the stars in the sky and watch the sun rise. I need to see the cows calve in the spring and watch the foals learn to use their legs. You have to come back here in the spring, Harriet. Promise me you will. You won't believe how this place bursts with life. *New* life. It gives me such a sense of blessing."

"I'd love to come back," she said, her throat tightening at the thought of having to leave. *This wasn't fair!*

"I wish I could show you some of the spring magic right now," he went on. "I wish I had a newborn foal for you to watch climb to its feet for the very first time. I wish..." He trailed off. "What's that?"

"What?"

He put a finger to his lips and cocked his head. "Do you hear that?"

Harriet shook her head.

"It sounds like a little peeping." Suddenly his long legs

were eating up the ground. Harriet had to break into a trot to follow him.

He walked straight for the pond, hearing something she couldn't. He reached the edge of the water, glanced around, then parted some tall grasses and looked down.

Harriet caught up with him, just a little breathless, and stared down into the shadowy hollow in the grass. Now she could hear the peeping that was coming from a pale ball of fuzz in the hollow.

"Baby ducks," Jeff said, squatting down. "Will you look at that? It's too late in the year. They'll never mature in time to fly south." He looked around and saw the parents swimming serenely on the pond. "They ought to be heading out any day now."

"Can we do something?"

"Sure." He scooped up one of the little ducklings, holding it near his face in gentle fingers. "Poor little guy, what are they doing hatching you now?"

The duckling peeped insistently.

"The parents don't look particularly concerned," Harriet remarked. "Shouldn't they be over here trying to get you away from the babies?"

"I would think so. Maybe they know it's hopeless." He looked at the small fuzzy ball in his hand. "But it's not hopeless, little guy." He set the duckling back with its siblings and let the grasses close over them. "Let's go sit over there," he said with a jerk of his head. "See if Mama and Papa come back to them."

They retreated to the shadows beneath a tree and watched until night began to darken the world. Neither of the adult ducks made any attempt to go to the babies. Instead they climbed out of the water on the other side of the pond and began preening.

"Maybe they're not the parents," Harriet said.

"Maybe. It sure is strange. Well, let's go rescue the little critters."

"Should we? What if the parents come back?"

Jeff shook his head. "It won't make any difference. These guys won't be able to migrate. Either they've already been abandoned, or they'll be abandoned in a few days. In any case, they need help."

He pulled off his shirt, spread it on the ground and gently put the six little ducks on it. Then he lifted it by the corners, making a little basket, and they started back for the house.

"We'll hand raise them," he told Harriet.

"I wouldn't even know how to begin."

"Oh, it's not so hard. I've done it before."

Sylvia was expecting them. Apparently she had known exactly how Jeff was going to deal with the ducklings. She already had a big box lined with some old rags to put the babies in.

With a pair of tweezers Jeff fed them bread soaked in milk. The ducklings sure seemed to like it. Harriet took a turn feeding them until their frantic little peeps began to quiet and their plump little bodies began to droop. Sylvia brought a tablecloth and put it over the top of the box. The ducks immediately fell silent.

"They'll sleep till morning now," Jeff said. "And considering that I'm really short on sleep, I think that's what I'm going to do myself."

"Me, too," Harriet said. It was as if fatigue had suddenly hit her like a sledgehammer.

"See you two in the morning," Sylvia said, settling down again at the counter with her cookbook.

Upstairs at the door of her bedroom, Jeff paused and looked down at Harriet. "Why don't you come with me," he said quietly. "My bed's big enough for two."

She wanted to. Oh, how she wanted to! But her eyes felt as if they were full of sand, and she was beginning to have flickering hallucinations as her brain tried to slip dreams in while she struggled to stay awake. "I really need to sleep."

"So do I. But I don't see why we can't do it together."

Which was how she came to be curled up in the big bed beside Jeff, with his arms around her. And for the first time in her life she fell asleep while someone held her.

Fifteen

Jeff awoke in the morning with Harriet curled up against his side, her head tucked on his shoulder. His arm was beneath her and had fallen asleep, but he didn't want to move. He wanted her to stay right where she was and wanted to stay right where he was. Never in his life had he awakened to find a woman in his arms.

He tilted his head a little so he could press his lips to her hair. She wore no perfume, and all he could smell was Harriet and baby shampoo. She smelled better than any woman he had ever known.

He heard the cock crow from the barnyard, his signal to rise and get to work. There was always plenty to do around the ranch, and even with the help he had, he still had all he could do to keep up. The time he had taken off lately to spend with Harriet had put him behind on his office chores, and he really needed to get downstairs and put his books in order. Hell, he hadn't even gotten around to listing the lost cattle, and there must be close to seven hundred head missing.

The cock crowed again, and he gave up pretending that he could stay here until Harriet's eyes fluttered open. If he had a woman like Harriet in his life on a regular basis, he'd hire even more help so he could make time to laze around with her in the mornings, so he could take time for trips to Denver or even more exotic places, like Europe and Mexico.

But he didn't have a woman like Harriet in his life. He was only borrowing her.

Remembering his stolen cattle had given Jeff an unpleasant jolt, and if he stayed here any longer, he was going to start stewing about all the things he didn't have and couldn't have. Work was all he had, and if he kept busy enough, he wouldn't start pining for other things.

Reluctantly, he slipped his arm from beneath Harriet and rolled carefully out of bed, trying not to disturb her.

Sometimes he felt as if he were wasting his whole life. Here he was, pulling on his jeans and boots, tucking in a shirt, reaching for a jacket the way he did damn near every morning. But this time he was leaving a warm woman alone in his bed, and it filled him with a pang of yearning.

What was the point? he wondered. He'd built this ranch into an extremely successful operation. He had cowboys, truck drivers, stable hands and an assortment of jobbers all depending on him for a paycheck.

But what did it mean? He had no one to share it with. And he had no one to leave it to. He sometimes shuddered to think what would happen to this place if it fell into George's hands. Leaving it to his niece and nephew hardly seemed a better solution, since the ranch would probably meet the same fate.

Although to be fair, he reminded himself, there was no guarantee that any children of his own would want to keep the place after he passed on.

And that's what made it all seem so pointless.

He paused a moment, looking back at Harriet, and felt a great well of sadness open in him. For a fact, life never gave you everything you wanted.

Harriet felt Jeff get out of bed, but she kept her eyes closed. She knew if she opened them and looked at him, she was going to ask him to stay. But he had things to do this morning, and besides, she didn't want to make herself that vulnerable. Asking for things left you open to disappointment.

She heard the door close behind him, then she buried her face in his pillow, breathing deeply of his scent and trying not to cry. Life could just be so damn unfair!

At eight, dressed in her habitual khakis, with a camera around her neck, Harriet went down for breakfast. She wanted to take some more pictures around the ranch, more for herself than anything else, and she was going to make her return flight reservations today.

She had to. She was already in over her head with Jeff and in serious danger of drowning. Prolonging the inevitable was only going to get her in deeper.

Jeff apparently heard her come down the stairs, because he emerged from his office and looked up at her with a smile. "Ready for breakfast?" he asked. "I waited for you."

"I wish you wouldn't do that," she replied grumpily.

He looked startled. "Why not?"

"Because I'm an unwanted guest, and you're already putting yourself out enough for me."

He hesitated, studying her with perplexity. Then, taking her by surprise, he caught her about the waist, lifted her the rest of the way down the stairs and gave her a big hug. "You're a very much *wanted* guest," he said softly in her ear, then gave her a hungry kiss.

When he set her on her feet, she felt dazed.

"Come on," he said, with a boyish grin. "Let's go see what Sylvia has for breakfast."

Sylvia had made blueberry pancakes, fried ham slices and hash browns. She even insisted on cooking their eggs to order, rather than allowing them to eat the scrambled eggs that had been standing in a chafing dish for the last hour or so.

They had just finished eating when Nate Tate arrived. Sylvia wanted to feed him, too, but he refused. "Gotta keep my waistline, Sylvia," he told her. "I had a good breakfast at home just an hour ago."

But he did accept a cup of coffee and joined Jeff and Harriet at the table. "Well," he said, when Sylvia had bustled back to the kitchen, "I've got some news. But first—Harriet, could you take a look at these pictures and see if you recognize any of these guys?"

He pulled a sheet of mug shots from a brown envelope and passed it to her.

Harriet looked down at the four pictures on the sheet and found her gaze drawn immediately to the third one. "That's one of the rustlers I saw."

"You're sure?"

"Positive." She passed the sheet back, pointing to the picture she recognized. "That's him. He didn't look much different through the lens of my camera."

"Well, his fingerprints were all over the steering wheel and rearview mirror of the car you found the body in, so it's my guess this is the guy who was killed out there. He's got a pretty good rap sheet. Burglary, armed robbery, battery on a law enforcement officer. He got out of prison just last spring." Nate tucked the photos back into the envelope.

"Three down," Jeff remarked. "I guess that means someone else is involved."

Nate nodded, looking none too happy. "How's the head count coming?"

"I figure about seven hundred head are missing so far. There might be more, but we haven't finished the roundup."

Nate shook his head. "Seven hundred." He sounded disgusted.

Harriet felt shocked. Even though they had figured that a hundred head must have been loaded on the trucks she'd seen, and even though Nate had mentioned the cattle that had been sold in—where was it? Omaha? Des Moines?—she hadn't really believed Jeff had lost that many cattle.

"Are you going to be okay?" Nate asked Jeff.

Jeff shrugged. "Sure. It's a financial blow, Nate, but I've got reserves. It's not like it's going to make or break me. I'm luckier than most. My net worth isn't all on the hoof."

Nate smiled at that and sipped his coffee. "You've done yourself proud, Jeff. I remember when you were a scrawny, stringy kid, trying your best to get your daddy's ranch through one more winter. Now look at you. Seven hundred head stolen and you're still going to be okay. That shows one hell of a business head."

"I've been lucky."

"Bull," Nate said emphatically. "You've worked your butt off and earned every dime you have. And I sure am glad to hear you've got more dimes than I thought you had. I've been worrying myself sick about what this might do to you."

"I'll be okay, Nate, really. It's a dent, but I'm far from totaled."

Nate sat for a few minutes, sipping his coffee and looking, Harriet thought, like a man who had more to say but was very reluctant to say it. He was different from other cops Harriet had known. In her experience, most cops didn't waste time worrying about people's feelings. Of course, Nate and Jeff had been friends for a long time.

Finally Nate put his mug down and leaned forward. "I had Gage Dalton do some research into the Overland Cattle Company. It's owned by a Denver holding company."

"Which one?"

"Something called Sundown Enterprises."

"Never heard of it."

"Neither had many other people. It's been around for the last ten years or so, has made a number of good investments. The cattle company is its newest venture. Gage had to do a little running around, but finally we got the records. Jeff, I hate to tell you this, but the principal stockholder of Sundown Enterprises is your brother."

"George?" Jeff looked stunned. "George?" he repeated. "I thought he wanted out of the cattle business. My God, Nate, he sold his share of the ranch to me nearly fifteen years ago."

"Well, apparently he wants another share of the ranch."

"But..." Jeff trailed off, then shook his head. "He wouldn't steal my cattle, Nate. I'm his brother!"

Nate nodded. "Maybe. We're still looking at where Overland got the cattle it took to market in July. Some friends of mine up in Montana are checking into it. Folks in the area were under the impression that Overland was leasing out grazing land, which explained why the cattle arrived in such big numbers, then moved out in big numbers. Nobody thinks Overland is raising them itself."

"It's possible."

"Anything's possible." Nate sighed and leaned back in his chair. "What doesn't add up is if Overland is merely leasing out grazing land, why was it paid for the cattle it took to market?"

"Maybe Overland bought a herd, fattened it, then shipped it out."

"Maybe."

But Jeff looked doubtful. As far as he knew, George didn't have enough money to buy that many head of cattle or enough money to buy a spread on which to fatten the cattle. "Are there any other shareholders in the holding company?"

"Just one. The guy used to own the land in Montana until he went bust three years ago. Story is, he sold to Overland for a song, for a lot less than the land is worth, and got to stay on as foreman." He reached for the insulated coffee carafe that Sylvia had left on the table and poured himself another steaming mugful. "Now, I may be suspicious by nature, but this sounds like a shady deal to me, Jeff. Why would a man sell his land for less than it's worth and take a job as foreman and stock in the holding company unless he stood to make some good money off it?"

"Maybe he just didn't want to leave his home."

"I know of plenty of foreign investors who would have snapped up the property at full value and still kept him on. Hell, it's happening all the time these days. He had to be offered something else, and I suspect he was offered a lot of easy money."

"Now, *that* sounds like George," Jeff said reluctantly. "He was always spinning pipe dreams about quick, easy money. *Lots* of quick, easy money."

"Yeah, that's how I remember him, too." Nate rubbed his chin, settled back in the chair and drummed his fingers on the tabletop. "It's thin evidence, I know, and I can't say anything for sure until I have more information. But the George I remember never wanted to do an honest day's work for an honest dollar. One get-rich-quick scheme after another."

"I still don't see how he could have come up with the money to buy a ranch," Jeff argued.

Nate shrugged. "God knows who else's cattle he may have rustled. And according to my sources, Sundown has had some investments turn out quite well."

"In which case," said Jeff heavily, "he ought to be paying his back child-support."

"He doesn't even do that?"

"Nope. He's always claiming poverty."

"Well, any guy who owns a ranch free and clear ain't poor in my estimation, not as long as he can sell the land."

"Maybe that's how he hid his assets from the court during the divorce," Jeff said. "Pumped it all into the holding company and bought the ranch, then didn't tell anybody about it."

Nate nodded.

Harriet was finding it hard to believe that both George and Jeff could have come from the same family. "What a sleaze," she heard herself say.

Both men looked at her. Nate's expression was amused, but Jeff's was sad. Harriet found herself wondering how many times over the years Jeff had envied his brother, first because George was the favored, pampered son, and then because George had left the ranch and gone to the big city to make a life.

"Maybe," Jeff said after a moment, "George never lost that money he made when I bought him out. Maybe the stories about bad investments were just stories, so I'd keep helping him out and so his wife wouldn't know what he was worth."

"It's a possibility," Nate agreed, "especially since he had the wherewithal to buy that ranch."

"But if he has that kind of money, why would he steal my cattle?"

Nobody had an answer for that—at least not an answer they were willing to say out loud. Harriet found herself thinking that it might be really simple. Maybe George had never made an honest dime in his life. Or maybe he just hated his brother's success.

Just then Sylvia entered the dining room through the swinging door. She was carrying the box of frantically cheeping ducklings and she set it down on the table in front of Jeff.

"I'm trying to make a cake for lunch," she said, "and I don't have the time to keep feeding these damn birds. You rescued 'em, boss, you feed 'em. I'll get you a bowl of bread and milk."

Harriet couldn't help it, she started to laugh. Jeff looked down into the box of squawking birds with a bemused expression, then he started chuckling.

"Nothing like a hungry baby of any breed to put things in perspective," Nate remarked with a smile. "Where'd you get them?"

"They were up by the pond. It's so late in the year they don't have a chance."

Nate leaned over and looked at the little ducklings. "I reckon not. You're going to hand raise them?"

"Apparently so."

"Better you than me. Eight or ten years ago, one of my girls rescued a baby crow that fell out of its nest. We were doing just fine for about a week, then one of the girls fed him a poisonous caterpillar. Talk about tragedy! I had six crying girls, and they all made me feel I was somehow to blame. Like I was supposed to know what a baby crow can't eat!"

Sylvia returned with a bowl of milk-soaked bread and a pair of tweezers. "There you go," she said, putting them down rather emphatically. "These birds are going to be the size of horses in another month. I've been feeding them almost non-stop since dawn!"

That said, she disappeared into the kitchen. Harriet looked at Jeff, and he looked at her.

"I'll feed them," she said.

"What I really need to do," he said, "is make some mash for them out of the bird feed. Bread can't be enough, and milk isn't a natural food for them."

"Well, you go do that while I shut them up with some of this."

"And I'll be on my way," Nate said, rising. "I'll let you know as soon as we have any more details, Jeff. For now, it's really all speculation."

Jeff walked him to the door but came back a few moments later to watch Harriet feeding the birds. "I don't want to believe it," he said finally.

"I can understand that." She looked up from all the wide-open beaks and tried to read his expression. He had retreated behind a stony facade. "He's your brother."

"But…" He shook his head. "I wish I could say it didn't sound like him, but unfortunately it does. Then there's the brand mark on the Overland cattle. It's too close for comfort to the Bar C."

"It does seem to stretch coincidence."

"And maybe that's all it is." He straightened, seeming to brace himself somehow. "I'll go get that mash. I don't want these birds to starve to death with full bellies."

Harriet stared after his departing back, wishing she could do something to make him feel better.

Times like this came to everyone, she reminded herself. There were times when life just went to hell, delivering one blow after another until you were reeling. And at times like that, there wasn't much anyone could do.

She thought about her promise to call for a plane reservation this morning and decided to postpone it just a little bit longer. One or two more days couldn't make that much difference, could they?

Jeff made the mash for the birds, grinding up feed with a mortar and pestle and adding a little water. The ducks gobbled it down almost faster than Harriet could believe, but it seemed to satisfy them more than the bread. Their cheeping trailed off, and presently they fell asleep.

A few moments after the birds fell asleep, Sylvia stuck her head through the kitchen door. "What's wrong? You didn't kill them, did you?"

Jeff laughed. "Nope. Believe it or not, they're sleeping. I'll make up another batch of this mash, then I've got to get out of here. Paco asked me to come out and take a look at a dead steer. He thinks the wolves did it.''

Sylvia frowned. "Things just keep going to hell, don't they? What are you gonna do about those wolves?''

"Not a damn thing, Sylvia. They've got a right to live, too. Besides, I don't think they did it, not unless that steer was already sick or injured.''

Sylvia shook her head. "Next thing you know, this place is going to be overrun by hungry wolves.'' She went back into the kitchen.

Jeff sighed and gave Harriet a rueful smile. "Sylvia and I are never going to see eye-to-eye on those wolves. The minute she heard they were up there, she wanted me to do something about it. Most ranchers would probably feel the same way, I guess, but I'm a long way from being hurt by the loss of a steer here and there. Since the wolves take down the sick and injured, I'm not losing a thing.''

He pushed back from the table. "I'll go make that mash now. Do you mind nursing the ducklings this afternoon?''

"Not at all. I'm kind of enjoying it.''

"You might want to take them out for a stroll around the barnyard when they wake up. They need the exercise.''

Which was how Harriet came to be walking around the yard early that afternoon with a column of six ducklings scampering along after her. Apparently the babies had decided she was their mother, because they tottered along behind her, cheeping excitedly. It was kind of fun, actually. She took pictures of them hurrying along in their little line after her, and when they reached the watering trough beside the corral, she decided to find out if they could swim.

She lifted one of the fuzzy little ducklings in her hand, smoothed its downy coat gently, then set it in the water. The little bird immediately began to swim, so she put the rest of the babies in with it.

At first they swam randomly, looking confused, but when

she hunkered down at the far end of the trough, they made a beeline straight for her, paddling with their little feet as fast as they could.

She found herself laughing with pleasure, thoroughly enjoying herself. One of the barn cats came strolling along the corral railing and watched for a few minutes before evidently deciding that the human present would not approve of duck-hunting cats. A little while later, one of the ranch dogs joined them, barking excitedly at the little birds. The babies appeared serenely unconcerned by the ruckus.

Finally, Harriet took the birds out of the trough, watched them shake themselves dry, then led them back to the house. The obedient little troop followed right on her heels.

"Well, quack-quack," Sylvia said as she watched them approach the house. She was smiling, though, drying her hands on her apron as she stood on the porch. "How are your babies doing, Mama Duck?"

"They went for a swim in the horse trough and had a wonderful time. They're probably hungry now, though."

"Well, if you want to sit out here and enjoy the afternoon, I'll bring the mash out to you along with your lunch."

Harriet decided to take her up on the offer. It was a perfectly gorgeous day, dry, sunny and in the low seventies. One by one she put her little charges back in their box, where they immediately resumed their hungry peeping.

Sylvia brought the mash and her lunch on a tray but excused herself from joining Harriet. "I'm gonna have a bunch of hungry cowpokes showing up at any minute. Maybe later we can have some iced tea together."

By midafternoon, Jeff still had not returned. Harriet began to feel impatient and lonely, and no matter how much she told herself to cut it out, the simple fact was that she was missing Jeff as if an essential piece of herself were missing. How, she asked herself, had she ever managed to get herself so deeply involved in such a short time? And in such hopeless circumstances?

The breeze whispered in the trees around the house, but it

offered no answers. The sun was sliding under the porch roof now, bathing her in warmth, and little by little she felt herself falling into a doze. Except for missing Jeff, she couldn't remember the last time she had felt so content.

"Miss Harriet?"

She opened her eyes groggily and looked around, finally noticing the cowboy who was standing at the foot of the steps, his hat in hand.

"Miss Harriet?"

She sat up straighter in her chair and blinked owlishly at him. The ducklings were still sound asleep in their box, apparently worn-out by their morning stroll and swim. "Yes?" His name was Sandy, she remembered, probably because of his sandy-colored hair. He was one of the cowboys who had shown up most often at supper in the dining room since she had come here.

"The boss sent me to get you."

"Me?" Harriet sat up even straighter, eagerness driving out the last of her sleepiness.

"Yes'm. He found a wolf cub what's been hurt. He sent me to get some bandages and said maybe as how you'd like to come see the cub before he lets it go agin."

"Sure." Although seeing Jeff ranked even higher on her list of inducements than the wolf cub.

"You need to dress for riding," he said, looking doubtfully at her khakis. "You got jeans, don't you?"

"I'll go put them on right now."

Passing through the kitchen, she told Sylvia she was riding out with Sandy to meet Jeff and see a wolf cub.

"Have a good time," was all Sylvia said. She was absorbed in cleaning the oven.

Harriet ran upstairs and changed, then ran back down, arriving just in time to see Sandy approaching with his horse and Maggie.

"Did you get the bandages?" she asked him.

"In my saddlebags."

She managed to mount without any assistance. Sandy seemed to think she knew how to ride, because he didn't offer to take a leading rein. And, Harriet thought as she rode out of the yard after him, she seemed to be doing pretty well on her own. Feeling proud and pleased, she was smiling as they headed out in the direction of Thunder Mountain.

What she didn't notice as they rode away was that Sylvia came out on the porch and stood staring after them. A few minutes later, she went back in, picked up the phone and dialed the stable. One of the stable hands answered.

"Pete," Sylvia said, "where did Mr. Jeff go?"

"He said he was going out toward Brenner Creek to meet Paco."

Sylvia hung up the phone and stood in the kitchen for several minutes, thinking about it. Brenner Creek was up north, but maybe she was just being too damn suspicious. He might have finished his business with Paco and ridden off to check out something else.

She shook her head and tried to brush aside the nagging uneasiness. But the more she thought about it, the uneasier she got. It was awful late in the afternoon to be asking that girl to ride out and meet him. Besides, she had never liked that Sandy since he started working here last winter.

Finally, unable to ignore her uneasiness, she called the stable again. "Pete, you send somebody out to get Mr. Jeff right now."

Sixteen

Jeff was already on his way back to the ranch house when Pete, the stable man, found him and told him Sylvia wanted him right away. He covered the last five miles to the house at a full gallop and found Sylvia waiting for him on the porch.

He drew his mount to a sharp halt and slid off, dropping the reins on the ground. "What's wrong?" he demanded as he mounted the steps. "Is someone hurt?"

Sylvia looked at him from pinched, worried eyes. "You didn't send for Harriet, did you?"

"No, of course not. What—" He broke off sharply. "Where is she?"

"She rode off with Sandy maybe an hour ago. He said you wanted her to come look at a wolf pup."

"I did no such thing." Anxiety rose in him, followed by a cold tendril of fear. He could think of only one reason Sandy would lie about such a thing. "Which way did they go?"

Sylvia pointed. "Toward Thunder Mountain. That's why I sent for you. Pete said you'd gone up toward Brenner Creek, and it just didn't add up."

Jeff swore and turned to look at his lathered mount. "I need a fresh horse." He called to Pete, who was just coming into the yard. "Pete, saddle Firefly for me! Sylvia, get me some warm clothes for Harriet, will you. I'm going to get my shotgun."

She reached out and touched his sleeve. "It's getting late, Jeff. You've only got another hour or so of decent light left."

He looked down at her, his eyes dark and unreadable. "I know. But morning may be too late."

She nodded and dropped her hand. "I told Ben I was worried. He went after them maybe a half hour ago. He'll mark the trail as best he can. You want me to call the sheriff?"

"What good will it do? He won't be able to get anyone to her any sooner than I can. I suppose you can let him know what's going on, but I can't wait for him."

"Of course not. I'll get Harriet's clothes."

Jeff got a shotgun from the locked gun case in his study and a box of shells. By the time he had his own jacket and was ready to go, Pete had saddled Firefly and Sylvia had a jacket and knit cap for Harriet. Sylvia's *own* jacket and cap, he noted. He bent to place a quick kiss on her cheek. "I'll find her," he said.

"See that you do," she said sternly. "And when you get her back, don't you let her go."

He didn't have time to wonder what she meant. He was in too much of a hurry to find Harriet before the early evening sunlight faded into twilight and then dusk.

He mounted up and discovered Pete and Orville were going with him. Both men carried shotguns in their saddle holsters, he noted.

"You might need some help, boss," Pete said almost shyly.

"Besides," Orville added, spitting a spray of tobacco juice to the ground, "extra eyes is always good when you're trackin'."

He nodded his thanks and led them toward Thunder Mountain. What he could not do, he told himself, was think of all the things that could have happened to Harriet. Worrying wouldn't help. He had to keep alert and move as fast as he could. It was all he could do.

"Could we slow down?" Harriet asked finally. She and Sandy had been moving at a rapid pace for more than an hour, and while she was more comfortable on Maggie than she would have believed possible just a few days ago, she still wasn't a good enough horsewoman to be able to handle this pace for long. Her legs were aching from the effort of balancing, and she noticed that foam was beginning to fleck Maggie's neck.

"We gotta get there before dark," Sandy said.

"That's great, but Maggie is getting tired and so am I. I only just learned to ride, Sandy."

He reigned his horse to a slower pace, and Maggie needed no urging to follow suit. "We'll ride slower for a few minutes," he said. "But then we gotta get going."

"Thank you."

They were heading toward Thunder Mountain in a straighter line than Jeff had taken her the other day, and since they were moving faster, they were covering the distance to the mountain more quickly. The mountain towered over them now, and they were already rising into the rugged country at its foot.

Sandy didn't seem inclined to talk, and Harriet didn't feel much like gabbing herself. When they had started out, she had wanted to question Sandy about the wolf pup, but his responses seemed to be limited to indifferent shrugs. Now she could care less what he thought.

Primarily because she was beginning to wonder what was going on here. They were in the mountain's shadow now, and the early twilight was further dimmed by the increasing numbers of trees that shadowed them. The diffuse, dim light flattened everything, and she found herself hoping that Maggie's eyes were better than hers, because it would be awfully easy to misjudge and step into a hole.

And the longer they rode, the more unlikely she thought it was that Jeff would have sent for her. Initially the trip had sounded like fun, but as they got farther from the ranch, and as afternoon turned into evening, the whole idea seemed more and more harebrained. Jeff wouldn't want her riding around out here after dark, she thought. And if he had known she was going to be out here at night, why hadn't he told her to bring a jacket? It was already getting chilly.

"Sandy?"

"Yeah?"

"Listen, I think I've changed my mind. Why don't we just go back to the ranch before it gets much darker?"

Sandy shook his head. "We're almost there, Miss Harriet."

"Oh. Well, that's good." His announcement reassured her. The wind snaked through the trees and wrapped around her, causing her to shiver. "It's getting cold out here."

"Won't be much longer," he said again, and lapsed into silence.

Harriet tried to ignore her aching legs and the goose bumps that were rising all over her. She wouldn't want Jeff to think she was a wimp, and the wolf pup did need those bandages. How could she have been so selfish as to have forgotten that?

Now, if she could just keep her seat in the saddle for a little while longer...

Jeff caught up with Ben Tweed just as the trail started to rise into the foothills. They were in the mountain's shadow now, and it was getting harder to see the marks left by Sandy and Harriet.

"Near as I can tell, they headed up the mountain," Ben said, pointing.

"Well, that narrows down the possibilities," Jeff said. "There aren't too many ways to go from here if you want to climb."

"Why in hell would he want to be taking her up there?" Ben asked.

Orville spit again. "That don't bear thinking."

"No, it doesn't," Jeff agreed. But he had some ideas, and every one of them came back around to the dead cattle rustlers. "Okay, we're going to have to split up. I figure they had to go up through the gorge there or by way of the trail to the left.'' He pointed. ''And I figure we'll save time if we don't have to keep trying to track them.''

Ben and the others nodded. ''Not much choice from here,'' Ben agreed.

''Pete and I will go up by way of the trail,'' Jeff decided. ''Ben, you and Orville go through the gorge. If you find them, signal with two shots once you have Harriet safe.''

Jeff rode off, faster now that he didn't need to read the trail, and with Pete hard on his heels. All Jeff could think about was what he was going to do to Sandy Brogan once he got his hands on him.

''We need to dismount here,'' Sandy said, the first words he had spoken in at least half an hour. ''Gotta walk this part.''

''I thought you said we were almost there.''

''Ten minutes more.''

Harriet hesitated. Sometime in the last half hour, she'd begun to think that Jeff hadn't sent for her. He wouldn't have done that. On the other hand, if Sandy had been sent to kill her like the rustlers, he'd had ample opportunity to do so since they'd left the vicinity of the ranch house. It just didn't make any sense. Maybe Sandy was lost. She clung to the hope, scary as it was, because the alternative was scarier. And for quite some time now, she'd known that she was lost herself. Even if she tried to get away from Sandy, where would she go?

Besides, if she tried to run from him, he would only come right after her, and she was willing to bet his horse was a lot faster than Maggie.

But she had to chance it, she realized. She'd been a fool to leave with Sandy in the first place, and an even bigger fool to follow him for so long after her first niggling doubts had appeared. In her eagerness to be with Jeff, she'd allowed herself to act stupidly. More than that, she'd deluded herself.

Sandy could have no good reason for bringing her so far into the wilderness. None at all. Maybe he was planning to make her death look like an accident. Maybe he'd brought her this far thinking no one would ever discover her body.

He certainly hadn't brought her here for a long evening ride.

"I can't move," she said suddenly to Sandy. "I'm not used to riding. You'll have to help me down."

He looked at her for a long moment, then shook his head and climbed down from his horse. As he did so, Harriet edged Maggie over beside his mount so that her left side was up against Sandy's horse.

"This ain't gonna work," Sandy said as he walked around his horse. "You gotta get down on the left side."

Harriet leaned forward, grabbing the pommel of her saddle with one hand, hanging on for dear life. Then, pulling her foot out of the stirrup, she kicked Sandy's mount in the side with every ounce of strength she could muster.

The horse reared, yanking the reins from Sandy's hand. At the same instant, Harriet heeled Maggie in the sides. Maggie, unaccustomed to such harsh treatment from her rider, bolted. Frightened, Sandy's mount took off in a different direction.

"Oh God, I've lost my mind," Harriet muttered as Maggie tore through the darkened woods, Sandy's curses ringing behind them. She couldn't get her left foot back in the stirrup and she could feel herself slipping to the side. Hanging on to the pommel with both hands, she started to pray.

Gradually, however, Maggie overcame her fright and began to slow down. Feeling around for the stirrup again, Harriet managed to get her foot into it and felt a huge sense of relief that she was no longer in danger of falling.

But her relief was short-lived. Straightening in the saddle, she looked around and realized the last of the light was almost gone and she had no idea where she was.

At a steady walk, she let Maggie choose her way. Sooner or later they had to come across a streambed, and if she followed it downhill, she would eventually get off this mountain, right?

But she was getting colder by the minute, until she began

to shiver, and as the last light faded from the woods, riding seemed to become more and more foolhardy. Maybe the more important thing would be to find somewhere she could shelter from the wind. Maybe a rock overhang or a little hollow. If she made it through the night, it would be easier to find her way in the morning.

Lightning arced across the sky, reminding her that this mountain made its own weather. Thunder growled long and low. She had to find some kind of shelter.

She found it at last, a rock overhang sheltered on two sides by brush and fallen tree limbs. She tethered Maggie to a nearby tree, then hunkered in the little space, pulling brush over her for warmth.

She listened for sounds of pursuit but heard none. Maybe Sandy had accomplished what he intended to, anyway. She could die from exposure by morning as easily as she could die from a gunshot. Shivering, she curled up and prayed for warmth.

She was lost on Thunder Mountain with nothing but the night—and maybe the wolves—for company.

Jeff and Pete came upon a sullen Sandy walking on foot back down the trail.

"Where the hell is Harriet?" Jeff demanded. He had to remind himself he couldn't kill the guy until he found out where he'd left Harriet.

"I don't know," Sandy said. "How the hell should I? Her horse bolted with her and mine ran off somewhere in the woods. She could be halfway home for all I know."

Jeff looked down at him, fingers itching to reach for the shotgun he carried. This wasn't the first time he'd gotten truly angry, but it was the first time killing a man actually sounded good to him. "What did you bring her up here for?"

Sandy shrugged. "To show her the wolves."

"You don't expect me to believe that!"

"Believe what you want. I was just gonna show her the wolves."

"Who the hell are you working for?"

"That's a funny question coming from the guy who signs my paychecks."

Jeff swung out of his saddle and walked over to the man. Grabbing the cowboy by the front of his shirt, he lifted him from his feet. "Look, you slime, you don't know how close you are to meeting an untimely end. Right now I'd find it a pleasure to blow your head off. Got it?"

Sandy rolled his eyes around and saw Pete pull his shotgun from its holster and point it his way. It was obvious that putting up a fight wasn't going to improve his situation.

"Now," Jeff said between his teeth, "tell me who you're working for while you collect paychecks from me."

"Overland Cattle," Sandy said. "They hired me."

"To do what?"

"Let 'em know where the hands were working when they asked."

"So they'd be able to tell where the herds were unattended."

"I don't know! I don't know why they wanted to know!"

"And I suppose you never put two and two together."

"Well, I kinda thought that might be it."

Jeff set him on his feet but didn't let go of his shirtfront. "What about Harriet? What were you supposed to do with her?"

"Kill her." He shrank back from the look on Jeff's face. "They wanted me to shoot her, but I didn't! I wasn't going to do that to no woman, no way! But they said I'd get the next bullet in the brain if I didn't get rid of her. So I figured I'd bring her up here. At least she'd have a chance!"

Jeff had to draw several deep breaths to regain control of himself. It would have been so easy to strangle the life out of this creep. Instead he said, "That's the only reason you're going to get off this mountain alive, Sandy. The *only* reason!"

He released the man's shirtfront. "Give me a rope, Pete."
Pete tossed his lariat down.

"I'm gonna tie you to a tree, Sandy," Jeff told him. "We'll come back for you after we find Harriet."

"Listen," Sandy said, "just let me go. I'll disappear, I swear!"

Jeff shook his head. "You're going to be talking to the sheriff before you disappear anywhere. Got it? Now, go sit over by that tree before I forget why it is I'm going to let you live."

Sandy took another look at Pete and saw the shotgun was still pointed at him. He sat where Jeff told him to.

After Jeff had him securely tied up, he asked where Harriet's horse had bolted and in what direction. "And don't lie to me, Sandy, because if I don't find that woman, you're going to be facing a murder charge."

"Okay. Okay. It was about two hundred yards farther up the trail. She bolted off to the north."

Lightning flickered overhead, and thunder rolled hollowly.

"How long ago did she bolt?"

"Twenty, maybe thirty minutes."

Jeff stood for a few seconds, his hands clenched into fists. "You'd better be here when I get back," he said. "And you'd better hope we find her alive, because otherwise I'm going to hunt you to the ends of the earth."

Then he swung up into his saddle again, heading up the trail. "Maggie wouldn't have run very far before she slowed down," he said to Pete. "I know that horse. Even a good scare won't make her run far."

Pete nodded. "And she was probably pretty tired by the time she got this far. She's an old horse, boss. Not much zip left in her."

The lightning made traveling more difficult. Each flare blinded them temporarily and made the horses shy. At least it didn't rain. Jeff kept praying that it wouldn't rain, right alongside his prayers that they'd find Harriet soon and that she'd be okay. If she got soaked out here tonight, cold as the wind was getting, she wouldn't survive the night. *Please, God, let her be okay.*

Lightning illuminated the trampled ground and the churned earth where Harriet had scared the horses into running. There Jeff and Pete turned north, riding steadily over rugged ground, having to trust their horses to find the way.

From time to time, Jeff lifted his head and called for Harriet. Other times, he whistled for Maggie, knowing the horse would whinny in response. He'd taught her to do that to amuse his niece and nephew, and now it might turn out to be a lifesaver.

Unless Harriet had been thrown and was lying unconscious somewhere in these woods. He didn't want to think about that possibility, but he couldn't help it. Harriet didn't really know how to ride, after all, and staying on a bolting horse could be difficult even for an experienced rider.

He couldn't stand the thought. Instead he called out again and whistled again, begging God for an answer to come out of the darkness.

But God didn't seem to be listening.

At some point Harriet felt warmer. She wasn't sure if it was the insulating brush she'd pulled over herself or hypothermia. And if it was hypothermia, there wasn't a thing she could do about it.

She tried to stay awake, though. Falling asleep could be deadly. On the other hand, she found herself thinking, dying in her sleep wasn't necessarily so bad, was it? Especially when she started thinking about leaving Jeff and going back to her life in New York.

Now, that was absolutely crazy, wasn't it? Here she was, facing death from exposure on the craggy side of a mountain in the middle of nowhere, and going back to her former life scarcely looked more inviting. What was wrong with this picture? she asked herself.

But she knew what was wrong with it. Her old life didn't

include Jeff. And the interesting thing was that, even after all she had suffered at the hands of these damn rustlers, she didn't want a life without Jeff, even if that meant staying here in the wilds of Wyoming.

Girl, she thought, *you are definitely out of your mind.* How could she even consider such a thing? Was she really proposing to spend the rest of her life hand raising baby chicks in the middle of nowhere? How could she seriously contemplate giving up the corner deli and all the other amenities of city life?

And for a *man?*

A man who didn't even seem to want to keep her? A couple of nights didn't begin to add up to a relationship. If she were crazy enough to tell Jeff she wanted to stay, he'd probably look embarrassed and say she'd misunderstood everything.

A sigh escaped her but was lost in the hammer blow of a crack of thunder. She found herself wondering if Jeff was out in this looking for her, or if he had any idea which way she'd gone. Maybe he wasn't even worried about her. Sylvia hadn't seemed to be listening too closely when Harriet had told her where she was headed. Maybe Sylvia thought she'd only gone out to look at wolves. Maybe Jeff figured she and Sandy had holed up somewhere to avoid the storm and would be back in the morning.

But even if he was looking for her, he'd have to stop in this storm. The lightning was far too dangerous. Nor was there enough light to see by. No, if he'd come out to look for her, he'd have had to stop. There was no hope she could get out of here before morning.

So what she had to do was stay alive until then. And that meant staying awake.

But sleep was persistent, trying to sneak up on her. She kept catching herself dozing, so she started playing mental games to stay alert. If she married Jeff, what changes would she make in the house? How would she keep her career going?

By the time sleep caught her unawares and carried her off,

she was beginning to think that none of the hurdles were insurmountable.

Except for Jeff himself, of course. Maybe he'd entered into a relationship with her only because he had known she was going to leave. Maybe he figured it was safe because it would end cleanly when she went back to New York. She tried to remember everything he'd said or done that might indicate he wanted her to stay but couldn't find anything.

Of course, her mind was growing fuzzy....

She slipped into sleep without even realizing it.

She awoke shivering to find tears running down her cheeks. She was uncertain how long she'd slept...twenty minutes or three hours? It was still night and the sky flickered with lightning, but the storm seemed to have moved farther away. The thunder sounded distant now, almost as if it came from the other side of the mountain.

And Maggie was stirring restlessly. Harriet felt guilty for leaving the horse saddled, but she didn't know what to do about it. Even assuming she could get the saddle off, she wouldn't know how to put it back on in the morning.

Boy, she thought miserably, she sure had a lot to learn if she was to make her life on the ranch. Not that she ever would.

Her tears felt hot on her cheeks, and she had the worst urge to curl up even tighter and just cry her heart out. She felt so depressed and lonely and afraid, so small and isolated and helpless. But crying wouldn't help, she told herself, dashing away her tears with the back of her hand and shivering again, this time with deep, racking shudders that told her how cold she had grown.

Maybe she needed to get out of this little cave and move around to warm herself up. Her stomach rumbled noisily, reminding her how long it had been since lunch. Her reserves were rapidly depleting, but moving around seemed to offer the only hope she had of getting warmer.

She pushed the brush aside and climbed out of her little

hole. Maggie stirred again, making a soft nicker, and thunder rang out in the distance.

Harriet made her way to the horse, guided by the flickering lightning, and stroked Maggie's nose the way Jeff had taught her to. A quiver seemed to run through the horse.

"Poor girl," Harriet murmured sympathetically. "You're cold, hungry and thirsty, too, aren't you?"

She stomped her feet, trying to warm them up, and began jogging in place, ignoring her stiff muscles, feeling the horse's warm breath against her cheek.

"We'll make it through the night, Maggie. You'll see. Then in the morning we'll find our way home. Somehow."

The horse nickered and tossed her head.

Just then, Harriet thought she heard the sound of a whistle before the wind tore it away. She tilted her head, wondering if it was just the wind, but Maggie chose that moment to lift her head and let out a long, loud whinny.

Harriet looked at the horse. "Did you hear it, too?"

Maggie whinnied again and began pulling at the reins that Harriet had tied around the tree.

"What is it, Maggie?"

But Maggie couldn't answer, and Harriet could only strain to hear what was disturbing the horse—and hope it wasn't Sandy coming after them.

Jeff reined Firefly sharply. "Did you hear that?"

"I shore did," Pete said.

"Could you tell where it came from?"

"Afraid not."

Jeff tilted his head back and whistled again, as loudly as he could.

Moments later, he heard the answering whinny. "Over there," he said, and urged his mount forward. "Harriet!" he shouted, straining his throat. "Harriet!"

And then, from a great distance, carried on the wind, he heard the faint response. "Jeff?"

He sent a prayer of thanksgiving winging heavenward.

Seventeen

Harriet was standing next to Maggie when Jeff found her, clinging to the horse's neck and fighting back tears of relief.

He leaped off his horse in one easy movement, dropping the reins on the ground. He closed the two paces between himself and Harriet and scooped her up into his arms, hugging her as tightly as he could, lifting her right off her feet.

"Thank God," he said. "Thank God!"

"I didn't think you'd find me," she said brokenly. "It's so dark and cold. I didn't know how I was going to find my way back...."

"I found you," he murmured, stroking her hair. "I found you. That's all that matters."

"I'm so cold...."

He wrapped her in Sylvia's jacket and pulled the knit cap onto her head until it covered her ears. He paused to chafe her frigid hands between his. "You'll warm up now," he said. "You'll see."

She tilted her head back, trying to see him in the dark, wishing her ridiculous tears would stop running down her cheeks. "I don't think I can ride."

"It's okay. We'll double up on Firefly. I'll take care of you, sweetheart. Trust me."

She did trust him. Wholly and completely. She managed a teary smile for Pete when he expressed his gladness at having found her. Then he fired two shots into the air with his shotgun.

"What's that for?" she asked Jeff.

"To let Ben and Orville know we found you. They can start heading home now, too."

A short while later, an answering shot came from the distance. "That's it," said Pete. "We'll probably run into 'em back where we separated."

"Probably." With gentle but strong hands, Jeff lifted Harriet into his saddle, then mounted behind her. His arms surrounded her, holding her steady and secure.

"Listen," Pete said as he bent over in the saddle and untied Maggie's reins from the tree, "I can go back and pick up Sandy if you want to take a shorter way back."

Jeff hesitated. He had several choices, and he *did* want to get Harriet back to the house as quickly as possible, but he shook his head. "No, I don't want to take a chance that that snake will pull something on you. Besides, given how dark it is, we'll all be safer if we don't separate. That way if anything happens, someone can go for help."

Harriet was past caring which way they went. Inside the depths of the down jacket, she was beginning to feel warmer. Shivers shook her from time to time, but as she rode, they lessened. She was exhausted, as much from fear and cold as anything else, but she didn't really care how fast she got back now. All she wanted was to stay right where she was, with Jeff's arms snugly around her.

She had lost all sense of time. She had no idea how late it was or how long they rode before they came upon Sandy, who was still tied to the tree and shivering miserably.

"I could have died trussed up like this," he snarled when he saw them.

"Isn't that what you intended for Harriet?" Jeff asked coldly. He pulled his shotgun from the holster and kept it leveled on Sandy while Pete untied him.

"Now, climb on Maggie," Jeff ordered. "Pete, tie his hands to the pommel."

Pete obliged, then led Maggie and Sandy down the trail.

Jeff and Harriet brought up the rear, with Jeff's shotgun cradled across her lap.

Funny, she thought wearily, but she never would have imagined herself riding through the night down a mountainside with a shotgun in front of her. She hated guns.

Except now it was a strangely comforting presence, as comforting as Jeff's solid body behind her. Nobody could hurt her now, not with Jeff cradling both her and the gun. Nobody would even try.

The sky was clearing by the time they met up with Ben and Orville, and as the sky cleared, the temperature dropped sharply. The five of them continued their journey whipped by a bitter wind that hinted of the coming winter. Jeff's body sheltered her from most of it, and Sylvia's jacket did the rest, although nothing could protect her cheeks.

At last the rugged slope gave way to a gentler one, and finally to the rolling acreage of the ranch. The moon came out briefly from behind the dissipating clouds, then set behind the mountain, leaving only starlight to guide them.

But at last the lights of the ranch became visible in the distance.

"Not much longer now, honey," Jeff said. "Just a few more minutes."

"I'm okay," Harriet insisted, her voice cracked with fatigue. She wasn't sure whether she was trying to convince herself or Jeff. Two attempts had been made on her life in a matter of weeks, and her exhausted mind wondered if she would ever be the same again. The mugging back in New York had left her feeling insecure on the city streets she had walked for years. Now maybe she would never be able to feel safe here. The thought filled her with infinite sadness.

The yard was full of sheriff's vehicles when they rode in, and all the ground-floor lights of the house were ablaze.

Jeff swung down, then helped Harriet to dismount, supporting her when her legs threatened to buckle. Just then the kitchen door opened, and Sylvia came out with the sheriff and two deputies.

"Oh, thank heaven," Sylvia cried, and dashed down the stairs to throw her arms around Harriet. "Oh, you poor, poor child. I had a feeling that man was up to no good. Come inside. I've made a huge pot of chicken soup, just the thing to warm you up and make you feel right again."

Harriet didn't want to leave Jeff, but Sylvia gave her little choice. Behind her she heard Jeff explaining what had happened and Sandy's role in it. Before the door closed behind her, she heard Nate telling Sandy he was under arrest.

Sylvia, fussing like a broody hen, helped her out of her jacket and guided her to a seat at the island. Then she placed a big bowl of steaming soup in front of her. "Eat, dear," the housekeeper said. "Once that soup hits your system, everything's going to look a lot better."

Fifteen minutes later, Jeff joined her. He looked almost blankly at the bowl Sylvia placed in front of him. Harriet, who was indeed feeling better as the soup filled her with warmth and energy, looked at him with growing concern.

"What's wrong, Jeff?"

"Oh, I don't know," he said almost bitterly. "I suppose it shouldn't be shocking to hear a man say that your brother ordered him to kill four people."

"Sandy did all the murders?"

"And George was the one who told him to do it."

Sylvia clapped a hand to her face, looking stunned. "I never liked that young man," she said, "but I didn't think he'd stoop that low."

Jeff sighed and reached for his spoon. "I've been afraid of it since I heard he was involved in the rustling. I should have expected it, I guess, but hearing Sandy actually say it—well, it hit me hard. I guess I was still nursing some little hope that George's partner was behind that part of it."

"I'm sorry," Harriet said, and truly she was. Her own fears seemed to pale by significance.

Jeff shook his head and ate a spoonful of soup. "You know, you think you know someone. After all, I grew up with him. He's been part of my life for thirty-five years. Then I hear something like this—" He broke off and shook his head again. "Damn fine soup, Sylvia."

A little while later, he insisted that he and Harriet had to go to bed. "Morning chores won't wait for me to wake-up," he said wearily.

Harriet followed him upstairs. When she stopped at her door, he took her hand and led her down the hallway to his bedroom.

"We'll take a hot shower," he said. "It'll get rid of the last of the chill."

Afterward, they climbed into his big bed and he held her close. Soon he started talking in a slow, pained voice.

"Back when I was in my early twenties, I fell in love with this girl. She was too young for me. Still in high school, as a matter of fact, but I took a real shine to her and figured that when she grew up, I'd ask her out."

Harriet nodded against his shoulder to let him know she was listening.

"Anyway, somehow George found out I was sweet on her, and he started dating her. He was still in high school at the time, and there wasn't much I could say, under the circumstances. He even asked her to marry him, but he bolted on the day of the wedding."

"You told me about that. But you didn't say that you loved her."

"I did, though. I even asked her to marry me when we realized George had run, but she turned me down. Understandably. She figured I was offering out of family honor or some such nonsense."

"What happened to her?"

"Oh, a while back she married a really nice guy. Then there was the woman in Denver. I told you she laughed in my face about living on a ranch? Anyway, part of the reason she laughed in my face was that she was seeing George.''

Harriet pushed herself up on her elbow. "George? He did it to you *again?*"

"It was what broke up his marriage finally. I can't hold him solely responsible for that one, though. After all, *she* was the one who was two-timing me.''

"But still!''

"But still,'' he agreed. "Anyway, he took what I wanted right from under my nose twice before, and now he tried to do it again tonight.''

Harriet felt a trickle of shock run through her. "What... what do you mean?''

"I mean that if anything had happened to you, I would have killed George with my bare hands. I mean he's damn lucky that he's going to get arrested, because if he ever comes within ten feet of me again, he's a dead man. I mean that—'' He broke off and drew her closer.

"I mean,'' he continued in a ragged whisper, "that I've never loved anybody in my whole life the way I love you, Harriet Breslin. I forgive George for everything else, but I'm never going to forgive him for what he tried to do tonight.''

"Jeff...'' Harriet didn't know quite what to say. Her heart was beating like a trip-hammer, and her throat squeezed so tight with emotion that it hurt.

"Oh, I know all the problems,'' Jeff continued. "Hell, if you want, I'll fly to New York every couple of weeks just so we can be together. I can't move there, but...Harriet, I love you so much I'm going to die if I can't be part of your life.''

"Jeff...do you really want a commuter relationship?''

"Hell, no,'' he said gruffly. "What I *want* is for you to find a way to move your job out here. What I want is for you to be able to find some way to enjoy living here with me. We wouldn't have to be here all the time, Harriet. We could travel. Visit all kinds of places. You could go back to New York anytime your job demands it. There ought to be some way we could work this all out!''

''But…'' Flabbergasted, she couldn't even marshal a response. Her mind seemed to be stuck on the wonderful news that Jeff loved her.

''I know you must hate this place by now,'' he said. ''After all that's happened to you, I really can't blame you. But I promise you, sweetheart, it's not like this here as a rule. Ordinarily you couldn't ask for a safer place to live. Could you at least hang around a little while longer and see what it's like now that all the bad guys have been taken care of?''

''I could probably do that,'' she managed to say finally. Joy and trepidation were both overwhelming her. Even as she exulted in the knowledge of Jeff's love, she could see all the hassles.

He turned on his side and tried to read her face in the darkness. ''Do we have a chance, honey? Do we?''

''We—'' She broke off and tried again, this time framing the words she most needed to say. ''I love you, Jeff. I truly, truly love you with my whole heart and soul.'' And for the first time in her life, she didn't feel she was cheating a little when she said it. She did love him. It was a rock-solid certainty in her heart.

He laughed with joy and kissed her repeatedly, hugging her so tightly her ribs ached.

''When I thought I might have lost you—'' He couldn't complete the sentence. ''I started to do some really heavy thinking about you, about us, about how we've been trying to avoid getting involved and just kept getting in deeper. I've never loved anyone as much as I love you, never needed anyone as much as I need you. I don't know how we're going to work out all the problems, but I honestly believe we can if we want to badly enough. Will you stay with me, sweetheart? Will you give us both a chance? Will you marry me?''

''I'll stay with you,'' she answered breathlessly. ''I'll stay. But, Jeff…Jeff, we've got to give it a trial period. In case. In case it doesn't work out for some reason. In case one of us discovers we were just carried away by the moment. In case…in case I discover I really can't live here indefinitely.''

He was silent a moment, then said, ''Whatever you want, Harriet. How long do you want? Six months? A year? Take whatever time you need to be sure, but believe this—I have never been surer of anything in my life than I am that I love you and want to spend the rest of my life with you.''

''Six months,'' she said shakily. ''Give me six months. If it didn't mean changing my whole life, I wouldn't even hesitate, Jeff, but it's so different out here.''

''Of course it is.'' He kissed her gently and brushed her hair back from her forehead. ''Six months. And if you need more, just say so. Believe me, I understand. If I were the one moving to New York, I'd want the time, too. It's just that— well, maybe I'm wrong, but it seems to me it would be easier to move your career than it would be to move mine.''

''Of course it would. I can hardly see you ranching in Central Park. No, I'm the one who has to make the move. I just want to be sure. I've been such a dyed-in-the-wool New Yorker for so long that I have to be sure the life-style change won't kill me. Although I don't think it will.''

''So, six months,'' he said again. ''I can wait six months. I can wait the rest of my life, as long as I have a chance.''

''You have more than a chance,'' she said. Her mind was already running over the things she would need to do to relocate her life, but he distracted her utterly and completely by kissing her senseless and making slow, gentle love to her.

He took her to the places she had only dreamed of before she met him, carrying her so high that she felt she could touch the stars. And later they fell asleep, twined together in the afterglow.

Life, thought Harriet as she drifted off to sleep, didn't get any better than this.

* * * * *

Epilogue

But life did get better. Six months later, in Good Shepherd Church, with gentle snow falling outside, Jeff and Harriet were married.

She had managed to move her career, and with Jeff's encouragement had begun to do the more artistic and creative work she had always yearned to do. The work gave her more freedom, and Marcie, after her initial objection to having to turn down commercial jobs, began to get excited about the possibilities. She was now predicting Harriet's photographic essays would be shown in major galleries.

But Marcie wasn't exactly ready to give up yet. As she fussed with Harriet's train and veil, trying not to trip over her own long burgundy skirt, she said, "You know, that publisher wants another set of cover photos from you. The first set is turning out to be a real success."

"I don't think so, Marcie."

"Look," Marcie said, "what more could you ask for? Heck, you don't even have to fly two thousand miles this time. You're already here. All you have to do is take the pictures."

"I'll think about it."

"Don't think too hard. It's good money. Not that you need money now, or anything, but...hey, it'll pay for a nice trip to Europe or something."

"I'll think about it, Marcie."

"You know, it could wind up being a long-term thing, working for this publisher. That's nothing to sneeze at."

But Harriet had more important things to occupy her right

now. As she walked down the aisle on her father's arm, past the smiling faces of friends new and old, past her beaming family, toward the man she was about to marry, she cherished the small secret now growing in her womb.

There would be pictures, and there would be babies, but most of all, there would be Jeff.

He was smiling broadly as he took her hand, and together they faced Reverend Fromberg. Jeff's dreams were coming true, too, Harriet thought with utter contentment.

Together they made each other's dreams happen. And sometimes he even took her to New York for the weekend so she could visit her friends and her favorite deli and have fresh bagels for breakfast and shrimp scampi for dinner. Who could ask for anything more?

Here's a preview of next month's

World's Most
Eligible Bachelors

Duncan MacNeill,
the sexy DEA agent from

DETECTIVE DAD
by
MARIE FERRARELLA

ONE

Fog descended around him with the suddenness of a gasp. It surrounded him, not like a virginal white veil but like an ermine wrap, thick, heavy and completely impenetrable. Visibility went from nominal on the dark road to nonexistent.

Just what he needed.

Duncan MacNeill bit off a curse. He was in a hurry to get home, in a hurry to put the day and its annoying details far behind him.

This fog wasn't helping his mood any.

Neither was the article in the magazine that sat next to him on the seat of his Mercedes. Everybody who'd seen it thought it was a hoot, except him.

The article that was such a sore point was courtesy of *Prominence Magazine,* which had selected him as this month's World's Most Eligible Bachelor, a title Duncan was certain the editors had dreamed up purely to raise sales.

Duncan didn't know whether to be insulted or amused. There was a case for both, so he settled for just being annoyed.

He gripped the steering wheel as he slowed his pace, but not his impatience. Lately everything seemed annoying to him. It was undoubtedly because he felt restless again. The undercover job was over and he'd been called back out of circulation. Politely put, he'd been placed at a desk and taken off field duty for his own safety until things blew over. Right now, it didn't seem as if they ever would.

He wasn't any good at waiting.

Duncan scrubbed a hand over his face as he wove his way

up the hill toward his house. Why was he letting himself get so maudlin tonight?

Maybe it had something to do with the fact that his birthday was less than a month away. Thirty-two. Somehow, he'd thought he'd be somewhere else in his life when he reached that age. It wasn't security he craved. He had more than enough of that. And it wasn't excitement, although that was part of what made him turn his back on the family business and go into law enforcement. He wanted to make a difference. Anonymously. After spending the first half of his life being photographed and hounded as the heir apparent of one of the country's richest families, he'd discovered the immense appeal of undercover work. He found he really liked anonymity.

But being the center of quite possibly the biggest South American drug bust of the decade had squelched that. If he'd had any doubts, there was the dubious honor of World's Most Eligible Bachelor to remind him that he was back in the limelight.

Which brought him back to his current melancholy. All the money he could ever want and a career he enjoyed still couldn't snuff out the restlessness that periodically descended on him out of nowhere and threatened to dissolve any peace of mind he might have earned.

He blinked as two tiny red embers emerged in the road up ahead.

What the—

Beams. They were beams, not embers. Two beams of light, cutting through the thick curtain of fog like the gleaming red eyes of some mythical creature in a long-forgotten fable.

The image barely had time to register before Duncan realized that he was driving straight into the back of a stalled car.

Swearing, he slammed on the brakes and turned the steering wheel sharply to the left to avoid slamming into the car, then to the right, fighting to regain control of his vehicle.

The impact rattled Duncan's teeth as the front right bumper of his car clipped the left rear of the stalled vehicle. The contact didn't seem to slow him down any as his car continued to slide wildly. Tires squealed as he skidded. An eternity later, it was over. The Mercedes came to a shaken halt, having completely turned around.

Shaken, angry, Duncan stormed out of his car. He left the door hanging open as he looked around for the other vehicle.

It had been shoved off the road by the impact of the collision.

Perilously close, he realized as he approached it, to the edge of the embankment.

If he had seen it just a moment later, or hit it any harder than he had, he would have sent the car and its occupants plummeting over the side, more than likely to their death.

Adrenaline pumped through him, ignited by the near miss. "What the hell do you think you're doing?" he shouted at the driver before he even reached the car. "I could have killed you!"

Duncan struggled to control his rage. Yanking the car door open, he was ready to haul the driver out and give him a piece of his mind.

Anger disappeared in the fog the moment he looked inside.

There was only one occupant in the car. A dazed, pale young woman. Her blond hair damp, plastered to her face as if the fog had found a way to seep through the sealed windows. There was a single, thin stream of blood oozing its way down the side of her cheek from a fresh cut at her temple. Pain was etched along her face.

Looking at her, Duncan had no idea how she had even managed to get behind the wheel of her car. There was absolutely no room for her to maneuver. Hugely pregnant, she would have been ripe enough to burst if she'd been a melon.

SPECIAL EDITION

Stories of love and life, these powerful novels are tales that you can identify with—romances with "something special" added in!

Fall in love with the stories of authors such as **Nora Roberts, Diana Palmer, Ginna Gray** and many more of your special favorites—as well as wonderful new voices!

Special Edition brings you entertainment for the heart!

SSE-GEN

SILHOUETTE® Desire®

Do you want...

Dangerously handsome heroes

Evocative, everlasting love stories

Sizzling and tantalizing sensuality

Incredibly sexy miniseries like **MAN OF THE MONTH**

Red-hot romance

Enticing entertainment that can't be beat!

You'll find all of this, and much *more* each and every month in **SILHOUETTE DESIRE**. Don't miss these unforgettable love stories by some of romance's hottest authors. Silhouette Desire—where your fantasies will always come true....

DES-GEN

INTIMATE MOMENTS®
Silhouette®

If you've got the time...
We've got the
INTIMATE MOMENTS

Passion. Suspense. Desire. Drama. Enter a world that's larger than life, where men and women overcome life's greatest odds for the ultimate prize: love. Nonstop excitement is closer than you think...in Silhouette Intimate Moments!

Silhouette®

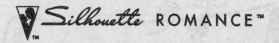

Silhouette ROMANCE™

What's a single dad to do when he needs a wife by next Thursday?

Who's a confirmed bachelor to call when he finds a baby on his doorstep?

How does a plain Jane in love with her gorgeous boss get him to notice her?

From classic love stories to romantic comedies to emotional heart tuggers, **Silhouette Romance** offers six irresistible novels every month by some of your favorite authors! Such as…beloved bestsellers **Diana Palmer, Annette Broadrick, Suzanne Carey, Elizabeth August** and **Marie Ferrarella,** to name just a few—and some sure to become favorites!

Fabulous Fathers…Bundles of Joy…Miniseries… Months of blushing brides and convenient weddings… Holiday celebrations… You'll find all this and much more in **Silhouette Romance**—always emotional, always enjoyable, always about love!

WAYS TO *UNEXPECTEDLY* MEET MR. RIGHT:

♡ *Go out with the sexy-sounding stranger your daughter secretly set you up with through a personal ad.*

♡ *RSVP yes to a wedding invitation—soon it might be your turn to say "I do!"*

♡ *Receive a marriage proposal by mail— from a man you've never met....*

These are just a few of the unexpected ways that written communication leads to love in Silhouette Yours Truly.

Each month, look for two fast-paced, fun and flirtatious Yours Truly novels (with entertaining treats and sneak previews in the back pages) by some of your favorite authors—and some who are sure to become favorites.

YOURS TRULY™:
Love—when you least expect it!

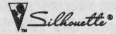